Wataru Watari
Illustration **Ponkan**⑧

Contents

MY YOUTH R♥MANTIC C☻MEDY iS WR∅NG, AS I EXPECTED

Wataru Watari
Illustration **Ponkan⑧**

VOLUME

1

YEN ON

NEW YORK

MY YOUTH ROMANTIC COMEDY IS WRONG, AS I EXPECTED Vol. 1
WATARU WATARI
Illustration by Ponkan⑧

Translation by Jennifer Ward
Cover art by Ponkan⑧

YAHARI ORE NO SEISHUN LOVE COME WA MACHIGATTEIRU.
Vol. 1 by Wataru WATARI
©2011 Wataru WATARI
Illustration by PONKAN⑧
All rights reserved.
Original Japanese edition published by SHOGAKUKAN.
English translation rights arranged with SHOGAKUKAN through Tuttle-Mori Agency, Inc, Tokyo.

English translation © 2016 by Yen Press, LLC

Yen On
1290 Avenue of the Americas
New York, NY 10104

Visit us at yenpress.com
facebook.com/yenpress
twitter.com/yenpress
yenpress.tumblr.com

First Yen On Edition: September 2016

Yen On is an imprint of Yen Press, LLC.
The Yen On name and logo are trademarks of Yen Press, LLC.

The publisher is not responsible for websites (or their content) that are not owned by the publisher.

Library of Congress Cataloging-in-Publication Data

Names: Watari, Wataru, author. | Ponkan 8, illustrator.
Title: My youth romantic comedy is wrong, as I expected / Wataru Watari ; illustration by Ponkan 8.
Other titles: Yahari ore no seishun love come wa machigatteiru. English
Description: New York : Yen On, 2016– | Summary: Hachiman Hikigaya is a cynic, but when he turns
   in an essay for a school assignment espousing this view, he is sentenced to work in the Service Club,
   an organization dedicated to helping students with problems in their lives.
Identifiers: LCCN 2016005816 | ISBN 9780316312295 (v. 1 : paperback)
Subjects: | CYAC: Optimism—Fiction. | School—Fiction.
   Classification: LCC PZ7.1.W396 My 2016 | DDC [Fic]—dc23 LC record available at
   http://lccn.loc.gov/2016005816

ISBN: 978-0-316-31229-5

10 9 8

LSC-C

Printed in the United States of America

MY YOUTH R♥MANTIC C☻MEDY iS WRØNG, AS I EXPECTED

Cast of Characters

Hachiman Hikigaya........... The main character. High school second-year. Twisted personality.

Yukino Yukinoshita........... Captain of the Service Club. Perfect and beautiful, but her personality is a disappointment.

Yui Yuigahama................. Hachiman's classmate. Tends to worry about what other people think.

Yoshiteru Zaimokuza......... Nerd. Thinks of Hachiman as his buddy.

Saika Totsuka................... Tennis club. Extremely cute. However...

Shizuka Hiratsuka............. Japanese teacher. Guidance counselor.

Report worksheet

Reflecting on my life in high school
by Hachiman Hikigaya, Class 2-F

Youth is lies. Youth is evil.

Those who incessantly celebrate their teenage years are lying both to themselves and to those around them. These people interpret everything in their environment as an affirmation of their beliefs, and when they make mistakes that prove fatal, they see those very mistakes as proof of the value of the teen experience, looking back on it all as part of a beautiful memory.

For example, when people like this dirty their hands with criminal acts like shoplifting or gang violence, they call it mere "youthful indiscretion." When they fail exams, they say that school is about more than just studying. They will twist any common sense or normal interpretation of their actions in the name of the word youth. In their minds, secrets, lies, and even crimes and failures are naught but the spice of youth. And in their wrongdoing and their failures, they discover their own uniqueness. They then conclude that these failures were all entirely part of the teen experience, but the failures of others are merely defeat. If failure is the proof of the teen experience, then wouldn't an individual who has failed to make friends be having the ultimate teen experience? But these people would never accept that as truth.

Their assertions are nothing but an excuse. Their principles are based entirely on their own convenience. Thus, their principles are deceit. Lies, deceit, secrets, and fraud are all reprehensible things.

These people are evil. And that means, paradoxically, that those who do not celebrate their teenage years are correct and righteous.

In conclusion:

YOU NORMIES CAN GO DIE IN A FIRE.

Anyway, **Hachiman Hikigaya** is rotten.

A vein popping out of her forehead, my Japanese language arts teacher, Shizuka Hiratsuka, read my essay aloud in a thunderous voice. Being forced to listen to it like that made me realize I still wasn't that great at composition. That essay was a pretty transparent attempt to string together a bunch of long words in an effort to sound smart. It was like something a novelist whose books wouldn't sell might do. So did that mean my poor writing skills were the reason she'd called me there, then?

Of course not. I knew that wasn't the reason.

Ms. Hiratsuka finished reading the essay, put a hand to her forehead, and sighed deeply. "Listen, Hikigaya. What was the homework I assigned you in class?"

"Uh, it was to write an essay on the theme of *reflecting on my life in high school.*"

"That's right. So why does this sound like the prelude to a school massacre? Are you a terrorist? Or just an idiot?" Ms. Hiratsuka sighed again, worriedly ruffling her hair.

You know, instead of calling her a teacher, wouldn't it be a lot sexier to call her a disciplinarian? Just as that thought crossed my mind, said disciplinarian whacked me over the head with a stack of papers. "Listen up."

"Yes, ma'am."

"That look in your eyes… You look like a rotten fish."

"You mean loaded with omega-threes? I must look pretty smart."

The corners of her mouth twitched upward. "Hikigaya. What exactly is the point of this smart-ass essay? If you have an excuse, I'll hear it now." The teacher glared at me so hard I could hear the sound of her gaze. She wasn't half bad looking, so her glare had an unusually powerful effect. I was overwhelmed. She's actually pretty damn scary.

"U-uh, well, I did reflect on my high school life, you know? High school students these days are lasically bike this, right?! It's basically all true!" I fumbled with my words. Just talking to another human being was enough to make me nervous, and this was an older woman, which was even worse.

"Usually for this kind of thing, you reflect on *your own* life."

"And if you'd indicated that beforehand, that's what I would have written! It's your fault for being vague when assigning the topic."

"Don't quibble with me, kid."

"Kid? Well, I guess to someone your age, I am."

A puff of wind went by.

It was a game of rock-paper-scissors, and her rock swung out with no warning. A splendid fist that held back nothing grazed my cheek.

"The next one will hit its mark." Her eyes were serious.

"I'm sorry. I'll write it over." The optimal choice of words to express apology and repentance.

But it didn't look like that was enough for her. Oh, crap. Was groveling on the floor really my only remaining option? I slapped my pants to try and get the wrinkles out, bent my right leg, and approached the linoleum. It was a graceful, fluid movement.

"It's not that I'm mad at you."

Oh, here it comes. This is it. It's so annoying when people say this. It's just like saying, *I'm not mad, so tell me, okay?* I've never met anyone who said that who wasn't actually mad.

But surprisingly enough, Ms. Hiratsuka genuinely didn't seem angry. Aside from that age-related stuff, at least. Returning the knee that had been on the floor to its former position, I looked at her.

Ms. Hiratsuka retrieved a Seven Star from a breast pocket that looked like it was about to burst and tapped the filter twice on her desk. It was something a middle-aged man would do. When she was done packing the tobacco, she flicked her cheap lighter and ignited the cigarette. She exhaled some smoke, an extremely serious look on her face as she fixed her gaze upon me once more.

"You haven't tried joining any clubs, have you?"

"No, ma'am."

"Do you have any friends?" she asked, knowing full well I don't have any.

"M-my motto is to treat everyone equally, so I have a policy of not keeping anyone particularly closer than anyone else!"

"In other words, you have no friends?"

"I-if you want to be that blunt about it...," I replied.

Ms. Hiratsuka beamed with motivation. "I see! So you don't after all! Just as I thought. I could tell the minute I saw those rotten, sordid eyes of yours."

You saw it in my eyes? Then why ask?!

Ms. Hiratsuka nodded to herself, satisfied, before giving me a sheepish look. "Do you...have a girlfriend or anything?"

"Or anything?" What was that supposed to mean? What would she say if I said I had a boyfriend? "Not right now." I tentatively included some hope for the future in my emphasis on the words *right now.*

"I see..." This time when she looked at me, her eyes were somewhat moist. I want to believe that it was just irritation from the cigarette smoke. *Hey, stop that. Don't point that tepid, patronizing gaze at me.*

But seriously, what's with this line of questioning? Does she think she's in some kind of inspirational teacher movie? Next, are we gonna hear some line or other from the rotten delinquent? Is the dropout going back to her old school as a teacher? I sure wish she would go back.

After Ms. Hiratsuka finished pondering, she expelled a smoke-filled sigh. "Okay, let's say this. You do your report over."

"Yes, ma'am." Sure, this time I'll just spew out some completely inoffensive paper, like something a pinup idol or a professional voice actress might write on her blog. Like *Today I had...**curry** for dinner!* What was the point of that ellipsis? Nothing that followed it was surprising at all.

Everything she'd said up until that point was to be expected. What came next was beyond my imagining.

"But still, you were callous, and your attitude toward me was hurtful. Were you never taught not to bring up a woman's age? So I'm ordering you to do some community service. Wrongdoing must be punished after all," Ms. Hiratsuka announced gleefully, her manner so perky I couldn't imagine she was remotely hurt—actually, wasn't she even perkier than usual?

Oh yeah...and the word *perky* just happened to remind me of another word—*breasts*. Much like my train of thought, my eyes strayed from reality and toward the teacher's boobs, pushing up from underneath her blouse. How depraved. But what kind of person gets so giddy about punishing someone, seriously?

"Community service? What do you want me to do?" I asked timidly. Based on her demeanor, I expected her to order me to clear ditches or stage a kidnapping or something.

"Come with me." She pressed her cigarette into an ashtray already filled to capacity and stood. She'd offered no explanation or preface to her order, so I paused. Noticing from the doorway that I wasn't moving, she turned back to me. "Come on, hurry up."

Flustered by her glare and furrowed brows, I followed.

× × ×

The layout of the Chiba City Municipal Soubu High School building is fairly convoluted. If you were to examine it from above, it would look a lot like the distorted square of the Japanese character for *mouth*—or the Japanese letter *ro*. If you add in the AV building poking out underneath, the bird's-eye view of our glorious school is complete. By the road stands the classroom building, and opposite that, the special-use building. Each facility is connected by a walkway on the second floor, and the whole thing forms the shape of a square.

The space surrounded on all four sides is the normies' holy ground: the quad.

During lunch hour, boys and girls get together to have lunch and then play badminton to help themselves digest. After school, with the buildings growing slowly darker behind them, they talk of love and gaze at the stars, caressed by the sea breeze.

It's all such bullshit.

From the sidelines, they were as cold as actors playing roles in some teen drama. And in that drama, I'd play a tree or something.

Ms. Hiratsuka was clicking briskly down the linoleum, apparently heading for the special-use building.

I've got a bad feeling about this. I mean, community service is a worthless activity, anyway. The word *service* isn't something that should be popping up in everyday conversation. I think it's a term that should be reserved for very specific situations—for example, a maid *servicing* her master. I'd welcome that kind of service with open arms, like, *Woo, let's party!* But that kind of thing never actually happens in real life. Or rather, not unless you pay. And if you do pony up the cash and get to do whatever it is you've got in mind, it's not exactly an activity bursting with hopes and dreams. Basically, service is bad.

On top of that, we were on our way to the special-use building. I was obviously going to be made to do something like move the piano in the music room or clean up garbage in the compost room or organize the book collection in the library. I had to take defensive measures before that happened.

"I've got a bad back, like…um…her…her…herpes? That's it…"

"I'm sure you wanted to say a 'hernia,' but don't worry about that. I'm not going to ask you to do physical labor." Ms. Hiratsuka regarded me with infuriating condescension.

Hmm. That meant that she wanted me to look something up or

do desk work. In a way, that sort of mindless busywork was even worse than manual labor. It was closer to that method of torture where you have to fill up holes in the ground and then dig them out again.

"I have this disease where I'll die if I go into a classroom."

"That's some long-nosed sniper material. Are you one of the Straw Hat Pirates or what?"

You read shonen manga?!

Well, I don't hate doing repetitive tasks on my own. I just have to turn off a switch inside me and say to myself, I'm a machine. Once I'm at that stage, I'll start looking for a mechanical body and then end up as a bolt.

"We're here."

The teacher stopped before a completely unremarkable classroom. There was nothing written on the nameplate by the door. I paused at that, thinking it odd, and the teacher slid the door open with a rattle.

Desks and chairs were stacked up casually in one corner of the classroom. Maybe it was being used for storage? The stack was the only thing differentiating this room from all the others. There was nothing special about it. It was extremely normal.

What made it feel so different, though, was that there was a girl there, reading a book in the slanting rays of the setting sun. The scene was so picturesque that I imagined that even after the end of the world she would still be sitting there, just like that.

The moment I saw her, my body and mind both froze. I was entranced.

When the girl noticed she had visitors, she bookmarked her paperback and looked up. "Ms. Hiratsuka. I thought I asked you to knock before entering."

Flawless visage. Flowing black hair. Even wearing the same uniform as all the faceless girls in my class, she looked completely different.

"Even if I knock, you never reply."

"You come in without giving me time to." She cast the teacher a dissatisfied glance. "And who's this addled-looking boy?" Her chilly gaze flicked toward me.

I knew this girl. Class 2-J, Yukino Yukinoshita.

Of course, all I knew was her name and face. I'd never spoken with her. I can't help it. It was a rare occasion for me to speak to anyone at this school.

Aside from the nine regular classes at Soubu High, there's also another class called the International Curriculum. The International Curriculum is two or three points higher than the regular classes on the bell curve and is composed mostly of kids who've spent time abroad or are looking to go on exchange.

Among that class full of standouts—or rather, people who just naturally drew the attention of others—Yukino Yukinoshita was particularly distinctive.

She was a straight-A student, always enshrined in the top rank on both regular and aptitude tests. And what's more, she was always showered with attention due to her uncommonly good looks. Basically, she was so pretty you could even say she was the prettiest girl in school. She was famous here, and everyone knew about her.

And then there's me. I'm so bland and ordinary, I don't even know if *anyone* knows I exist. So there would be nothing to be offended about if she didn't know me. But the word *addled* hurt a bit. Enough to make me start escaping reality by remembering that candy from a long time ago with a similar name. I haven't seen it in a while.

"This is Hikigaya. He wants to join the club." Prodded forward by Ms. Hiratsuka, I bowed lightly. I assumed she wanted me to introduce myself or something.

"I'm Hachiman Hikigaya from Class 2-F. Um…hey. What do you mean, 'join the club'?" *Join what club? What club was this?*

Ms. Hiratsuka opened her mouth in anticipation of my question. "Your punishment will be to participate in this club's activities. I won't accept any arguments, disagreements, objections, questions, or back talk. Cool your head for a bit and think about what you did." She handed down my sentence with the force of crashing waves, leaving me no room for protest. "Well, then, I think you can tell by looking at him, but he's rotten to the core. That's why he's always alone. He's such a pitiful soul."

You can tell just by looking?

"If he learns how to be around people, I think he'll straighten himself out a little. I'll leave him with you. My request is that you correct his twisted, lonely character," the teacher said, turning back to Yukinoshita.

Yukinoshita opened her mouth, looking annoyed. "If that's the issue, I think you should just knock some discipline into him. Kicking would also work."

What a scary girl.

"If I could, I would, but these days they make a little bit of a fuss about that. Physical violence isn't allowed." The way she said that, it was as if she were saying that *psychological* violence *was* allowed.

"I refuse. Seeing those lewd eyes of his brimming with ulterior motives, I feel a threat to my person." Yukinoshita straightened her collar (though it hadn't really been out of place) and glared in my direction. *I'm not even looking at your overly modest chest. No, really, it's true, okay? Really, really. I'm seriously not looking. It just happened to be in my field of vision and caught my attention for an instant.*

"Relax, Yukinoshita. His rotten eyes and shady character are precisely what give him a good grasp of self-preservation and calculating risk versus return. He'll never do anything that would get him arrested. You can trust in his mild, low-level creepiness."

"None of that was complimentary in the slightest," I protested. "You don't mean all that, right? It's not about calculation of risk versus reward or self-preservation. Why can't you just tell her that I have common sense?"

"A low-level creep... I see..."

"She's not even listening, and she's convinced!"

Perhaps Ms. Hiratsuka's persuasion had borne fruit, or perhaps my low-level creepiness had won her trust. Either way, Yukinoshita communicated her decision in a very undesirable manner. "Well, if it's a request from a teacher, I can't just refuse... I will comply." She acquiesced as if the idea was *really* unpleasant.

The teacher smiled in satisfaction. "I see! Then I'll let you take it from here," she said, excusing herself briskly.

Then there was me, left behind, standing there.

Frankly, I would have been much more at ease if she had left me all alone. My usual solitary environment calms my soul. The *tick, tick, tick* sound of the second hand of the clock seemed awfully slow and excessively loud.

Come on, come on, is this for real? Suddenly a rom-com development? This is making me royally anxious here. I'm not complaining about this situation as a premise, though.

Unintentionally, some bittersweet memories from my middle-school days came back to me.

It was after school, and two students were alone together in a class-room. A gentle breeze rippled the curtains, slanted sunlight flowing in, and there was a boy who had worked up his courage to confess his love. Even now I can remember her voice in every detail.

Can't we just be friends?

Oh man, what a crappy memory. And forget being friends—I'd never even spoken to her after that. In the aftermath, I'd developed an impression that friends are people who don't even talk to each other. I guess what I'm trying to say is, even if I were to end up alone with a beautiful girl, I'd never be part of a rom-com.

But having endured such advanced training for this very situation, I'm not falling into that trap again. Girls only ever show interest in hot guys (LOL) and normies (LOL), and once they have, they engage in impure relations with said individuals.

In other words, they are my enemies.

I've gone to a lot of trouble to avoid ever feeling that way again. The easiest way not to get involved in a rom-com plot is to make girls hate you. Sometimes you must lose the battle to win the war. If you want to protect your pride, you don't need people to like you!

And that's why instead of greeting her, I decided to threaten her with a glare. *I'll kill her with my wild-beast eyes! Grrrrr!*

Yukinoshita looked at me like I was a piece of garbage. She narrowed her large eyes and let out a cold sigh. And then, in a voice like the murmuring of a clear stream, she spoke to me:

"Don't just stand there growling like some animal. Sit down."

"Uh–ah–okay. Sorry."

Whoa, what was that look in her eyes? Was *she* a wild beast? She'd definitely killed five people, just like those animals that chomped on Tomoko Matsushima. She even made me reflexively apologize. I didn't have to go so far as to try to intimidate her. She already considered me an enemy. Terrified to the core, I deposited myself in an empty chair.

Yukinoshita left it at that and, without showing any interest in me at all, had at some point opened her paperback again. I heard the soft slide of a turning page. She had a book cover on it, so I couldn't see what she was reading but figured it was something literary. Like Salinger or Hemingway or Tolstoy or something. That's the kind of impression I got from her.

Yukinoshita sat there like a princess, looking very much the top student and also in no way less beautiful than her reputation purported. However, as is usual with people of that race, Yukino Yukinoshita was an individual who lived apart from the crowd. Living up to her name, she was the snow under the snow. No matter how beautiful she was, she was untouchable and unattainable: You could only fantasize about her beauty.

Frankly, it had never occurred to me that I would be able to get close to her through an unfathomable series of events like this. If I bragged to friends about this, they'd be envious for sure. Not that I had any friends to brag to.

So what was I supposed to do with this gorgeous princess before me?

"What?" Perhaps in reaction to all my staring, Yukinoshita furrowed her brows in displeasure and looked up at me.

"Oh, sorry. I was just wondering what's up here."

"What?"

"Well, I got dragged here with no real explanation," I replied.

Instead of clicking her tongue at me, she showed her ill humor by vigorously snapping her paperback shut. She glared at me as if she were looking at an insect, gave a sigh of resignation, and spoke.

"Okay. Then let's play a game."

"A game?"

"Yes. A game to guess what club this is. Okay, so what club is this?"

Playing a game alone with a girl...

Now this was coming off as some kind of kinky setup, but Yukinoshita radiated no aura of temptation. She was more like a honed knife, sharp enough that if you lost, it might cost you your life. Where did that rom-com atmosphere go? This is a gambling apocalypse!

The force emanating from her bested me, and I broke into a cold sweat, casting my eyes around the classroom for clues. "There're no other club members?"

"No."

Could you still have a club without any members? I had serious doubts about that.

Honestly, there were no hints. No, wait. If you were to look at it from another angle, there were *only* hints. I'm not bragging or anything, but having been almost entirely devoid of friends since I was little, I'm pretty damn good at games you can play on your own.

I've got a fair amount of confidence in my skill with puzzle books, riddles, and things of that nature. I think I could win the All-Japan High School Quiz Championship. Well, okay—I couldn't gather enough members for a team, so I couldn't go to the event...but still.

There were a number of clues I'd managed to discern already. Assembling my hypothesis based on that, the answer should have presented itself.

"A literature club?"

"Hmm? How did you come to that?" Yukinoshita replied with mild interest.

"It wouldn't need a specialized room or any kind of equipment, and even with only a few members, the club wouldn't be disbanded. In other words, it's a club that doesn't need financial support. Furthermore, you were reading a book. You were showing me the answer all along."

Perfect deduction, if I do say so myself. Even without some bespectacled elementary school student to tell me, "Huh? Something's not right!" I could figure out this sort of thing before breakfast.

Even Princess Yukino seemed impressed as she made a quiet *mm-hmm* noise. "Wrong." Her laughter was brief and derisive. Ooh, that kind of got on my nerves! ☆ Who'd called her a paragon of good conduct, a flawless Superhuman? More like Demon Superhuman.

"Then what is it?" I asked, my voice tinged with irritation.

But Yukinoshita, seemingly unperturbed, announced that the game would continue.

"I'll give you the biggest hint. Me being here, doing this, is a club activity."

So she'd finally given me a hint. But that didn't give me any answers. In the end, it only led me to back to my same conclusion—that this was an arts and literature club.

No, wait. Wait, wait, calm down. Stay cool. Stay cool, Hachiman Hikigaya.

She'd said, *There are no club members aside from myself.*

But the club still existed.

In other words, that had to mean that there were ghost members, right? And so the punch line was that the ghost members were *actual ghosts.* And in the end, it would be a setup for a rom-com between me and a beautiful ghost girl.

"An occult research society!"

"I said it was a club."

"A-an occult research club!"

"Wrong. Haaa...ghosts? What nonsense. There's no such thing." The way she said it wasn't even slightly cute. Not like *Th-there's really no such thing as ghosts! I-I'm not saying that just because I'm scared, okay!* She considered me with eyes that held me in the deepest and most sincere contempt. Eyes that said, *Go to hell, moron.*

"I give in. I have no idea." How could I figure out something like this? *Give me something easier!* "*Why's a raven screwing around with a writing desk?*" *Anyway, that's not trivia; that's a riddle.*

"Hikigaya. How many years has it been since you last talked to a girl?"

The question came completely out of the blue, destroying my train of thought.

She's so rude.

I'm pretty confident in my memory. I remember the minute details of conversations that anyone would forget. So much so that girls in my class have treated me like a stalker. According to my superior hippocampus, the last time I'd talked to a girl had been in June, two years earlier.

> *Girl: It's seriously hot right now, huh?*
> *Me: More like humid, eh?*
> *Girl: Huh? Oh…yeah, sure, I guess.*
> The end.

Something like that. I mean, she hadn't been talking to me. It had been a girl sitting diagonally behind me.

I remember people to an uncomfortable degree. Even now, every time I remember that in the middle of the night, I want to yank the covers over my head and scream, *Aahhhhhhh!*

While I'd been off on that particular bad trip down memory lane, Yukinoshita had launched into a loud proclamation. "*Haves* giving things to *Have-nots* out of the goodness of their hearts is known as *volunteering.* Giving aid to developing nations, running soup kitchens for the homeless, and letting unpopular guys talk to girls… Lending a helping hand to people in need. That is what this club does." At some point, Yukinoshita had stood and, from that vantage, was naturally looking down on me.

"Welcome to the Service Club. We're happy to have you."

Her words didn't sound in the least bit welcoming, and hearing her made me tear up a bit. She hit hard, right where it hurt, and kicked me while I was down.

"As Ms. Hiratsuka says, great people have an obligation to help the less fortunate. I have been entrusted with this and will fulfill my responsibility. I will correct your problems for you. Be grateful."

I guess what she was implying some sort of noblesse oblige? Which meant something about the duty of nobles to help the poor or whatever.

Yukinoshita, standing there with her arms crossed, was the picture of an aristocrat. And actually, when you considered her grades and her appearance and all that, calling her an *aristocrat* wouldn't even have been an exaggeration.

"You broad…" I just had to say something. I had to explain to her using the best words I could that I was not someone to be pitied. "Listen, this might be weird to say about myself, but I'm not so shabby at academics, either, you know? On the aptitude test for humanities, I was ranked third in Japanese in my grade! I'm one of the smart ones! If you leave out the part about me not having a girlfriend or *any* friends, I've got pretty high specs, basically!"

"That part at the end included some rather fatal deficiencies, you know… But your ability to deliver it in all confidence is somewhat amazing in its own right…you weirdo. I'm creeped out already."

"Shut up! I don't want to hear that from you! You freaky chick."

She really was a freak. At the very least, she was nothing like the Yukino Yukinoshita I was acquainted with through hearsay. Though having never actually spoken to anyone, I'd really just overheard it…

I guess I considered her an aloof beauty. At that moment, she wore a cold smile. To elaborate, it was sadistic. "Hmph. Based on what I've seen, the reason you're all alone is that rotten personality and those twisted sensibilities of yours."

Yukinoshita clenched her fist as she spoke passionately. "First, since you clearly feel so uncomfortable here, let's give you a place to belong.

Did you know? Just having somewhere you belong can save you from a tragic end like becoming a star and burning out of existence."

" 'The Nighthawk's Star'? How obscure can you get?" Someone with lesser academic prowess than myself, ranked third in Japanese, would never have gotten that reference. Plus, I like that story, so I remember it well. It's so sad, it actually brings a tear to my eye. Especially the part where nobody likes him.

Yukinoshita's eyes widened in surprise at my retort. "That's unexpected. I didn't think an average, mediocre high school boy would be reading Kenji Miyazawa."

"Did you just slip in a remark implying my inferiority?"

"I'm sorry. That was going too far. It would be correct to say below average."

"You meant you were going too far in the positive direction?! Didn't you hear the part about me being ranked third in my grade?"

"Bragging over a mere third-place ranking alone marks you as an inferior individual. Trying to demonstrate your cognitive abilities through your grades in a single class alone is imbecilic."

How rude could you get? She was treating a boy she'd only just met as an inferior being. The only other person I can think of who does that is a Saiyan prince.

"But 'The Nighthawk's Star' suits you. The appearance of the nighthawk in particular."

"Are you saying I'm disfigured?"

"I couldn't say that. The truth can be too painful to hear sometimes after all..."

"You basically just said it..."

Yukinoshita's expression turned serious as she patted me on the shoulder. "Don't avert your eyes from the truth. Look at reality...and a mirror."

"Hey, hey, hey! It might be weird for me to say this about myself, but my face is well proportioned. My own sister's even told me, 'If you only kept your mouth shut...' It would be more accurate to say that my face is the only good thing about me." That's my sister, all right. She's got sharp eyes. The girls at this school really have no taste compared to her!

Yukinoshita pressed her hand to her temple as if she had a headache. "How dumb are you? Beauty is an entirely subjective measure. In other words, here, where you and I are the only people present, what I say is the only truth."

"Y-your logic is ridiculous, but for some reason, it kind of makes sense..."

"And even without taking into consideration your difficulties, when a boy has rotten fish-eyes like you do, it's inevitable he'd give off a bad impression, anyway. I'm not commenting on your individual features. It's your expression that's ugly. It's proof that your heart is twisted."

Says the girl with the cute face and all that nasty stuff on the inside. She had a look in her eye like that of a hardened criminal. Maybe we were both what they call the *utterly uncute.*

But for real, were my eyes really that fishlike? If I were a girl, I'd spin that into something positive, saying something like *Huh? Do I look that much like the Little Mermaid?*

While I drifted through my escapist fantasy, Yukinoshita swept back the hair on her shoulders and announced triumphantly, "I don't like people who boost their egos through such superficial metrics as grades or looks, anyway. Oh, and I don't like that rotten look in your eyes, either."

"Enough about my eyes already!"

"Indeed. There's nothing you can do about them at this point, anyway."

"It's about time for you to apologize to my parents." I could feel my face twitching all over the place.

Yukinoshita's expression fell as if she regretted her words. "You're right. That was a mean thing to say. Your parents are surely suffering the most."

"Fine! My bad! Or rather, my face is bad." When I pleaded to her on the verge of tears, Yukinoshita finally sheathed her sharp tongue.

I was now enlightened to the fact that there was no point in saying anything to her anymore. And while I indulged a vision of myself meditating cross-legged at the foot of a linden tree and attaining nirvana, Yukinoshita continued the exchange.

"Now your practice conversation with an actual person is complete. If you can speak with a girl like me, you should be able to speak to most ordinary people."

Smoothing down her hair with her right hand, Yukinoshita's expression beamed with accomplishment. And then she smiled. "Now with this wonderful memory in your heart, you'll have the strength to go live your life alone."

"Your solution to my problem is beyond bizarre."

"But that in and of itself isn't sufficient to satisfy the teacher's request... I have to address the root of the matter... What if you quit school?"

"That's not a solution. That's just like putting a Band-Aid on a pimple."

"Oh, so you're aware that you're a pimple?"

"Yeah, because everyone calls me a pain in the butt—and shut up!"

"You're so annoying."

I smiled at last, having said something witty, and Yukinoshita glared at me with eyes that asked, *Why are you alive?* I'm telling you, she's got a scary look.

Then it got quiet enough to make my ears hurt. In actuality, they probably also hurt from all of Yukinoshita's insults. The rude sound of the door being roughly pulled aside rang through the room, breaking the silence. "Yukinoshita. Sorry to interrupt."

"A knock..."

"Sorry, sorry. Oh, don't worry about me—do go on! I just dropped by to see how things were going." Ms. Hiratsuka leaned against the wall of the classroom, smiling coolly at an exasperated Yukinoshita. She looked back and forth between the two of us. "I'm glad you two seem to be getting along."

Why and where the hell did she get that idea?

"You keep working on fixing that twisted character of yours and correcting those rotten, sordid eyes. I'm going back now. Go home by the time school is over, you two."

"H-hold on a minute, please!" I reached for the teacher's hand, trying to stop her. Immediately, I was wailing, "Ow! Ow, ow, ow, ow! Uncle! Uncle, uncle!" as she twisted my arm. I frantically tried tapping out until she finally let me go.

"Oh, that was you, Hikigaya? Don't stand behind me like that. I'll end up using my moves on you rather ungently."

"Are you Golgo or what?! And you meant *accidentally*, right? Don't do it *ungently*!"

"You sure have a lot of questions for me right now. Is something wrong?"

"There's something wrong with you! What do you mean, *correct* me? You're making me sound like a juvenile delinquent! What the heck is with this place, anyway?" I demanded.

Ms. Hiratsuka went *hmm* and put a hand to her chin, briefly adopting a thoughtful expression. "Yukinoshita didn't explain it to you? In short, the goal of this club is to stimulate personal transformation and resolve people's worries. I guide students here who I believe are in need of change. Think of it as the Hyperbolic Time Chamber. Or would it be easier to understand if I just called it *Revolutionary Girl Utena*?"

"That's needlessly difficult to understand, and those examples give away your age."

"Did you say something?" She shot me a murderously cold look.

"No." I muttered quietly, hunching my shoulders.

Seeing me like that, Ms. Hiratsuka sighed. "Yukinoshita. It seems you're having trouble correcting him."

"The problem is he isn't even aware of his own issues," Yukinoshita replied, indifferent to our teacher's pained countenance.

Why did I suddenly feel like I wanted to bolt? It felt like that time in sixth grade when my parents found out I had a porno mag and lectured me over and over about it.

No, that's not what I should be thinking about right now.

"Um...you keep talking about my correction or transformation or reformation or girl revolution or whatever and having fun chattering away together without me, but I don't really want any of that," I said.

Ms. Hiratsuka tilted her head to the side, dubiously. "Oh?"

"What are you talking about? If you don't change, you'll be in deep trouble, socially speaking." Yukinoshita regarded me as if her argument were as sound as *No more war! Abandon nuclear weapons!* "From what I can see, you are markedly lacking in humanity. You don't want to change that? Have no desire to improve yourself?"

"That's not what I mean. Like...um...I'm saying I don't want to talk about myself to people who are telling me, 'Change! Change now!' If I changed just because someone told me to, that new person wouldn't even be me, anyway! And besides, the self is just—"

"You just can't see yourself objectively," Yukinoshita interrupted, preventing me from snatching a quote from Descartes in an attempt to sound deep. It would have been a great line, really. "You're just running away. You can't move forward if you don't change." She cut me down in a single stroke. Why was she so sharp? Were her parents sea urchins or what?

"What's wrong with running? You keep saying, 'Change, change!' like the village idiot who only knows one word. What'll you do next? Face the sun and say, 'The brightness from the west is too harsh and keeps bothering everyone, so today, please set in the east!'?"

"That's just sophistry. Don't shift the conversation. The sun isn't even what's moving, anyway—it's the Earth. Do you not know Copernican theory, either?"

"It was obviously a metaphor! If you're calling that sophistry, then what you're saying is sophistry, too! In the end, I would only be changing to escape reality. Who's the one running now? If you're really *not* running, then you wouldn't change. You'd make a stand right there. Why can't I affirm who I am at present and who I was in the past?"

"...If that were true, then no worries could be solved and no one could be saved." The moment the words *no one could be saved* came out of her mouth, Yukinoshita's outraged expression became truly blood-curdling. Reflexively, I flinched. I was almost ready to break into an apologetic *S-s-s-sorry!*

In the first place, words like *save* aren't really something a high schooler usually says. I had no idea what it was that drove her to feel so strongly about this.

"Calm down, both of you." The sound of Ms. Hiratsuka's level voice relieved the current stormy atmosphere...or rather, the storm that had been there from the start. I looked at the teacher's face, and she was honestly grinning and joyful. She looked like she was having fun.

"This has gotten entertaining. I love developments like this. It's sort of like *Shonen Jump!* Great, right?" She was getting *excited* about this for some reason. Though a grown woman, her eyes sparkled like a little boy's. "Since time immemorial, the way of *shonen* manga has been to resolve a clash of perspectives on justice by means of competition."

"Uh...what are you talking about?" I was talking, but she wasn't listening.

Our teacher unleashed a boisterous laugh, faced us, and loudly proclaimed: "So let's do this. You're going to guide the lost lambs who come to you. Save them according to your individual principles and prove their veracity as much as you see fit. Who can serve others the best? Gundam Fight! Ready? Go!"

"No." Yukinoshita refused bluntly. Her gaze conveyed an iciness equivalent to what she'd been leveling at me a moment earlier. Well, I felt the same way, so I figured I'd nod. Plus, G-Gundam is old.

Discovering her students' shared feelings on the matter, the teacher bit her thumbnail in frustration. "Ngh... It would have been easier to understand if I'd said 'Robattle,' huh?"

"That's not the issue here..." Medabots? *That's way too obscure.*

"Teacher, please stop getting carried away in a manner unbefitting your age. It's really painful to watch." Like hurling an icicle, Yukinoshita flung her sharp, frigid words at our instructor.

That seemed to cool Ms. Hiratsuka down, and after the color of shame faded from her face, she cleared her throat as though it had never happened. "A-anyway! The only way you can prove that you are righteous is through action! I told you to compete, so you're going to have a competition! You have no right to refuse."

"This is complete tyranny…"

She's an utter child! The only adult part of her is her chest! Oh well, I just have to pretend I give a crap about this competition and then be like, "Tee-hee! Aw, I lost! ☆ " Participation counts, as they say. What a wonderful and convenient idea.

But that horrid little-girl-on-the-inside, giant-boobs-on-the-outside womanchild continued spewing her absurdities. "In order to make you two fight with all you've got, I'll give you an incentive. How about the victor being able to order the loser to do anything?"

"Anything?!" Anything means, you know, *that*. That is to say, anything. *Gulp.*

There was the sound of a chair scraping as Yukinoshita drew back two meters and adopted a defensive stance. "With *him* as my competition, I feel a threat to my virtue, and so I refuse."

"That's prejudice! Second-year boys aren't necessarily *always* thinking obscene thoughts!" *We're thinking of, um…lots of other things! Like… world peace? Yeah…we're not thinking of much else.*

"So even Yukino Yukinoshita is afraid of something… Are you that unsure of your ability to win?" Ms. Hiratsuka asked, her face adopting a nasty semblance.

Yukinoshita looked a little sullen. "Fine. Though I find it rather vexing to give in to such cheap provocation, I will accept your challenge and deal with him while I'm at it."

Whoa, Yukinoshita sure hates losing! What gave me that impression, you ask? Only an extremely competitive person would have added that I can tell you're provoking me part. But what did she mean by *dealing with me? That's scary. Cut it out.*

"So it's settled." The teacher smiled smugly, ignoring the mental daggers Yukinoshita was tossing at her.

"Huh? What about what I want?"

"From that leer on your face, I don't even have to ask."

Well, yeah, but…

"I will be the judge of this competition. My judgment will be arbitrary and biased, of course. Don't overthink it; just do whatever… I mean, do your best to be reasonable and appropriate."

Tossing that line over her shoulder, our instructor exited the classroom. In her wake stood myself and a very unhappy-looking Yukinoshita. Of course, we weren't talking to each other.

In the silence, I heard a crackling as if from a broken radio. It was the precursor to the bell ringing. When that very synthetic-sounding melody rang out, Yukinoshita shut her book with a snap. It was time to go home. Taking that as her signal, Yukinoshita briskly began preparing to leave. She tucked the paperback she'd been holding neatly in her bag and stood. Then she glanced at me.

But she just looked at me and then left without a word. Sparing not so much as a *bye* or *later*, she strode briskly out the door. Her demeanor was so frigid, I didn't even have a chance to say anything to her.

And then I was left there, all alone.

What an unlucky day it'd been. I got called to the teachers' room, press-ganged into joining some mysterious club, verbally abused by a wastefully cute girl… I'd suffered a lot. Wasn't talking to a girl supposed to make your heart leap? My heart'd done nothing but sink! I'd rather have talked to my usual conversational partner, a stuffed animal, than endure all that! A stuffed animal doesn't give you any lip. It smiles at you kindly. Why couldn't I have been born a masochist?

And what's more, how'd I get forced into this incomprehensible competition? *I don't even think I can beat Yukinoshita.*

But, like…club activities and competitions and all that stuff sounds all right from an outsider's perspective, doesn't it? Personally, when it came to club activities, my idea of participating was just watching some DVDs of girls in a rock-band club. *This* turn of events was not going to make us friends. More likely, Yukinoshita would just calmly tell me, *Your breath smells, so could you please not breathe for three hours?*

Youth really is a lie.

Losing the sports tournament in your final year and then making it all out to be some beautiful thing by crying… Failing your university entrance exams and then taking a year off to try and study to take the test again the next year, all the while fooling yourself by saying that failure is life experience… Bragging about how you're just being considerate of your crush and letting her go so you can pretend it's not just about you being unable express your feelings—

And one more thing. That's right. Thinking that haughty, rage-inducing girl's a tsundere—*all hard candy shell on the outside with a gooey center that'll ultimately expose itself and lead to a rom-com? Never gonna happen.*

I won't accept that my essay needs revision. Youth really is false, fraudulent, and fictitious nonsense.

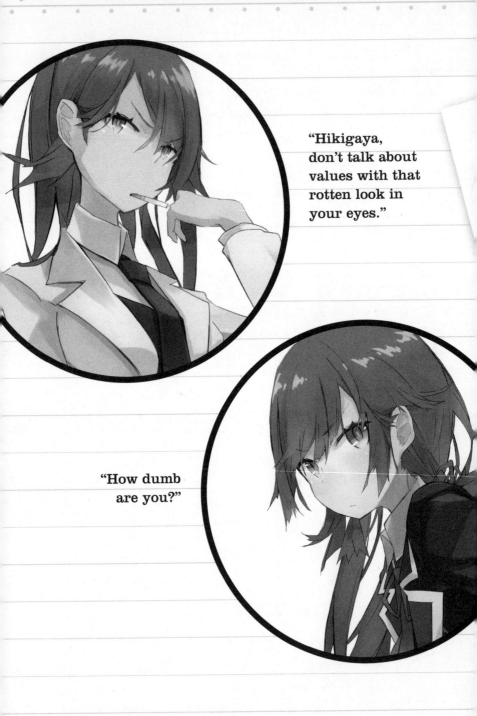

"Hikigaya, don't talk about values with that rotten look in your eyes."

"How dumb are you?"

Guidance Counseling Survey

Soubu Secondary School   Grade: 2nd Year   Class: F

Name: **Hachiman Hikigaya**

(M) / F

Attendance no. 29

What is a personal value you hold dear?

Values or mottoes or beliefs or whatever aren't things you go out of your way to declare. They're things you should hide inside yourself. That's my personal value.

In your grad yearbook, what did you write as your dream for the future?

I didn't have space to write anything.

What are you doing now to prepare for your future?

Forgetting my past trauma.

Teacher's comments:

I'm so relieved to see such a fittingly rotten personal value. Was that incident with the yearbook traumatic, too? In your case, you keep causing your own daily high school traumas, so it's like a vicious cycle of suffer and forget. Maybe you should give up?

Yukino Yukinoshita always stands firm.

I left class after homeroom to find Ms. Hiratsuka waiting for me. Her arms were crossed, and she was drawn up to her full height, looking exactly like a prison guard. A military uniform and a whip would suit her to a T. Well, school is basically like a prison, so it's not really much of a leap to imagine her wearing that. She's like something out of Alcatraz or Cassandra. Why couldn't a Savior of Century's End show up right about now?

"Hikigaya. It's club time," she announced, and I suddenly felt my blood drain away. *Oh, crap. She's taking me to the slammer. If she's escorting me to the clubroom, I'm really gonna start despairing about my life at this school. Yukinoshita is a natural-born condescender. She doesn't just have a sharp tongue. What she says is verbal abuse, plain and simple. She's not* tsundere. *She's just an unpleasant woman.*

But Ms. Hiratsuka exercised no sympathy for me as she gave me a cold, robotic smile. "Let's go," she said, trying to take my arm. When I deftly dodged her grab, her arm shot out again, and I slipped away from that, too.

"Um, you know, on the grounds that a school education values students' autonomy and promotes their independence, I think I really must object to this show of force."

"Unfortunately, school is actually a place where you're trained to conform to society. Once you go out into the world, your opinion means nothing. Get used to compulsion now." No sooner had she said that than her fist flew at me. It hit me in the stomach with a penetrating thud, knocking the wind out of me.

Taking advantage of my immobility, Ms. Hiratsuka grabbed my arm. "You know what'll happen the next time you try to run, right? Don't cause any more trouble for my fist."

"You've already decided to punch me again?" *I can't handle any more pain.*

Once we started walking, the warden opened her mouth as if just remembering something. "Oh yeah. If you run away again, I'll declare your competition with Yukinoshita forfeit, period, with additional punishment tacked on for good measure. Don't fool yourself into thinking you'll be able to graduate on time."

She's totally screwing with both my future and my mental health.

Heels clicking on the floor, Ms. Hiratsuka strode along beside me. Looking at the two of us in a certain way, though, her hand on my arm kind of made her look like a call girl cosplaying as a teacher as we left a club where she'd picked me up for a date.

There were three ways in which this scenario wasn't like that. First, I hadn't paid her. Second, she wasn't resting her hand on my arm; she was twisting my elbow as far as it would go. Finally, I wasn't happy or in the least bit excited. The tip of my elbow was brushing the teacher's boob, but even that wasn't doing it for me. She was taking me to that clubroom.

"Um, I'm not gonna run away or anything, so I'm okay on my own. I mean, I'm always alone, anyway. I'm totally fine on my own. I can't relax if I'm *not* on my own."

"Don't say such lonely things. I want to go with you." She gave a sudden—verging on kind—smile. It was completely different from her usual leering smirk, and this abrupt departure from the norm set my heart beating a little faster. "I'd rather escort you, no matter how much you hate it, than end up grinding my teeth because you got away. It's less psychological stress for me this way."

"What a terrible reason!"

"What are you talking about? If you don't want to go, there's nothing I can do about that, but I'm taking you to this club right now for *your* sake. So you can be corrected. This is the beautiful love between a teacher and her student."

"This is love? If *this* is love, I don't need it."

"Despite that sad excuse you used to try to get away, you really are twisted. Maybe you're so twisted up, it reversed all your meridians. Don't go building a Holy Emperor Cross Mausoleum or something."

You like your manga just a little too much, don't you?

"You'd be cuter if you were a little less contrary. It can't be very much fun, having such a backward view of the world."

"Life isn't just about fun. If it were, there wouldn't be any sad Hollywood movies. There *is* such a thing as finding pleasure in tragedy, you know."

"Classic Hikigaya. Many young people have a distorted worldview, but *you* take it to a pathological level. It's like that special affliction kids get after their first year of high school… You have a full-blown case of *second-year head swell.*" Beaming, Ms. Hiratsuka diagnosed my condition.

"Wow, that's kind of mean, treating me like I'm diseased. And what the heck is 'second-year head swell' even supposed to mean?"

"You like manga and anime, right?" Ms. Hiratsuka changed the subject, ignoring my request for an explanation.

"I guess I don't hate them."

"Why do you like them?"

"Well…they're part of Japanese culture and recognized as a form of pop culture we can take pride in on a global level, so it would be unnatural to *not* acknowledge their relevance. The market for it has expanded, too, so they're also important from an economic perspective."

"Mm-hmm. So what about regular arts and literature? Do you like Keigo Higashino or Koutarou Isaka?"

"I read them, but frankly, I prefer their work from before they got popular."

"What light novel imprints do you like?"

"Gagaga and Kodansha BOX. Well, I don't know if the latter counts as an imprint or not. What's with the interrogation?"

"Mm-hmm… It's just as I expected—and I mean that in a bad way. You've got a serious case of second-year HS." My would-be diagnostician regarded me with dismay.

"Like I said, what the heck is that?"

"Second-year head swell is just what it sounds like. It's a frame of mind common among high school students. They think that being twisted is cool and have a tendency to parrot ideas popularized on the Internet, like 'Get a job and you lose!' and the like. They claim they were fans of popular authors 'before they got famous.' They disparage things everyone else loves and applaud the obscure. What's more, they look down on their fellow nerds. They wield twisted logic while simultaneously projecting an aura of having achieved a bizarre sort of enlightenment. In a word, they're dicks."

"I'm a dick…? Damn it! It's basically all true! I can't even argue!"

"Oh, that was a compliment, though. Students these days are really good at separating themselves from reality. As a teacher, I can't manage it all. I feel like I'm working in a factory."

"Students these days, huh?" A sarcastic smile slipped out of me. Here come the clichés. I considered casually overturning her argument out of boredom.

Ms. Hiratsuka looked me right in the eye and shrugged. "You look like you have something to say about that, but that kind of behavior is exactly what indicates you have the disease."

"Is that right?"

"Don't get the wrong idea here. This is all sincere praise. I like you. You haven't given up on thinking. Even if it is twisted thinking."

Hearing the words *I like you* got me a little choked up, putting me at a loss for words. I struggled to come up with a retort to that unfamiliar phrase.

"So from your twisted perspective, how do you see Yukino Yukinoshita?"

"She's a jerk," I replied instantly. I believed so strongly that she was a jerk that it was as if she'd told me, *I think you should give up on "Concrete Road."*

"I see." Ms. Hiratsuka smiled wryly. "She's an incredibly gifted student, though… I suppose the elites of the world must have their own problems to deal with, too. But she's a very nice girl."

In what universe?! I mentally clicked my tongue.

"I'm sure she's ill in some way, too. She's kind and generally in the right. But the world is unkind and full of wrongs. It must be hard for her to live in it."

"Aside from the part where she's kind and in the right, I'm mostly in agreement with you about the world," I said, and my teacher gave me a look that said, *I know, right?*

"You…you kids really are twisted after all. There are parts of you that I don't think will conform well to society, and that worries me. That's why I want to gather all of you in one place."

"That club is an isolation ward?!"

"You could say that. I like watching you students; you entertain me. So perhaps I just want to keep you close at hand."

Smiling merrily, she twisted my arm, which was becoming habitual. Maybe she'd gotten that MMA-esque move from some manga. My elbow occasionally touched her voluptuous bust while emitting a horrible creaking noise.

Phew… With my arm twisted so far, even I'd have had trouble slipping away from her. It was frustrating, but I had no choice but to placate myself with the sensation for a little while longer.

Yes, indeed. It really was too bad.

It occurred to me that boobs came in pairs, so shouldn't *bust* be a plural, like *busts*?

X   X   X

Once we got to the special-use building, I guess Ms. Hiratsuka wasn't worried about me running away anymore, so she finally released me.

But even then, as she was walking out, she glanced back at me. Her look didn't say she wanted to see me a little longer or that she didn't want to leave me. There was no trace of any of that. No, the impression I got was one of pure murderous intent as though warning, *If you even try to run, you know what'll happen, right?*

Smiling bitterly, I walked down the hallway. The corner of the special-use building was as still as death, with a chilly draft flowing through it.

Though there had to have been other clubs engaging in their activities at the time, their noise apparently didn't carry this far. I don't know if that was because of the location or a result of the mysterious aura emanating from Yukino Yukinoshita.

I put my hand on the door to slide it open. To be honest, my heart felt heavy, but it would have bothered me to run away simply because of that. Basically, I just had to not give a crap about anything she said. I wouldn't think of us as two people in a room together. It was instead one person and one other person. I wouldn't feel awkward or uncomfortable if she were a total stranger to me.

Today I would be initiating "Being Alone Isn't Scary" strategy number one: If you see a stranger, think of them as a stranger. By the way, there is no strategy number two. Essentially, I think that awkward feeling is caused by looming thoughts like *I have to talk about something* or *I have to be friends with this person.* I mean, when you sit down on a train next to someone, you'd never think, *Oh man, we're all alone! This is so awkward!* If I approached it that way, she'd give up. She would just sit quietly and read her book.

When I opened the door to the clubroom, Yukinoshita looked exactly the same as she had the day before, sitting there reading.

I opened the door but didn't know what to say to her. I just made a small bow and walked toward her.

Yukinoshita regarded me briefly and then went back to her paperback.

"I'm this close, right here in front of you, and you're going to ignore me?"

She was so committed to ignoring me, I wondered for a moment if I'd turned into air. This was exactly how I felt in class every day.

"What a strange greeting. What tribe are you from?"

"…Good afternoon." Unable to endure her sarcasm, the greeting drilled into me since preschool popped out of my mouth, and when it did, Yukinoshita smiled.

I think this was the first time she'd ever smiled at me. It taught me some useless factoids—like that when she smiles, she gets dimples and her canines poke out a little bit.

"Good afternoon. I thought you wouldn't come again."

Frankly, I think that smile was foul play. Foul play on the level of Maradona's Hand of God. In other words, in the end, I had no choice but to accept it. "I-I just came because if I'd run away, I'd have lost the competition! D-don't get the wrong idea!" That was a slightly rom-com-ish exchange. But usually, the positions of the guy and the girl are reversed. This wasn't right.

Yukinoshita didn't appear particularly offended by my statement. Rather, she just kept on talking as if unconcerned that I'd replied at all. "I think getting dressed down that badly would stop the average person from ever coming again. Are you a masochist?"

"No!"

"A stalker, then?"

"Not that, either! Hey, why are these guesses based on the assumption that I like you?"

"You don't?" The jerk just nonchalantly tilted her head to the side, a baffled expression on her face. It was kind of cute but not worth the cost of this exchange.

"No way! Even I'm turned off by your massive ego."

"Oh? I got the impression that you liked me," she said, her expression cold and neutral as always, showing no surprise.

It's true: Yukinoshita did have a cute face. She was so cute that even someone like me, who didn't have a single friend in this school, knew about her. There was no doubt she was one of the hottest girls in school.

But even so, her ego was abnormal.

"What kind of upbringing makes you believe such naive bullcrap? Was every day your birthday? Was your boyfriend Santa Claus?" It would've had to be something like that for her to have developed such a relentlessly optimistic brain. If she continued down this path, she was sure to meet a sorry end. She had to correct that trajectory before she did something that couldn't be undone.

Against my better judgment, the human kindness inside me stirred. I chose my words carefully to soften the blow. "Yukinoshita. You're abnormal. Don't think otherwise. Get a lobotomy or something."

"You should be a little more tactful. For your own good." Yukinoshita snickered as she looked at me, but her eyes weren't smiling… Terrifying. To her credit, she didn't call me garbage or trash or whatever. Frankly, if her face wasn't so cute, I would most certainly have been punching it. "Well, from the perspective of an inferior being such as yourself, I may seem abnormal, but to me, this is the epitome of common sense. Experience has taught me that I am right." Yukinoshita proudly threw out her chest and chuckled smugly.

It's funny. That bearing is quite attractive on her.

"Experience, huh…?" Her putting it that way made me think she must indeed have had a Santa Claus boyfriend. Her appearance alone was enough to convince me of it.

"You must be having such a fun time at school, then," I muttered with a sigh.

Yukinoshita twitched. "I-indeed I am. Quite frankly, my time here has wanted for neither too much nor too little of anything. It's been a very placid experience," she said, but for some reason, she was facing the other way. And thanks to that pose, I gathered another fatally useless factoid: the gentle line from her chin to her neck was rather beautiful.

Watching her, I belatedly realized something. I think if I'd been calmer, I would have noticed it right away, though. It was completely impossible for such a naturally condescending egotist to construct normal human relationships, and thus, it was impossible that her life at school could be going as smoothly as she claimed.

Let's just ask her about that...

"Hey. You have any friends?" I inquired.

Yukinoshita averted her gaze. "Well, first, can you define exactly what constitutes a 'friend'?"

"Oh, never mind. Only someone who has no friends would ask that."

Source: me.

Honestly, though, I didn't know what exactly counted as a friend, either. I think it's about time someone explains to me how it's different from an acquaintance. Are you friends if you meet someone once and siblings if you see them everyday? Mi-Do-Fa-Do-Re-Si-So-La-O? Why is "O" the only part of that name that isn't a note in the musical scale? Details matter, damn it!

The designations used to differentiate friends and acquaintances are pretty suspect to begin with. It's especially striking with girls. Even when you're in the same class, I feel like you have to rank them as classmates, friends, or best friends. So then where do you draw the line between those categories?

But let's get back on topic.

"Well, I can see you having no friends, so yeah, never mind."

"I didn't say I have none, now did I? Even if I didn't have any, it wouldn't necessarily be disadvantageous."

"Oh, okay. Of course. Yeah, yeah." I smoothly brushed aside her excuse as she glowered at me. "But, like, how do you have no friends if everybody likes you?"

Yukinoshita looked indignant. Then she turned away, seemingly displeased, and opened her mouth. "I'm sure you wouldn't understand." Her cheeks were slightly puffed out as she fixed her gaze in the opposite direction.

Well, Yukinoshita and I are completely different individuals, so I wouldn't understand what she was feeling, not in the slightest. Even if she were to tell me, I'm sure it would be difficult to grasp. No matter how far you go, in the end, people can never really understand one another.

But on this subject, on solitude… This is the one area in which I think I could relate to her.

"Well, it's not like I don't see your point. You can have fun on your own. I'm actually disgusted by the idea that a person can't be alone."

…

Yukinoshita considered me for an instant before flicking her gaze away again and closing her eyes. She seemed to be thinking about something.

"You're alone because you want to be, so it's irritating when people pity you for it. I get that, I get that."

"Where does an inferior entity like you get off treating me like one of your own? It's quite vexing," she complained, trying to dispel her irritation by combing back her hair.

"Well, though you and I are people of a very different caliber, I can sympathize with the sentiment of being alone because you want to be. Though it pains me to say so," she added, grinning in mild self-deprecation. It was a slightly dark but also peaceful smile.

"What do you mean, 'people of a different caliber'? I have a very informed opinion on the art of aloneness. I'm so informed, you could even call me the Master Loner. The idea that someone like you could preach about being a loner is actually absurd."

"What's this…? Suddenly you come across as such a strong, reliable—if slightly sorrowful—man." Yukinoshita gaped at me with shock and surprise on her face.

Satisfied to have elicited that reaction from her, I continued triumphantly, "You can't call yourself lonely. Everyone loves you. You're a disgrace to real loners."

Suddenly, Yukinoshita's expression morphed into a derisive smile. "What a simplistic notion. Do you operate purely off reflexes from your spinal cord? Do you even know what it's like, having people like you?

Oh, I forgot. You've never experienced that. I should have taken that into consideration. I'm sorry."

"If you're going to bother being considerate, at least see it through to the end." *I guess this is what they call fake politeness. She really is a serious jerk.*

"So what's it like having everyone like you, then?" I asked.

Yukinoshita closed her eyes briefly to consider. With great effort, she cleared her throat and opened her mouth. "As a person whom no one likes, you hearing this may be unpleasant."

"Everything that comes out of your mouth is unpleasant, anyway, so don't worry about it," I reassured her, and Yukinoshita took a small breath.

There was no way I could feel worse than I already did. Our last exchange had left me feeling like I'd had more than enough already—like that time I ordered unlimited ramen.

"I've always been cute, so most boys who approach me are attracted to me."

Uncle.

This was filling like double veggies and extra spices.

But now that she'd made such an impressive declaration, I couldn't leave my seat. I would suck it up and wait for her to continue.

"I think it was from about fifth or sixth grade. Ever since then…" She tapered off, her expression growing rather melancholy compared to before.

That was just under five years. I wondered what on earth it was like to be constantly showered with attention from the opposite sex. Frankly, as someone who's been showered with loathing from the opposite sex for just under about sixteen years, I can't imagine it. As a guy who doesn't even get Valentine's chocolate from his own mother, I don't understand that world. The way I see it, she's a member of that smugly smiling team of winners at life. She's just gonna force me to endure more ridiculous bragging.

But…it's also true that because her vector in that area is positive while mine's deeply in the negative, it was difficult for me to handle an open expression of emotion from her. It was like standing stark naked in the ravaging winds of a storm. It was as bad as being denounced by a classroom kangaroo court. It was very much the hell of being made to stand alone in front of the chalkboard, surrounded by your classmates on all sides as they clap in unison, chanting, *Apologize! Apologize!*

That really did suck. That was the only time I've ever cried at school. But that's enough about me for now.

"Well, it's got to be a lot better than being constantly hated right and left. You've been pampered. Pampered!" The unpleasant memories surfacing in my mind set off my mouth.

At that, Yukinoshita heaved a short sigh. She summoned something very closely resembling a smile but was clearly a different expression altogether. "I never asked people to like me," she declared, before adding, "Or perhaps, I would have rather had someone like me for real."

"What?" My response was entirely involuntary. Her comment had been delivered in a vanishingly quiet whisper.

Yukinoshita turned to me again, her mien serious. "How would you feel if you had a friend who was always popular with girls?"

"What a dumb question. I don't have any friends, so it's not something I'd worry about." What a strong, masculine retort! I'd surprised even myself with my instantaneous-to-the-point-of-interruption improv rejoinder.

Yukinoshita must have shared my surprise. She was left speechless, her jaw hanging slack. "For an instant, I entertained the delusion that you might have said something cool." She gently touched her hand to her temple, as if beset by a headache or something, and cast her eyes down. "Just give me an answer, speaking hypothetically."

"I'd kill him."

Seemingly satisfied with the immediacy of my reply, Yukinoshita nodded. "See? You would attempt to exclude that individual, wouldn't you? Just like an irrational animal…no, inferior to one, even. At the schools I've attended, there were a lot of people like that. I suppose they were all just pitiful souls who employed that sort of behavior as self-validation." Yukinoshita snorted.

A girl hated by other girls. There was indeed a category of that nature. I've learned *something* from my ten years at school. I wasn't necessarily immersed in it, but I got that much just by watching from the sidelines. No, I understood it precisely *because* I was watching from the sidelines. I'm sure that Yukinoshita had always been in the middle of it, and that was exactly why she was surrounded by enemies. I could imagine what would happen to someone like that.

"In elementary school, my indoor shoes were hidden about sixty times, and for about fifty of those incidents, girls in my class were responsible."

"I want to know about those last ten times."

"Boys hid them three times. Teachers bought them from me twice. The dog made off with them five times."

"That's a high dog statistic." That bit had surpassed my expectations.

"That's not the part that's supposed to shock you."

"I deliberately ignored the lead."

"Thanks to that, I went home with my indoor shoes every day, and I even took to carrying my recorder home, as well." Yukinoshita's expression conveyed the tedium of these trials.

Unintentionally, I found myself sympathizing with her. It was just, you know...*not* because her story rang a bell or because I felt guilty because back in elementary school this one time I'd figured out the period early in the morning when no one was in the classroom and had switched the tips of our recorders. I just felt genuinely sorry for her. Honestly, honestly. Hachiman tells no lies!

"It must have been hard."

"Yes, it was. Because I'm so cute." She laughed in a mildly self-deprecating way, and this time the sight of her wasn't nearly as irritating as before. "But I don't think it can be helped. Nobody's perfect. They are weak, with ugly hearts, and they quickly turn to jealousy. They try to knock others down. It's so odd... In the world we live in, the greater a person is, the more difficult his or her life becomes. Don't you find that strange? That's why I'm going to change this world and everyone in it." Yukinoshita held a clear sincerity in her eyes—eyes as cold as dry ice. Cold enough to burn.

"That's an incredibly bizarre direction to channel your efforts."

"Is that so? Even if you're right, I think it's a much better choice than to end up withered and exhausted like you. I hate the way you... regard your own weaknesses as virtue," she snapped, casting her gaze out the window.

Yukino Yukinoshita is a beautiful girl. At this point, this was an indisputable fact. I was forced to accept it, however regrettable that was.

She appeared on the outside to be a paragon of flawless conduct—academically peerless and generally impeccable. But her personality had a massively fatal flaw.

No one found things like that cute.

But there was reason for the flaws. I wasn't taking Ms. Hiratsuka's words as gospel, but being an elite, Yukinoshita did have her own troubles.

I'm sure it wouldn't have been difficult to hide it. To cooperate with everyone, to use every trick in the book, excelling at everything, while fooling the world around you. Most people do that.

Just like how someone good at studying, when they get good grades on a test, will say it was a fluke, that they were guessing, or just got lucky. Or when a bunch of plain girls are jealous of a pretty girl, the pretty girl makes a big show of her own ugliness by talking about her subcutaneous fat.

But Yukinoshita doesn't do that.

She never lies to herself. I can respect that. Because I'm the same way.

Yukinoshita redirected her attention to her paperback, as if to signal the conversation was over.

Seeing that, an odd feeling caught me off guard. It occurred to me that she and I were alike, in a way, though it was very unlike me to think so. At that moment, I even started feeling as though the silence between us was somehow comfortable. My blood pressure increased ever so slightly. It felt as if my heart rate had surpassed the speed of the clock's second hand and was telling me it wanted to go even faster.

So…

So her and me…

"Hey, Yukinoshita. Can we be frie—?"

"I'm sorry. That's impossible."

"What? I didn't even finish my sentence!"

Complete and utter rejection. And plus, the look on her face said, *Eww…*

There's nothing cute about her. Rom-coms can go die in a fire.

Yui Yuigahama is perpetually glancing around furtively.

"So, what, you have some cooking-related trauma, then?"

I'd been assigned a make-up report for home economics because I'd skipped cooking class, and for some reason, I got called to the faculty office after I handed it in. This was giving me some serious déjà vu. *Why must I have your lectures inflicted upon me, Ms. Hiratsuka?*

"Aren't you supposed to be teaching Japanese?"

"I'm also responsible for guidance counseling. Mr. Tsurumi foisted the job off on me." I glanced at a corner of the faculty office to see the aforementioned Mr. Tsurumi watering a potted plant. Ms. Hiratsuka regarded the other teacher before turning back to me. "First, I'll ask why you skipped practice. Make it brief."

"Well, you know... I don't really see the point of practicing cooking with the whole class."

"I don't see the point of that excuse, Hikigaya. Is group activity that painful for you? Or did none of the groups let you join?" Ms. Hiratsuka studied my expression with fairly sincere worry.

"No, no, what are you talking about, Sensei? It's supposed to be *practice cooking*, right? In other words, there's no point doing it unless it closely resembles the real thing. My mother cooks alone, you know? In other words, cooking *alone* would be the correct way to do it! Paradoxically, it's practicing cooking in groups that's wrong!"

"Those are two completely different things."

"Sensei! Are you telling me that *my* mommy is *wrong*?! That's going too far! There's no point in continuing this conversation! I'm leaving!" I retorted, turning on my heel and attempting to leave.

"Hey. Don't try to confuse the issue by flying off the handle when you're clearly in the wrong here."

So she could tell. Ms. Hiratsuka stretched out her arm, tugged the collar of my uniform from behind, and spun me around by the scruff of the neck, just like how you'd pick up a kitten. *Nghh.* Maybe going *Tee-hee! ♪ I'm so naughty! ☆* and sticking my tongue out would have been a better strategy to get away with it.

Ms. Hiratsuka sighed, thumping my report with the back of her hand.

"You're fine up to 'How to make good curry.' The problem is the part after that. 'First slice the onion into wedges. You slice them thinly and then season them. Just as the shallower a person is, the more easily they are influenced by their environment—the thinner you slice the onions, the more the flavor will soak into them.' Who told you to make it so salty? You're ruining the dish!"

"Sensei, please stop being so smug and acting like you said something witty. It's embarrassing to watch."

"And I don't want to read this kind of essay. I shouldn't have to say this, as it should be obvious to you already, but you're doing it over." The teacher put a cigarette in her lips with an expression of utter disgust.

"Can you cook?" Ms. Hiratsuka asked me as she flipped through reports. The look on her face said she expected the answer to be *no.* That was unfair. High schoolers these days could all make curry, at least.

"Yes. Thinking about my future, it's obvious that I should know how."

"So you've reached the age where you're thinking about moving out?"

"No, that's not what I meant."

"Oh?" *Then why?* Ms. Hiratsuka asked with her gaze alone.

"Because cooking is a vital skill for a househusband," I replied.

Ms. Hiratsuka's large eyes, bordered moderately with mascara, blinked twice, three times. "You want to be a stay-at-home husband?"

"I see it as one of my future options."

"Don't give me that rotten look while you talk about your dreams for the future. Your eyes should be sparkling, at the very least. Just for my knowledge, what exactly do your plans for the future entail?"

I had a hunch it would be a bad idea to reply with something like *Actually, you should be worrying about your* own *future,* so I resigned myself to giving her a reasoned answer. "Well, I'll go on to some decent university."

Ms. Hiratsuka nodded and made listening noises. "Mm-hmm. What about your career following that?"

"I'll pick out a beautiful and talented girl and marry her with the intention of having her support me in the end."

"I said *career*! Give me a career for an answer!"

"I said *househusband*."

"That just makes you a leech! And that's an absolutely terrible way to live. Men like that dangle marriage in front of women like bait, and then before you know it, they've crawled into your house and have even made a duplicate key, and soon enough they start bringing in their things, and once we broke up, that useless good-for-nothing even went so far as to take my furniture!" Ms. Hiratsuka's rant contained way too many specifics. She got so into it, she ran out of breath, tears welling up in her eyes.

Too sad... She looked so pitiful, I just had to say something to make her feel better.

"Sensei, it's okay! I won't be like that. I'll do housework properly and be the best leech ever!"

"What kind of super-leech logic is that?!"

My aspirations for the future denied, I was forced to stand at the crossroads of my life. On the brink of having my dreams crushed entirely, I scrounged up a good argument with which to arm myself. "It does sound bad if you call it being a leech, but I don't think being a stay-at-home husband is such a bad decision."

"Mm-hmm?" Ms. Hiratsuka shifted in her chair, making it creak, and glared at me. Her posture said, *I'm listening. Try me.*

"Thanks to the gender equality movement and all that, it's already taken as a given that women will go on to have careers. You being a teacher is proof of that, Ms. Hiratsuka."

"Well, that's true." It looked like she had accepted that much. Now I could take it a step further.

"But now that a large number of women have joined the workforce, it's only rational that an equal number of men are going to be crowded out. In any given time and place, there have always been a limited number of jobs, isn't that right?"

"Hmm..."

"For example, let's say that fifty years ago at a given company, there were a hundred workers, and they were one hundred percent male. If they then hire fifty women, obviously fifty of the men that were originally there have to go elsewhere. This is a simplified analogy, but you get the idea. Add in the recent recession, and it's becomes quite apparent that the number of positions available for men has decreased dramatically."

At that point, Ms. Hiratsuka put her hand to her chin, adopting a thoughtful posture. "Continue."

"There's also the fact that companies don't need as much personnel as they did in the past. With the spread of computers and the development of the Internet, we've become more efficient, and the productivity of a single individual has grown by leaps and bounds. In fact, from a societal perspective, you start to get the message that *Yeah, I know you badly want to work, but we can't manage that.* Look at stuff like work sharing."

"True, those concepts do exist."

"Plus, with the remarkable development of consumer electronics, anyone can do the same work and put out a standard level of quality. Men can do housework."

"Wait, hold on a second," she said, interrupting my fervent argument. She cleared her throat quietly and peered at my face. "Th-those things can be pretty hard to use, though… Men might not necessarily manage, you know."

"No, that's just you."

"What was that?" Spinning her chair, she kicked my shin. It *really* hurt. I carried on with my reasoning, hoping she'd forget that last bit.

"I-in other words! We've desperately endeavored to create a society where you don't have to work, so it's completely absurd to be saying things like, 'You have to work!' or 'There's no jobs!' "

A flawless conclusion. Work and you lose; work and you lose.

"Aaagh. You're still rotten to the core." The teacher unburdened herself of a massive sigh but then smirked as if she'd thought of something. "If a girl were to cook for you just once, maybe you'd think differently," she said, standing and shoving me along from behind, pushing me out of the faculty office.

"H-hey! What are you doing? *Ow!* That hurts, I said!"

"Go to the Service Club and learn the importance of labor." With a viselike grip, she tightened her hand on my shoulder before following up with a strong whap to shove me out of the room.

I turned back to voice a protest of *What was that for?* or something of that nature, only to find the door slamming shut cruelly in my face. That was the aforementioned rejection of any "arguments, disagreements, objections, questions, or back talk."

I considered for a moment perhaps skipping out of club time, but the instant the thought crossed my mind, the shoulder she had just been squeezing throbbed with pain. She'd probably punch me again if I ran away. I couldn't believe she'd managed to imprint that delayed-action agony in my body within such a small window of time. What a terrify-ing woman.

I decided to show up at the mystery club I'd recently been forced to join—the Service Club or whatever it was called. That was its name, but I had no idea what we actually did. I was even more perplexed by the head of the club. What the hell was her deal?

X   X   X

Yukinoshita was reading a book in the clubroom, as usual. We casually exchanged hellos, and then I carried a chair over to a spot a little ways away from her and sat down, pulling a few books from my bag. Now the Service Club had entirely transformed into a Youth Reading Club.

So what were we actually supposed to do in this club, in the end? Where'd all that talk about a competition go? The answer to my ques-tions arrived suddenly in the form of a visitor's faint knock.

Yukinoshita's page-turning hand paused, and she precisely inserted a bookmark into her paperback. She then turned to the door and called: "Come in."

"P-pardon me!" squeaked a nervous voice. The door slid aside with a light scrape, opening barely a few inches. A girl entered, almost squeez-ing through sideways. The way she moved, it seemed as though she didn't want to be seen. Her chestnut-brown hair flowed down to her shoulders in loose waves, and with every step she took, they swayed. Her eyes darted about as if she was scouting out the area, her gaze never stopping to rest, and when her eyes met mine, she let out a tiny squeal.

Was I some kind of monster?

"Wh-why is Hikki here?"

"Uh, I'm in this club." *And wait, does "Hikki" mean me? Who is this girl, anyway? Quite frankly, I have no recollection of her at all.*

I didn't remember her because she was such a stereotypically mod-ern high school girl. I saw her ilk all the time. Basically, she was one of those fashionable teenage girls. All of her clothes flagrantly disregarded the school dress code: the short skirt, the three buttons open on her blouse, the necklace sparkling on the chest peeking out of said blouse, the heart charm, and the tawny hair bleached bright.

I didn't associate with girls of that sort. Because I didn't associate with girls of any sort.

It seemed like she knew me, though, and I didn't feel I could just ask, *Excuse me, who are you?* But then I noticed the color of the ribbon on her chest was red. In our school, each of the three grades were assigned different ribbons, and that was how you could tell someone's year. Red meant she was a second-year, like me. The reason I noticed her ribbon straightaway wasn't because I was looking at her chest—it just happened to enter my field of vision, okay? By the way, it was pretty big.

"Well, sit down." I casually pulled out a chair and motioned for her to sit. I wasn't being all gentlemanly to disguise my impure intentions. I want to emphasize that it was, naturally, all out of sincere kindness.

Really, I'm a super gentleman. I mean, I dress like one all the time.

"Th-thanks…" She looked a little flustered, but she nevertheless plopped herself down in the seat I'd offered.

Yukinoshita, who was sitting opposite her, met her gaze. "Yui Yuigahama, right?"

"Y-you know me?" Hearing her own name, Yui Yuigahama's expression suddenly turned bright. It seemed she regarded Yukinoshita's recognition as a mark of status.

"You know her name? Do you know all the students in this school or what?"

"Not at all. I didn't know you."

"Oh…"

"It's nothing to get upset about. I should have. I only didn't because I was disinterested in your stunted character. I had a strong, subconscious desire to avert my eyes from you, but that was my weakness and my fault."

"Hey, was that supposed to make me feel better? That's a pretty terrible way to comfort someone. That last part basically makes the whole thing my fault!"

"I wasn't trying to make you feel better. I was just being sarcastic." Without even giving me a glance, Yukinoshita flicked back the hair that had fallen to her shoulders.

"This club seems…kinda fun." Yuigahama observed our interaction with something of a sparkle in her eyes. Maybe she had a few screws loose.

"This experience isn't particularly pleasant for me… In fact, that assumption of yours is incredibly unpleasant." Yukinoshita shot her a chilly glare.

When the look hit Yuigahama, she became flustered, fidgeting and shaking her hands wildly in front of her. "Oh! Well, um, like… I just thought you guys seemed like you were really natural with each other. You know, um… Hikki's acting totally different from how he usually does in class, so I was like, *Wow, he talks!*"

"Of course I talk." *Do I come off* that *lacking in communication skills?*

"Oh, yes, I remember now. You're in Class F as well, Yuigahama?"

"Huh? Is she?"

"You *were* aware of that, weren't you?" Yukinoshita said, and Yuigahama twitched in response.

Oh, crap.

I knew better than anyone else what if feels like when someone in your own class doesn't remember you at all. So, in order to spare her that pain, I decided to lie.

"O-of course I was!"

"So why'd you look away?" Yuigahama cross-examined me intently. "Isn't that sort of thing why you don't have any friends in our class? You act so weird, it's creepy."

Oh, that condescending gaze was so familiar. There was indeed a girl in my class who sometimes looked at me the way you'd look at something dirty. She was part of the clique that often hung out with the soccer club or whoever. *Oh, I see. She's my enemy, huh?* My consideration had been wasted on her.

"Slut," I muttered.

Yuigahama snapped back at me. "Huh? What do you mean, *slut*? I'm still a vir—Uh… Ah-ha-ha! N-nothing!" Her face flushed bright red as she flailed her hands in an attempt to erase the word that had almost escaped her lips. What a dumbass.

Yukinoshita butted in to save Yuigahama from her fit of panic. "That's not something you need to be embarrassed about. At your age, being a virg—"

"Hey, hey, hey! What are you talking about?! Not having done it in your second year is embarrassing! Yukinoshita, what does that say about my hotness level?!"

"What a superficial system of values." *Whoa, I don't know why, but Yukinoshita's frigidity just turned up a notch.*

"*Hotness level?* Sounds like something a slut would say."

"You said it again! I can't believe I'm being called a slut! You're such a creep, Hikki!" Yuigahama moaned in frustration as she looked at me through teary eyes.

"Me calling you a slut has nothing to do with my creepiness. And don't call me Hikki." She was making me sound like a *hikkikomori*—one of those shut-ins who never comes out of his room. Oh, so that was supposed to be an insult. It was probably a derisive nickname the class had given me. *What the hell? That's kind of mean.* It almost made me want to cry. Talking behind people's backs is rude. *So say it straight—right to my face. I can't get hurt if I don't hear it myself.* "You slut."

"You…you really are a pain in the butt! And you're seriously creepy! Why don't you just die?!"

I'm a pretty mild guy, and I never snap at anyone. I'm like a safety razor. But that was enough to make even me go quiet. There are a lot of things out there you just shouldn't say to people. Words relating life and death, in particular, can be particularly impactful. If you aren't prepared to take someone's life with your own hands, then you should never say you will.

So after a brief silence, as a warning to her, I said gravely and with palpable anger in my tone, "Don't use stuff like *Die!* or *I'll kill you!* as casual insults. I'll kill you if you do that again."

"Oh…s-sorry. That's not what I…huh?! You just said it! You super-said it!" As I'd noted earlier, Yuigahama is a dumbass. But surprisingly, she was also capable of making a sincere apology.

I realized my initial impression of her hadn't been entirely accurate. I'd thought her head was filled with nothing but partying, sex, and drugs—just like everyone else in her clique, the soccer club crowd, and the people who hung out with them. What was this, a Ryuu Murakami novel?

Apparently tired of bouncing around, Yuigahama breathed a short sigh. "Hey, I heard from Ms. Hiratsuka that this place grants students' wishes?" she asked, breaking the brief silence.

"Did she?" I'd been under the impression this club was for reading books and wasting time.

Yukinoshita completely ignored my dubious expression and responded to Yuigahama's question. "Not quite. The Service Club is really only for helping people. Whether or not your wishes are granted depends on you."

"How is that 'not quite'?" Yuigahama asked, perplexed. That was exactly what I'd wanted to ask, too.

"It's the difference between giving a starving person a fish and teaching them how to fish. Volunteer efforts are, at their core, about putting that ideal into practice, and not just about producing results. Perhaps the best way to describe it is that we encourage self-reliance."

That sounded like something out of an ethics textbook. So it looked like we were basically in agreement that the point of the club was putting self-reliance and cooperation (the same bullcrap held up as virtuous in any school) into practice. I guess the teacher had babbled on about labor or whatever… So in other words, the club was about working to help other students.

"Th-that's kind of amazing!" Yuigahama had this look in her eyes like she'd just had a revelation, like *Whoa, you just convinced me!* It made me a little worried that one day she might get suckered in by a cult.

There's absolutely no scientific basis for this idea, but there is this common belief that girls with big boobs are a little…you know. I think this example could be added to the list.

And then there was Yukinoshita with her flat-as-a-board chest, her clear intellect, and her wisdom. As usual, she was smiling coldly. "I may not actually grant your wish, but I will help you as best I can."

Apparently reminded of what she'd originally come here for, Yuigahama piped up. "Oh! Um, um…listen, so…cookies…," she began, glancing at my face.

I'm not empty carbs. People in class treat me like empty *air*, and though those sound similar, they're different.

"Hikigaya." Yukinoshita jerked her chin, gesturing toward the hallway. It was a sign telling me to get lost. She didn't have to signal me like that. She could have kindly said, *You're an eyesore, so would you be so kind as to please leave that seat, though it would make me very happy if you never come back.*

If it was something they could only talk about between girls, then there was nothing I could do about it. Stuff like that was a thing. The hints were *health and physical education*, *boys not included*, and *a class for girls only in a different classroom*. In other words, that was what they were going to talk about.

I do wonder what they talk about during those classes. It still bothers me.

"…I'm gonna go get a Sportop." I'm too nice, if I do say so myself. I read the room and casually took action. If I were a girl, I'd fall for me for sure.

When I got up, Yukinoshita apparently thought of something, so she called after me as I put my hand on the door. "I'd like a Vegetable Lifestyle 100 Strawberry Yogurt Mix."

She doesn't even think twice before using me as her errand boy. Yukinoshita, you're a piece of work.

×　×　×

Making a round trip from the third floor of the special-use building to the first floor took less than ten minutes. If I took my time strolling along, maybe the girls would be done with their conversation. No matter what kind of person she was, she was still our first client. In other words, the competition the teacher had set for Yukinoshita and I had begun. Well, I doubted I was going to win, so all I had to worry about was minimizing the amount of damage the whole affair would deal me.

In a suspicious-looking vending machine in front of the school store, there was a mysterious beverage in a juice box that you never really see at convenience stores. It tasted quite similar to something else, but it actually wasn't bad, so I kept an eye out for it. Sportop's candy-like taste in particular flew in the face of current "no-calorie, no-sugar" trends, and I liked that rebellious spirit. It tasted all right.

The vending machine rumbled like a sky fortress when I inserted a hundred-yen coin. Once I'd secured some Sportop and a Vegetable Lifestyle, I deposited another hundred yen. Just buying drinks for two out of three would have been kind of awkward, so I decided to pick something up for Yuigahama, too, pressing the button for Men's Café au Lait. In all, it totaled three hundred yen. I'd just blown about half my net worth. I was so broke.

×　×　×

The first thing Yukinoshita said when I got back was "You took too long," snatching the Vegetable Life out of my hands before jamming in the straw and taking a sip.

That left me with the Sportop and the Men's Café au Lait. Yuigahama apparently realized whom the latter was for. "Here," she said, pulling a hundred yen from a change purse that looked like a pocket.

"Oh, it's okay." Yukinoshita hadn't paid, and I'd bought this extra drink without asking Yuigahama if she wanted one. Even if there was a reason for Yukinoshita to pay me, Yuigahama was under no such obligation. So instead of taking her hundred-yen coin, I put the café au lait in her hands.

"B-but...I can't..." She stubbornly kept trying to hand me the money. Not wanting to go through that annoying *I'll pay! No, it's okay!* routine, I just went over beside Yukinoshita. Yuigahama huffed and reluctantly put the coin away. "Thanks." She expressed her gratitude quietly and took the café au lait in both hands with a *tee-hee*, looking happy and bashful.

I thought that was probably the greatest show of thanks I'd received ever. That smile might have been too much in exchange for just a hundred yen.

Satisfied, I tried to catch Yukinoshita's interest. "Are you two done talking?"

"Yes, things went quite smoothly thanks to your absence. Thank you."

And that was the worst show of thanks I'd ever received.

"Well, that's good. So what're we doing?"

"We're going to the home ec room, and you're coming, too."

"Home ec?" That meant...*that* place. That iron-maiden-like classroom where you grouped up with friends of your choice and underwent the agony that was cooking practice. There were knives and gas stoves and stuff in there! It was dangerous! That stuff should have been restricted, seriously!

Along with gym class and field trips, home ec stood out as one of my top three trauma-inducing activities, and who'd subject themselves to such an environment of their own free will? My intrusion on one of those settings—with all those cliques and their merry chattering—produced an unbearable silence.

"Cookies... We're baking cookies."

"What? Cookies?" I didn't remotely get what she was talking about, so all I could say was *What?*

"Yuigahama wants to make cookies for someone, but she requested our help because she lacks confidence in the enterprise," Yukinoshita explained to dispel my confusion.

"Why do you need us for something like that? Just ask your friends."

"Erk...w-well, um...," Yuigahama stammered, her eyes darting everywhere. "I don't really want people to know, and if my friends found out, they'd make fun of me... This sort of...serious stuff isn't really like them."

I let out a small sigh.

Frankly speaking, there was nothing I cared less about than peoples' love lives. My time was far better served remembering one word of English vocabulary than remembering who liked who. To say nothing of helping her. That was out of the question. So yeah, those were my feelings on the matter, so you can tell how scant my interest is in the language of love.

When they said they wanted to talk alone, I figured it was something really serious. And this was it? Well, I guess it was a relief. Frankly, when someone asks for romantic advice, all you have to say is *Go for it! You can do it!* or whatever. And if things don't go well, you just have to be like, *That guy is such a jerk, huh?* "Hmph." A derisive snort slipped out of my nose.

Yuigahama met my gaze. "U-uh..." At a loss for words, she looked down, clutching the hem of her skirt. Her shoulders shook a bit. "Ah... aha-ha! It's weird, huh? Someone like me going on about handmade cookies... It's like, why am I acting like such a kid, huh? Sorry, Yukinoshita. Never mind."

"If you say so. I'm not deeply concerned one way or the other, but... Oh, don't feel like you have to pay this boy any mind. He has no human rights. He's compelled to be here."

Apparently, the Japanese constitution doesn't apply to me. What kind of shady outfit is this?

"No... It's fine, it's fine! It's not really like me. It's weird...and I heard from Yumiko and Hina and stuff that it's not in right now, anyway," Yuigahama said, glancing my way again. She looked wilted and despondent.

Yukinoshita opened her mouth to kick her while she was down. "…Indeed. It really isn't the kind of thing you'd expect from someone with a party-girl aesthetic like yours."

"Y-yeah…it'd be weird, huh…?" Yuigahama laughed as if trying to gauge our opinions of her. Her mostly downcast eyes caught mine. Based on her behavior, I got the impression that she wanted some kind of reply.

"…No, I'm not trying to say that it's weird, or unlike you, or that it doesn't suit you, or not something you would do. I honestly just don't care."

"That's even meaner!" Yuigahama smacked the table indignantly. "You're unbelievable, Hikki! Augh, you're pissing me off. I'm the type of girl who can do whatever I put my mind to, y'know!"

"That's not the kind of thing you should be saying about yourself. It's more like something my mom would say to me, her eyes all sincere and tearful: *I thought you were the kind of boy who could do things when he put his mind to it…*"

"Your mom has already given up on you!"

"That's a reasonable assessment."

Yuigahama's eyes welled up, and Yukinoshita said something or other while nodding vigorously.

Leave me alone.

It's true, though; having someone give up on you is a sad thing. And Yuigahama was really into this plan, so I felt bad about raining on her parade. And we did have that competition going on… Reluctantly, I voiced my cooperation. "Well, I can really only make curry, but I'll help."

"Th-thanks." Yuigahama looked relieved.

"I'm not really expecting you to cook anything. You just have to taste it and tell us what you think."

If I was only there to give my opinion as a guy, as Yukinoshita described, I should have been capable of that, at least. Lots of guys don't like sweet stuff, so I could help her learn to cook for a masculine palate. Plus, I was no picky eater, so most things tasted good to me.

Wait, is that even useful?

X   X   X

The home ec room was filled with the sweet scent of vanilla extract.

Yukinoshita, as comfortable as if it were her own home, opened the refrigerator and took out some eggs, milk, and other items. She secured a scale and bowls and such, as well, and started preparing and rattling around with a ladle and some other mysterious cooking implements I didn't recognize.

Apparently, this flawless superwoman was also an expert cook.

She quickly finished laying out everything she would need and then put on an apron as if to say, *Now it's time for the real deal.*

Yuigahama put one on as well, but she didn't seem used to it, as the way she tied her string was a mess.

"That's crooked. Can't you even put on an apron right?"

"Sorry, thanks... Huh?! I can put on an apron, at least!"

"Oh? Then put it on right. If you don't even try to do it properly, you'll end up past the point of no return, just like him."

"Don't use me as your cautionary tale. What am I, a hairy *nama-hage* demon looking for naughty children?"

"You should be glad. This is the first time you've ever been useful to someone. Oh, though I may be treating you like monster, I wasn't trying to imply anything about your scalp. Don't worry."

"I wasn't worried. And stop looking at my hair with that patronizing smile on your face." I swiftly hid my hairline behind my hand in an attempt to shield it from Yukinoshita's rare smile. I heard a voice giggling at me. Yuigahama, still in her sloppily tied apron, watched us from the side.

"You still don't have it on? Or is it that you can't put it on after all? …Ahhh, I'll tie it for you, so come over here." Exasperated, Yukinoshita beckoned the other girl over with a flick of her hand.

"You don't…mind?" Yuigahama mumbled with the slightest bit of hesitation. She looked like an anxious child who didn't know where she was supposed to go.

"Come on." The icy sound of Yukinoshita's voice broke her indecision. Yukinoshita seemed kind of angry, and it was a little scary.

"S-s-s-sorry!" Yuigahama zipped right over to Yukinoshita. *What are you, a puppy?*

The vexed girl moved behind the source of her annoyance and firmly retied her apron.

"Yukinoshita…you're kind of like a big sister."

"There's no way my little sister could be this incompetent." Yukinoshita sighed, looking disappointed, but I felt as if Yuigahama's comparison was surprisingly not far from the mark. Yukinoshita, with her air of maturity, and Yuigahama, with her baby face—together, the two rather resembled a pair of sisters.

They really gave off a warm household vibe.

Also, only old men are into that whole girl-wearing-nothing-but-an-apron thing. Me, I thought the school-uniform-plus-apron-combo was the ultimate.

I felt my heart growing warm and let slip a leer.

"H-hey, Hikki…"

"Wh-what is it?" Whoops. That might have been a creepy smile. My voice went shrill, too, kicking the creepiness factor up a notch. I'd set off a chain reaction of creep factor.

"Wh-what do you think of domestic girls?"

"I think they're okay. I think all guys are attracted to them to a degree."

"O-oh…" Hearing that seemed to put her at ease, and she smiled. "Okay, let's do this!" Rolling up the sleeves of her blouse, she cracked open an egg and beat it. She added other ingredients like flour and then sugar, butter, and vanilla extract.

Yuigahama's skills were so far from the norm that even someone like me who didn't really know a lot about cooking could tell. Maybe this is much ado about cookies, but I believed that precisely *because* they're so simple to make, they clearly display the baker's skill level. You could see a person's real ability, the kind you couldn't fake.

First of all, the beaten egg: There was shell in it.

Next, the flour: It was all clumped up.

And the butter: It was still hard.

She exchanged sugar for salt like it was the obvious thing to do and poured in a ton of vanilla extract. The milk sloshed around dangerously inside the bowl.

When I happened to glance over at Yukinoshita, she was holding her forehead and looking green. Even I, with my poor cooking skills, felt a chill run down my spine. Yukinoshita, with her talents, must have been shuddering in horror.

"Well, then…," Yuigahama said, taking out some instant coffee.

"Coffee, huh? Well, food goes down easier when you have something on hand to drink. That's thoughtful of you."

"What? That's not what this is for. This is for subtle seasoning. Don't lots of guys hate sweet stuff?" Yuigahama cocked her head over her shoulder at me as she worked. I took my eyes off her hands for a moment to consider her face, and by the time I looked back there was a black mountain inside her bowl.

"That doesn't look subtle at all!"

"Huh? Oh. Then I'll adjust it by adding more sugar," she said, constructing a white mountain next to the black. A giant tsunami of beaten egg engulfed them both, creating a true hell.

Let me get right to the point: Yuigahama lacked cooking skills. It wasn't a question of those skills being poor or underdeveloped. She had absolutely none to begin with.

Not only was she clumsy, but she was imprecise, dangerously creative, and altogether unsuited for cooking. I'd never want to do chemistry experiments with this girl. She was the type who'd kill you with a mistake.

By the time those things came out of the oven, for some reason, they looked like coal-black pancakes. Judging by the smell, they were bitter.

"Wh-why?" An expression of shock on her face, Yuigahama gazed at the mystery substance.

"I can't comprehend it… How can you make so many errors all at once?" Yukinoshita mumbled. Her voice was quiet, so Yuigahama probably couldn't hear. But even so, it sounded like something that she couldn't hold in—words that had just popped out.

Yuigahama put the mystery substance on a plate. "It looks a bit odd, but…you don't know until you taste it, right?!"

"That's true. And we have a taste tester right here."

"Aha-ha-ha! Oh, Yukinoshita. It's so rare that you err in your choice of vocabulary. The term you're searching for is *food taster*—someone who *tests for poison*."

"What poison?! Oh…poison… Hmm, I guess it is poison after all?" For someone who'd initially taken such vigorous offense, Yuigahama suddenly seemed quite unsure, tilting her head to the side and giving me a look that said, *So what do you think?*

That didn't even warrant a reply, did it? I shook off Yuigahama's puppy-dog eyes and tried to get Yukinoshita's attention.

"Hey, am I seriously supposed to eat this? This is like the charcoal they sell at a hardware store."

"She didn't use any inedible ingredients, so you'll be fine. Probably. Plus…" Yukinoshita paused and moved to whisper in my ear. "I'll eat some, too, so it's okay."

"For real? Are you maybe actually a good person? Or do you like me?"

"Actually, you can eat them all and die after all."

"Sorry. I was so shocked, I got a bit kooky."

Because they were cookies, get it? I wasn't sure you could honestly say the things before us counted as cookies, though.

"Your job was supposed to be taste testing, not refuse disposal. Plus, I'm the one who took on her request. I'll take responsibility for that," Yukinoshita said, pulling the plate over to her side.

"I can't properly dispose of them without grasping exactly what the problem is. And there's no way to avoid exposing myself to danger in order to find out."

Yukinoshita picked up one of the blackened objects. Had I been told those things were actually iron ore, I might have believed it. She looked at me, her eyes tearing up a bit.

"Will this kill me?"

"That's what I'd like to know," I said, glancing at Yuigahama who was regarding us like she wanted to be one of the gang. *Go ahead. You have one, too. Know our pain.*

×   ×   ×

I somehow managed to grind away at Yuigahama's cookies.

I didn't throw up and keel over the minute I ate one, like they do in manga. I just tasted a bitter awfulness so intense that I felt like losing consciousness would have been a mercy. If only I could have passed out, I wouldn't have had to eat any more. The level of workmanship in those cookies made me wonder what the heck she'd put in them—mackerel guts? That was about where they ranked on the scale, but at least eating them didn't mean instant death. But still, I wouldn't have been surprised to learn that ingesting this substance had increased my risk of cancer over the long term and that I'd start seeing symptoms in a few years.

"Ugh! These are so bitter! And gross!" Yuigahama wailed tearfully as she crunched away.

Yukinoshita immediately passed her a teacup. "It's better if you avoid chewing as much as possible by swallowing quickly. Take care not to let it touch your tongue. It's much like drinking a nasty medicine."

She really didn't hesitate to say the meanest stuff.

The kettle came to a rolling boil, and Yukinoshita poured out some black tea for us. Having all consumed our assigned quota, we washed it down with tea. Finally able to relax, I sighed.

Yukinoshita opened her mouth to snap us out of our momentary reprieve. "Okay, now let us reflect on how we might improve them."

"Yuigahama never cooking again."

"You're telling me they're that bad?!"

"Hikigaya, that's our final solution."

"That's a solution?!" Yuigahama went from shock to dejection. Her shoulders drooped, and she sighed deeply. "I guess I'm just not cut out for cooking after all… I've got no…talent, or whatever you call it."

Yukinoshita heaved a deep sigh in return. "I see. I've come up with an answer."

"What do I do?" Yuigahama asked, and Yukinoshita replied calmly:

"You just need to put in the effort."

"That's your answer?"

In my humble opinion, effort is the worst solution.

Saying that you just have to *try hard* and that no other factors matter was just another way of saying *There's nothing else you can do now.* Quite frankly, it was no different than proceeding without a plan at all. It would have been much better just to say, *You've got no chance, so give up.* There's nothing more pointless than wasted effort. It's better to give someone the boot so they can devote their time and toil to something else.

"Effort is a great solution if it's done right," Yukinoshita declared as if she'd just read my mind. *Are you an esper or what?*

"Yuigahama. You said earlier that you have no talent, didn't you?"

"Huh? Oh yeah."

"You must revise that way of thinking. People who don't put in the minimum amount of effort have no right to be jealous of people with talent. Those who fail do so only because they cannot imagine the effort it takes to be successful at achieving their goals." Yukinoshita's words were both sharp and so utterly correct that they allowed no counterargument.

Yuigahama's voice caught in her throat. She'd probably never been slapped in the face with such a sound case before. Confusion and fear flitted across her face. She covered them up with a flippant smile. "B-but, like, lately everyone's saying they don't do stuff like this. It's just not the thing to do right now." Yuigahama smiled shyly, and the moment it seemed her smile might disappear with a chuckle, the sound of a cup clinking on the table resounded through the room. Though it was a very small and quiet noise, it reverberated like clear ice. The sound forcibly drew one's attention to its source, Yukinoshita, who emitted an aura of crisp shrewdness.

"Could you stop trying to conform to your surroundings? It's terribly unpleasant. Aren't you ashamed, pointing at others as the root of your own clumsiness, awkwardness, and foolishness?"

Yukinoshita's tone was stern. Obvious loathing bled into it, and it made me cringe so hard I let out a whispered *"Wh-whoa!"*

Yuigahama was overpowered into silence. Her face was downcast, so I couldn't quite tell, but her hands clenching the hem of her skirt were enough to show her feelings.

I was sure she possessed strong communication skills. Strong enough to be a member of the A-list after all, which took more than just looks—she'd have needed to know how to play nice with others. But seen from another angle, it really only meant that she was good at integrating herself. In other words, she lacked the courage to risk loneliness in order to be herself.

On the other hand, there was Yukinoshita, a veritable my-way-or-the-highway personality. Her brash character was the real deal. She acted as if she was actually proud of being alone. They were two completely different types of girls. On the power scale, Yukinoshita was clearly the stronger. She was right after all.

Yuigahama's eyes watered up. "You're so…" *So mean*, I assumed she was going to say. Her voice was feeble, as if she was about to burst into tears. Her shoulders trembled uncontrollably, and her voice trembled unreliably with them: "…so cool…"

" "What?!" " Yukinoshita and I said in unison. What the hell was she talking about? The two of us exchanged glances.

"You're always so real… It's, like…really cool." Yuigahama gazed at Yukinoshita, admiration etched on her face.

Yukinoshita, on the other hand, stiffened up and retreated a couple steps. "Wh-what on earth is this girl talking about? Were you listening to me? I believe I was being very harsh."

"No, not at all! Oh, well, it's true what you said was mean, and honestly, hearing it did kind of make me flinch, but…" Yeah, that sounded about right. I honestly didn't think Yukinoshita would go that far berating a girl. I hadn't just flinched; I'd been cringing halfway out the door. But apparently for Yuigahama, that diatribe had only been flinch-worthy.

"But it felt like you were being honest. And when you talk to Hikki, you only ever say terrible things to each other, but…you're actually talking. I only ever go along with what everyone else is doing, so this is the first time I've ever seen something like that…" Yuigahama didn't run away. "Sorry. I'll do it right next time," she apologized, looking right back at Yukinoshita.

This time Yukinoshita was the one left speechless, silenced by Yuigahama's unexpected gaze. This was probably a first for her. Surprisingly few people will apologize after being rationally and logically informed that they are wrong. Most people would just turn bright red and snap.

Yukinoshita looked off to the side and combed her hair back with a hand. She had an air that said she was looking for the right words but couldn't find them. Man, she sucked at ad-libbing.

"Teach her how to do it right. And you listen to what she says, Yuigahama," I said, breaking the silence between them, and Yukinoshita exhaled a short sigh and nodded.

"I'll show you how to do it first, so try doing it exactly as I do." Rolling up the sleeves of her blouse, she cracked an egg and beat it. She sifted out a precisely measured amount of flour and mixed it thoroughly so as not to let it clump up. Then she added in the other ingredients: sugar, butter, and vanilla extract.

Her skills were simply incomparable to those demonstrated by Yuigahama a moment earlier. The batter was done in a flash, and Yukinoshita started cutting out the shapes of hearts, stars, and circles with cookie cutters. There was already a sheet of wax paper on the cookie tray. She carefully laid the dough onto it and slid the tray into the preheated oven.

After a short wait, an indescribably sweet aroma began wafting out.

If the prep work is perfect, the results should be, too. And sure enough, the freshly baked cookies were a beauty to behold.

Transferring them to a plate, Yukinoshita swiftly presented them to us. The cookies, baked to a pretty golden brown, were each no doubt worthy of being called cookies. They were very well made, just like Aunt Stella brand cookies. I took one gratefully.

Depositing it in my mouth, I couldn't help but break into a broad smile. "These are so good! What color is your patisserie?!" My honest opinion slipped out.

My hands wouldn't stop. I put another in my mouth. Delicious, of course. I'd probably never get another chance to eat a girl's handmade cookies, so I took advantage of the opportunity to toss yet another one down the hatch. Those things Yuigahama had made hadn't been cookies, so they didn't count. "These are so good... You're amazing, Yukinoshita."

"Thank you." Yukinoshita smiled without a trace of irony. "But you know, all I did was stay true to the recipe, so I'm sure you can make them just like mine, Yuigahama. If you can't, I think there's got to be something wrong with you."

"Why can't she just give that guy these?"

"There wouldn't be any meaning in that. Come on, Yuigahama. Let's give this a shot."

"O-okay. Do you really think I can pull it off? Can I really make cookies like you do, Yukinoshita?"

"You can, if you stick to the recipe." Yukinoshita did not neglect to add that warning.

And so began Yuigahama's revenge.

Yuigahama went through the very same process and the very same steps that Yukinoshita had with her dough-over... Get it, dough-over, because they're cookies? That was some sweet wordplay. The cookies would likely be sugary when they were done, too... Get it? Because I made a sweet pun?

But...

"Yuigahama, not like that. When you sift the flour, draw a circle with your hands. A *circle*. Do you understand? Didn't you learn that properly in elementary school?

"When you mix it, hold the bowl firmly. The entire bowl is spinning, so it's not mixing at all. Don't spin it around. Move it like you're cutting *through* the batter.

"No, not that! Forget the 'subtle flavoring.' Put in the canned peaches and such another time. And if you add that much water, it will kill the batter. It'll be liquidated!"

Yukinoshita, *the* Yukino Yukinoshita, was stumped. She was exhausted. When they somehow got the dough in the oven, her shoulders sagged in a heavy grief. There was no sign of her usual attitude, and sweat beaded on her forehead.

When they opened the oven, a fine smell that much resembled the one that had come before wafted out. But...

"It's not quite the same..." Yuigahama's shoulders drooped in dejection.

Upon tasting, they were indeed clearly different from the ones Yukinoshita had just baked. But they were good enough to be called cookies. They were a lot better than the briquette-like objects she'd produced before. I would've been quite willing to eat them like normal cookies.

But it seemed as though neither Yuigahama nor Yukinoshita was satisfied.

"How can I teach you in a way you'll absorb?" Groaning to herself, Yukinoshita tilted her head.

Watching them, I suddenly realized what this meant. Yukinoshita was a bad teacher.

Put simply, Yukinoshita had talent, but because of her talent, she didn't have the slightest understanding of how the talentless felt. She couldn't comprehend their failures.

Saying *Just follow the recipe* was like telling a math student *You just have to use the formula*. Someone bad at math doesn't even get what the formula is for in the first place. They can't grasp how the formula will help them reach the answer. Yukinoshita couldn't understand why Yuigahama didn't understand. Putting it that way makes it sound as if Yukinoshita was at fault, but that wasn't the case. Yukinoshita had done everything possible. The problem was the other girl.

"Why won't it go right? I did it just like you told me!" An expression of sincere bafflement on her face, Yuigahama reached out to take a cookie.

To say that really smart people always make good teachers or that they can reliably explain things in a way that any idiot could understand is a lie. No matter how you instruct a disappointment of a human being, they're still a disappointment, so they won't get it. No matter how many times you do it over, you can't shore up that deficit.

"Hmm... They really are different from the ones Yukinoshita made." Yuigahama slumped, and Yukinoshita held her head in her hands.

I took a bite of another cookie as I watched them. "Look, I've been wondering this the whole time, but…why are you trying to make such good cookies?"

"What?" Yuigahama gave me a look that said, *What're you talking about, you virgin?* It was so disdainful, it kind of ticked me off.

"You don't even get it, even though you're a slut. How dumb are you?"

"I *said* don't call me a slut!"

"You don't get guys at all."

"Th-there's nothing I can do about that! I've never dated one! I-I mean I have a lot of friends who are dating…b-but copying them is what got me into this, so…" Yuigahama's voice got quieter and quieter to the point where I couldn't hear her at all. *Speak clearly. Clearly!* She was acting just like me when I get called on in class!

"I don't really care about Yuigahama's intimate liaisons, but what ultimately is your point, Hikigaya?"

Come on, 'intimate liaisons'? I don't even see that phrase on the hanging ads on trains lately. How old are you?

After an appropriate pause for effect, I smiled triumphantly. "Phew, it looks like you two have never eaten *actual* handmade cookies. Come back in ten minutes, please. I'll feed you the *real thing*."

"What did you say? Fine! I'm looking forward to it," Yuigahama said, and apparently angry at having her cookies disparaged, she dragged Yukinoshita out into the hallway and disappeared.

Now, then. It was my turn in this game. In other words, this was the ultimate battle to decide the supreme, most extreme solution to her problem.

× × ×

A few minutes later, the home ec room was enveloped in an aura of suspense.

"These are *real homemade* cookies? They're lopsided and uneven sizes. Plus, some of them are burned. These are…" Yukinoshita gazed at the objects on the table dubiously.

Yuigahama peeked at us from off to the side.

"Bwa-ha! You talked big, but these are nothing! What a laugh! They're not even worth eating!" Yuigahama burst into derisive laughter. She was actually cackling her head off. *I'll remember this, you jerk.*

"C-come on, don't say that. Just give them a try, please." I held back the twitches tugging at the corners of my mouth and didn't let my unperturbed smile falter. I would let my smile show them that I'd set everything up perfectly, was ready to turn the tables, and positive I would win.

"If you say so…" Yuigahama tentatively put a cookie in her mouth. Yukinoshita plucked one from the plate without a word.

Pleasant crunching sounds rang out, followed by a moment of silence.

"Oh! W-wow." Yuigahama's eyes opened wide. The flavor had arrived at her brain, and she struggled to find the appropriate words to describe it. "It's not like they're anything special, though, and it's also kinda gritty. Frankly, they're not that good!" She veered wildly from shock over to anger. The violent swing from one pole to the next made her grimace in my direction.

Yukinoshita said nothing, but she looked at me suspiciously. Apparently, she'd noticed.

I tolerated both glares for a moment before gently dropping my gaze. "Oh… They're no good, huh? I tried my best, though…"

"Oh… Sorry." When I cast my eyes down, Yuigahama awkwardly lowered her eyes to the floor as well.

"Sorry. I'll throw them out," I said, snatching the plate away and turning from them.

"W-wait a second!"

"What?"

Yuigahama took my hand, stopping me. Instead of replying, she picked up one of the lopsided cookies and tossed it into her mouth. She made a crunching sound, chewing up the gritty thing. "Th-they're not so awful you'd have to throw them out… I couldn't call them bad."

"Oh… So you're satisfied with them?" I smiled at her, and Yuigahama nodded wordlessly before immediately spinning around to look away. The setting sun was flowing in through the windows, making her face look red.

"Well, they're the cookies you just made."

"What?"

I smoothly and casually let her in on the truth. I'd never said *I* was the one who'd made them, so I'd never lied.

"…Ehh?" Yuigahama repeated stupidly. Her eyes had turned to dots, and her mouth hung entirely, exaggerating the effect of her foolishness.

"Huh? Huh?" Blinking and wide-eyed, she turned from me to Yukinoshita and back again. She didn't even remotely grasp what had just happened.

"Hikigaya, I don't quite understand. What was the point of this farce?" Yukinoshita sized me up, clearly displeased.

"There's a certain saying… 'If you have love…love is okay!'" I gave her a thumbs-up with a big grin on my face.

"That's so old!" Yuigahama reacted quietly. Well, that show *did* air back when I was in elementary school. Yukinoshita didn't appear to have gotten it, and she tilted her head to the side with a look like *Question mark?*

"You set the bar too high." A smile slipped onto my face. Ooh, what was this? This feeling of superiority? This feeling like I was the only one with the correct answer? It was too much. I couldn't help but blab on about it. I chuckled. "The goal of hurdling is not to jump over the hurdles. It's to reach the finish line with the best time. There's no rule saying you have to jump to get there. It do—"

"I get what you're trying to say. That's enough."

—*esn't matter if you knock over the hurdles or send them flying or try to crawl under them.* Was what I was going to say when Yukinoshita interrupted me.

"You're saying we've mistaken the means for the goal." She didn't seem quite convinced. But that was just what I'd been about to say, so I had no choice but to nod and then continue.

"She went to all that trouble to make some handmade cookies. If you don't play up the *handmade* part, then there's no point. A guy isn't going to be happy if you hand him something exactly the same as store-bought. It's actually better if they taste a little bad," I said, but Yukinoshita still didn't look convinced.

"It's better if they're bad?" she asked.

"Yeah, that's right. If you emphasize that, while you couldn't do it perfectly, you *tried your best!* then he'll get the tragically false impression that *oh, she tried so hard for me!*"

"It can't be that simple…" Yuigahama looked at me, doubtful, as if to say, *What are you talking about, you virgin?*

I sighed. I had no choice. I'd have to tell her a story to persuade her.

"This story is about a friend of a friend of mine, from back when he'd just started eighth grade. It was the beginning of a new year, so they had to pick a class representative in homeroom. But, this being eighth grade, none of the boys wanted to be class rep. So of course, they had to draw straws. And this guy was born with no luck at all, so of course, he was picked to be class rep. So the teacher gave him his assignments, and then they had to decide on the female class rep. He was a shy, bashful, and timid guy, so it was really hard on him."

"All those words mean the same thing. And you're taking way too long to get to the point."

"Shut up and listen. And that's when a girl volunteered as a candidate. She was cute. And thus, auspiciously, the boy and girl class reps were decided. The girl said shyly, 'I'm looking forward to working with you this year.'

"After that, she would come and talk to him from time to time. He started to go, 'Huh? Does she like me? Now that I think about it, she volunteered after I was chosen as the boys' rep. She comes to talk to me a lot, so she must like me!' It didn't take him long to come to that conclusion. About a week."

"That's fast!" Yuigahama, who had been nodding and hmming, voiced her surprise.

"You moron. Time and age gaps or whatever, none of that has anything to do with love. So anyway, after school one day, when they were handing out papers like the teacher told them to, he resolved to confess his feelings for her:

" 'U-um, hey… Do you have a crush on anyone?'

" 'Huh? No!'

" 'Come on, if you're saying it like that, I know you do! Who is it?'

" 'Who do you think?'

" 'I don't know! Come on! Give me a hint!'

" 'I don't know if I can…'

" 'Oh, then his initials! Tell me his initials! Or just the first letter of his last name or first name is fine, c'mon!'

" 'Hmm, well then, I guess I can do that.'

" 'For real?! Yes! So what's the letter?'

" 'H.'

" 'Huh? Is that…me?'

" 'Huh? What're you talking about? Of course not. What? Huh? That's so gross. Just stop.'

" 'Ah-ha-ha. Of course… I was just kidding.'

" 'Who in their right mind would… We're done here, so I'm going.'

" 'O-okay…' And as I was left alone in the classroom, I watched the setting sun, tears rolling down my face. What's more, when I went to school the next day, everyone knew about what had happened."

"So it was about you, Hikki…," Yuigahama mumbled awkwardly, averting her eyes.

"Hey! Don't be dumb. No one said it was about me! The first person was just, y'know, a mode of storytelling."

Ignoring my explanation, Yukinoshita let out an annoyed sigh. "It was suspicious from the moment you said 'a friend of a friend.' You don't have any friends."

"What?! You bastard!"

"Your trauma is irrelevant. What was your point?"

It wasn't irrelevant. That incident had made the girls hate me even more and had prompted the boys to start teasing me left and right, giving me the nickname 'Egogaya,' and, well, I guess it was irrelevant.

I pulled myself together and went on.

"In other words, you know…guys are depressingly simple. We'll get the wrong idea if you do so much as talk to us, and just getting handmade cookies is enough to make us happy. So…"

I paused and looked intently at Yuigahama. "Cookies that are nothing special, sometimes gritty and not that good, are still good enough."

"Ngh…! Shut up!"

Her face tinged red in anger, she threw everything she had at hand at me—plastic bags, wax paper, and so on. How kind, to choose things that wouldn't hurt if they struck home. *Huh? Does that mean she likes me? Ha-ha, just kidding. I'm not going through* that *again.*

"You really piss me off, Hikki! I'm leaving!" Yuigahama glowered at me, grabbing her bag and standing. She turned her head away with a *hmph* and began walking toward the door. Her shoulders were shaking.

Oh, crap, maybe I'd gone to far. I really wasn't keen on the prospect of nasty talk about me flying around the class again. I'd have to amend that statement. "Look, it's like…if you can get across the fact that you tried, you'll sway him."

Yuigahama turned around at the door. The light was coming from behind her, and I couldn't see her face. "Would it sway you, Hikki?"

"Huh? Oh, I'm already swaying like crazy. I'm so bad, you just have to be nice to me to make me fall for you. And hey, don't call me Hikki!"

"H-hmph," Yuigahama replied indifferently to my flippant remark before immediately looking away again. She put her hand on the door and moved to leave.

Yukinoshita spoke to her back. "Yuigahama, what are you going to do about your request?"

"I don't care about that anymore. I'm gonna try doing it my own way next time. Thanks, Yukinoshita." Yuigahama turned around, smiling. "See you tomorrow. Bye." She waved and left for real this time, her apron still on.

"Is that really a good idea?" Yukinoshita mumbled, still looking at the door. "I think that if you have room to improve, you should push yourself to the limit. That would be better for her, in the end."

"Well, that's true. You'll never betray yourself if you put in effort, but you may end up betraying your dreams."

"How are those two things different?"

The wind stroked Yukinoshita's cheeks as she turned around, her two braids swaying.

"Even if you do make an effort, your dreams won't necessarily come true. It's actually more likely that they won't. But the fact that you tried alone is comforting."

"That's just something you tell yourself to feel better."

"Even so, you aren't betraying yourself."

"You're so naïve... It's disgusting."

"Both you and the rest of society are hard on me. I at least have to be kind to myself. Everyone should pamper themselves more. If everyone's a failure, then no one's a failure."

"This is the first time I've ever seen someone argue pessimism as an ideal. If your ideas were to become popular, the world would fall to ruin." Yukinoshita looked disgusted, but I was quite fond of my ideology. One day I'd like to found Neetoria, a government of the NEETs, by the NEETs, for the NEETs... I guess it would probably crash and burn within three days after all.

X   X   X

I finally understood what this Service Club or whatever did.

In short, it was apparently for advising students and helping them solve their problems. But its existence wasn't particularly advertised. I mean, I hadn't known about it. And it wasn't just because I was disconnected from the campus hive-mind. Yuigahama hadn't been aware of it, either, so that meant that we needed someone to connect us to the students, and that someone was Ms. Hiratsuka. Students went to her with their problems from time to time, and she'd send them on to us.

So in other words, the club was an isolation ward.

In that sanatorium, I was, as usual, reading a book.

Receiving counseling on your worries was basically just exposing your insecurities. High school students are sensitive, so telling them to talk to other students from the same school about their problems was probably just too much to ask. Yuigahama had come because Ms. Hiratsuka had introduced her to us. Without the teacher's involvement, nobody would ever visit.

There were no guests today, either. The shop was open for business, but none was forthcoming. Both Yukinoshita and I were comfortable with silence, so it was very quiet while we focused on our reading, which was why the hard rap on the door rang out so loudly.

"Yahallo!" She pulled open the sliding door with her insipid, concentration-killing greeting. It was Yui Yuigahama. I averted my eyes from the legs protruding from her short skirt and switched instead to gape at the widely open blouse on her chest. Slutty as usual.

Seeing her, Yukinoshita let out a grand sigh. "…What is it?"

"Huh? What? That's not much of a welcome… Yukinoshita, do you…hate me?"

Yuigahama's voice was subdued, but Yukinoshita heard her nonetheless. When the girl's shoulders began trembling, Yukinoshita gestured as if deep in thought before annoucing in her usual monotone, "I don't hate you. I just…find you difficult, maybe."

"That means exactly the same thing in girl speak!" Yuigahama flailed. It seemed she really didn't want to be hated. She looked like a prostitute, but her reactions were very much akin to those of a normal girl.

"So? Why are you here?"

"Well, I'm super into cooking right now, aren't I?"

"You are? This is news to me."

"So this is, like…thanks for the other day? I made some cookies, so I was wondering if you wanted some."

Yukinoshita went pale as a sheet. If someone brought up Yuigahama's cooking, the first thing that came to mind was those charred, iron-like cookies. Just remembering them, both my throat and heart dried up.

"I don't really have much of an appetite, so it's okay. I appreciate the sentiment." Most likely she'd only just lost her appetite following the mention of Yuigahama's cookies. Not calling attention to that part was probably her way of being kind.

Indifferent to Yukinoshita's firm refusal, Yuigahama hummed as she plucked a cellophane-clad package out of her bag. The cutely wrapped thing was, indeed, pitch-black. "Man, trying it was so fun, you know! I'm thinking I'll try making a bento lunch or something later! Oh, so, Yukinon, let's have lunch together!"

"No, I like eating alone, so that would be a little much. And 'Yuki-non' is creepy, so stop it."

"No way! Aren't you lonely? Where do you eat, Yukinon?"

"In the clubroom…and were you listening to what I just said?"

"Oh, so, like, I'm free after school, so I'll help you with your club stuff. Oh, geez, this is, like…a thanks? This is my thanks, so don't worry about it at all!"

"Are you listening?" Yukinoshita, clearly stunned by Yuigahama's surging, all-out attack, glanced in my direction. It seemed as though she wanted me to do something about Yuigahama.

There's no way I'm helping you.

You're always spitting venom at me, you didn't pay me back for the Veggie Lifestyle…and she's your friend.

Seriously, though, I thought Yuigahama was coming to thank her like this because Yukinoshita had sincerely tried to help her with her problem. Yukinoshita was both entitled and obligated to accept that thanks. It would have been wrong for me to get in the way of that.

I shut my paperback and quietly stood. Offering a parting, inaudible "Bye" in my wake, I attempted to leave the clubroom.

"Oh, Hikki!" I heard my name, and when I turned, a black object was flying at my face. Reflexively, I grabbed it.

"Consider that my thanks, I guess? 'Cuz you helped me, too, Hikki."

I examined the package of black, heart-shaped somethings. They smelled ominous and looked vaguely sinister, but if this was her thanks, I'd accept them with gratitude.

But don't call me Hikki.

Shizuka Hiratsuka

Hachiman Hikigaya

Birthday

Private
(Don't ask a woman
for her date of birth.)

Special skills:

Hand-to-hand fighting techniques

Hobbies:

Driving, bike touring,
reading (manga, Harlequin romances)

How I spend my weekends:

Drinking until morning,
sleeping until noon,
waking up to drink some more,
sleeping

Birthday

August 8
(It's during summer vacation,
so my friends have never
celebrated it once. I have been
cursed before, though.)

Special skills:

Trivia, riddles, and things you
can do alone. Talking to myself.

Hobbies:

Reading

How I spend my weekends:

Lying around reading,
lying around watching TV,
lying around sleeping

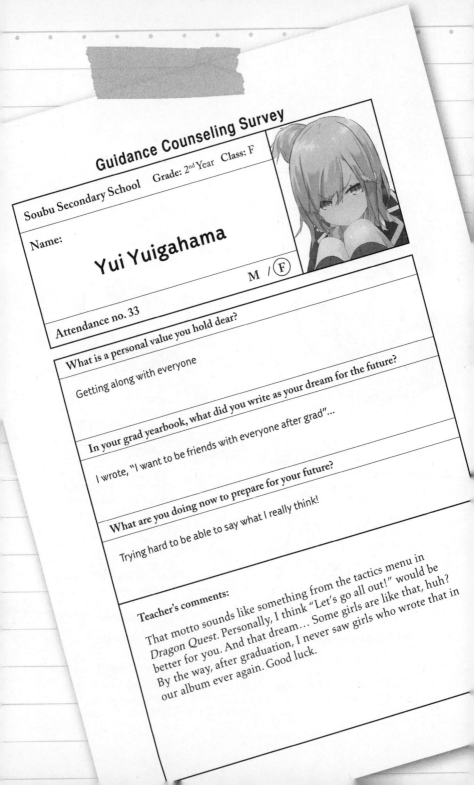

Guidance Counseling Survey

Soubu Secondary School   Grade: 2nd Year   Class: F

Name:

Yui Yuigahama

M / (F)

Attendance no. 33

What is a personal value you hold dear?

Getting along with everyone

In your grad yearbook, what did you write as your dream for the future?

I wrote, "I want to be friends with everyone after grad"...

What are you doing now to prepare for your future?

Trying hard to be able to say what I really think!

Teacher's comments:

That motto sounds like something from the tactics menu in *Dragon Quest*. Personally, I think "Let's go all out!" would be better for you. And that dream... Some girls are like that, huh? By the way, after graduation, I never saw girls who wrote that in our album ever again. Good luck.

"Yuigahama,
are you listening?"

"......You slut."

Even so, **the class** is doing well.

The bell rang, and fourth period ended. All at once, an air of relief began flowing through the class. Some students dashed off to the school store, some rearranged their desks and spread out their lunch boxes, and others went off to other classrooms. Lunch on this particular day in Class 2-F was bustling and noisy, as usual.

On days like today, when it rained, I had nowhere to go. I had the perfect spot where I usually went to eat my lunch, but obviously, I wasn't interested in getting soaked while I ate. Left with no alternative, I munched on my convenience store pastry alone in the class.

Usually, on rainy days like this, I would spend my lunch reading a novel or some manga, but I'd left the book I was reading in the clubroom the day before. Maybe I should have gone to get it during our ten-minute break period. It was a little too late for that now, though. "Too little, too late," as the Americans would say. *Wait—that's basically what I just said!*

I'm playing both sides of a comedy duo all on my own here. That's how bored I am. You know, I've always thought that when you spend long periods of time by yourself, you just naturally end up doing things without requiring other people.

When I'm at home, I talk to myself a lot. I sing loudly by myself. So often, when my sister comes home, I'll be like "MORE! MOR–welcome home." Obviously, I don't sing at school.

So instead, I think a lot.

I'd even say that to be a loner is to be a master of contemplating. As man is a thinking reed, he ponders things without even realizing. And precisely because the loner does not expend mental resources thinking about other people, his thoughts become that much deeper. This means that loners come to have different thought patterns than more social types, and sometimes that leads them to unique ideas that ordinary people wouldn't come up with.

It's difficult to convey a large amount of information through the limited method of expression that is conversation. It's just like how a computer works. It takes time to upload a huge amount of data to a server or to send it via e-mail. That's why loners tend to be somewhat lacking in conversation skills. That's all it is. I don't think that's necessarily a bad thing. Computers aren't just for sending e-mails. There's also the Internet and Photoshop. What I'm saying is, don't judge people based on that sole trait.

I used a computer as a metaphor there, but I don't actually know a lot about them. The ones who did were those guys crowded together in the front row of the classroom. And by "those guys," I was referring to the ones who'd brought their PSPs for a hunt on their ad-hoc Wi-Fi. I think their names were, like, Oda and Tahara or something.

"Hey! Use the hammer!"

"The gun lance was more than enough to waste him. ^ ^"

They seemed to be having very much fun indeed. I play that game, too, and honestly, I'd have liked to join them. It wasn't too long ago that manga, anime, and games were the province of loners. Lately, however, they've been turning into a sort of communication tool, and communication skills would be required in order to join people like them. Sadly, because I'm not quite as ugly as I could be, if I were to try to join them, they'd start saying stuff behind my back like *He's not for real* and *What a faux-taku*. What do you guys expect me to do about it, seriously?

When we were in middle school, I saw those guys talking about anime, so I tried to join in, but when I did, they both fell conspicuously silent. It was painful. Ever since then, I'd given up on trying to ingratiate myself with them.

I was never the kind of kid who'd burst out with *Let me play!* so I'm not about to start now. When we played kickball on recreational days, there was this rule that two of the leader types among the boys would play rock-paper-scissors to decide who got first pick for his team. I was always left for last. As a ten-year-old, I'd think to myself, *I wonder when I'm gonna get picked?* So pathetic you could cry, am I right?

As a result, though I'm reasonably athletic, I became bad at sports. I like baseball and stuff, but I have no one to play with. So when I was little, I played baseball all by myself, doing nothing but bouncing balls against walls and doing solo fielding practice, making liberal use of ghost runners and ghost defense men.

But there was another race in class quite adept at that sort of communication. The crowd sitting in the back were of that variety. There were two guys from soccer club, two guys from the basketball club, and three girls. One glance, and you could tell by their fashion-conscious appearances that they were the top caste in this classroom. By the way, Yuigahama was one of them.

Two among this herd were particularly dazzling. First, Hayato Hayama. That was the name of the clique's alpha. He was the ace of the soccer team and would soon be a candidate for captain. He was not someone who'd make you feel good about yourself after staring at him for a long time.

Basically, he was good-looking and stylish in a casual way. Fuck that guy.

"Man, I don't think I can make it today. I've got club and stuff."

"C'mon, you can skip one day, right? There's, like, a two-scoop sale today at Thirteen and One Flavors. I want a chocolate and cocoa double scoop."

"Both of those are chocolate. (LOL)"

"Huh? They're *totally* different! And I'm, like, *so* hungry." That loud voice was Hayama's other half, Yumiko Miura.

Her blonde hair was arranged in ringlet curls, and her uniform top was deliberately pulled down to show so much shoulder that I was like, *What are you, a samurai-era prostitute?* Her skirt was so short you had to wonder what was the point of wearing it at all. Miura had a pretty and shapely face, but she dressed so slutty and acted so stupid, I wasn't fond of her. Actually, I was genuinely scared of her. I felt like anything could come out of her mouth.

But Hayama apparently didn't see Miura as someone fearsome. Rather, from what I could tell, he regarded her as a friend who was as outgoing and affable as he was. This was exactly why I didn't understand the guys on the upper rungs of the food chain. No matter how you looked at it, she only acted that way because she was hanging out with him. In my presence, she would have killed me with a single snort. Well, there was no reason for her to associate with me, so she'd never talk to me, anyway, and I was fine with that.

Hayama and Miura continued to shoot the breeze.

"Sorry, not today," Hayama said, taking control of the conversation again. Miura stared at him, nonplussed.

Then the blond beside her ruffled up his hair and piped up with, "We're serious about going to Nationals this year."

What? Nationals? I mean, the city of Kunitachi uses the same characters as the word *nationals*, so maybe he was referring to Kunitachi, as in a location in the Tokyo Metropolitan Area that you could reach via the Chuo line. Because there was no way he could seriously think his team was going to Nationals.

"Bwa-ha…" An involuntary chuckle welled up in my throat. Oh man, he had this look on his face like *I am so cool for saying that.* It was so bad. The worst. Inexcusable.

"Plus, Yumiko…if you eat too much, you'll regret it."

"I don't get fat, no matter how much I eat. Aw, there's just nothing to do today but eat! Right, Yui?"

"Yeah, it's true, it's true. You've got a great figure, Yumiko. But I've got some plans today, so…"

"I know, right? There's just nothing to do but stuff our faces!" Miura said, and everyone laughed as if they'd been ordered to. It was just like the kind of hollow laughter you hear on a variety show laugh track. It was awfully loud, as if they'd just been cued to [laugh here] by the teleprompter.

I wasn't really trying to eavesdrop on their conversation. They were just so loud, I couldn't help but overhear. Actually, both nerds and normies tend to get loud when they're gathered in a group. There was no one near where I was seated, enthroned in the center of the room, but everything around me was a total commotion. It was as though I were in the eye of a hurricane.

From the middle of his group, Hayama flashed that smile that everyone loved. "Don't eat too much and make yourself sick."

"I *told* you, I'm fine no matter how much I eat. And I don't get fat. Right, Yui?"

"Yeah, like, Yumiko has, like, the figure of a goddess, for real. Her legs are *so* pretty. So, I, um…"

"What? I dunno… There's that girl, Yukinoshita or whatever her name is. Don't you think she's got it going on?"

"Oh, that's true. Yukino's totally got it."

Silence.

"Oh, well, but you've got better style, Yumiko," Yuigahama quickly continued when Miura went quiet, her eyebrow twitching. They were like…a queen and her maid or something.

But apparently, Yuigahama's backpedalling was insufficient to placate the queen's bruised feelings, and Miura's eyes narrowed in displeasure.

"Well, I guess it's no big deal. If you don't mind going after club's over, I'll come with you," Hayama offered casually as if sensing the tense atmosphere.

That appeared to placate the queen, who chirped, "Okay! Then text me, okay?" with a smile, and the conversation recommenced.

Yuigahama, who'd been looking like she was trying to hide, breathed a sigh of relief.

Hey, hey, that looked really rough. What is this, a feudal society? If you have to tiptoe around like that in order to become a normie, I'm fine being a loner forever.

When Yuigahama raised her head, our eyes met. When she saw my face, she took a deep breath, as if having made up her mind about something.

"Um, I…I've got somewhere to go during lunch, so…"

"Oh, do you? Then buy one of those things on your way back…a lemon tea. I forgot to bring a drink today, and I'm eating a pastry, so it's hard to eat without some tea, y'know?"

"H-huh? But, like…I'm coming back when fifth starts…like…I'll be gone all lunch, so I kinda sorta dunno if I can…" Yuigahama hesitated, and in an instant, Miura's face stiffened. Her expression mirrored the betrayal one might expect to see on a dog owner who'd just been bitten by her pet. Yuigahama, who'd probably never disputed anything Miura had ever said before, was suddenly denying a request.

"What? Uh…wait a minute. Huh? Like, didn't you say the same thing a while ago and bail on us after school? You're not being very social lately."

"Well, that was, like, sort of circumstances beyond my control, and I'm sorry, but I've got some personal business to attend to…" Yuigahama's reply rambled along. What was she, some white-collar office flunky?

But Yuigahama's explanations actually had the opposite effect intended, and Miura began tapping her nails on the desk in irritation. The queen's sudden explosion silenced the entire class. The Oda and Tahara (or whoever) I mentioned earlier deliberately switched off the sound on their PSPs. Hayama and hangers-on all dropped their gazes awkwardly to the floor. The sole sound audible in class was the restless, repetitive tapping of Miura's long nails atop the desk.

"I don't get what that's supposed to mean. If you've got something to say, then out with it. We're friends, aren't we? And you're, like…hiding stuff like that? How is that good?"

Yuigahama drooped, downcast.

The things Miura was saying were superficially nice, but in reality, she was just using their friendship to impose her will on Yuigahama. They were *friends*, Yuigahama was *one of them*, giving Miura free rein to say anything and do anything. That was what Miura really meant. And behind her words lurked a hidden threat of *If you can't spit it out, you're not one of us, and therefore our enemy.* This was an inquisition, and Yuigahama was being forced to step on a cross to test her faith.

"Sorry...," Yuigahama repented timidly, looking down.

"Don't just tell me '*sorry.*' You have something you want to say, don't you?"

Nobody would be capable of spitting out what they had to say after hearing that. This wasn't a conversation, and that wasn't a question. Miura was just attacking her and forcing her into an apology.

How moronic. Go ahead and destroy each other.

I turned my head away from the girls and took a bite of my pastry while fiddling with my phone. I munched a bit and then swallowed. But there was still something...something that wasn't bread stuck in my throat.

What was it?

Meals should have been more joyous and fun than this. If you subscribed to the ideology of the Lonely Gourmet, anyway. I didn't have the slightest desire to save her, though. It just gave me a mild stomachache to see a girl I knew crying in front of me. The sight would have ruined my meal. I really just wanted to have a nice meal. Plus, it was my job to get bullied around here, and I wouldn't let anyone else steal that role from me so easily.

Oh, and also...because I really didn't like that broad.

I pushed back from my desk with a rattle and sharply stood. "Hey, that's—"

"Shuddup."

—*enough.* The moment I attempted to finish saying that, Miura glared at me with snakelike eyes that practically hissed. "—a good reminder that I was thinking of buying myself a drink! B-but I guess I'll pass."

That was terrifying! Was she an anaconda or what? I'd nearly stammered an apology on reflex alone!

I sat down, dispirited, and Miura ignored me completely, instead looking down on the shrunken Yuigahama. "Listen, I'm saying this for your sake, but that sort of vague crap really pisses me off."

She insisted she was doing this for Yuigahama, but everything else she'd said had been about her own feelings and her own interests. She hadn't even finished her sentence and was already contradicting herself. But to Miura, that sort of thing wasn't a contradiction. She was the queen of this clique, and in a feudal society, the ruler's authority was absolute.

"Sorry…"

"That again?" Miura snorted vigorously in anger and disgust. That was all it took to make Yuigahama wither even more.

Just cut it out. This is annoying. You're making everyone in the classroom tiptoe around the scene you're making. I can't handle this kind of nasty atmosphere. Don't be dragging us all into your coming-of-age theater piece.

I screwed up what meager courage I had one more time. Nobody could possibly hate me any more than they already did, anyway. It's not a bad idea to play a game when you've got nothing to lose.

I stood to face them, and at the same time, Yuigahama turned to me with tear-laden eyes.

"Hey, what're you looking at, Yui? You've been doing nothing but apologizing," charged Miura in a chilly tone, as if carefully targeting that moment.

"She's not the one you should be apologizing to, Yuigahama," interrupted a voice apt to ring much colder than Miura's. It was a voice like the arctic wind, a voice that could make people cower, but it was as beautiful as the northern lights. Everyone's eyes were drawn to the door of the classroom, and even though it was in the corner of the room, it was as if it were the center of the world.

That voice could only belong to one person: Yukino Yukinoshita.

I was frozen in a half-upright position as if paralyzed. Miura's earlier threats were child's play compared to this. I mean, taking on Yukinoshita was so scary, you just couldn't keep your cool, you know? She went past scary to a point where you start thinking she's angelic.

Yukinoshita entranced everyone in the class. At some point, the sound of Miura's clicking on the desk had stopped, and all noise had dissipated. The only thing cutting through the silence now was the sound of Yukinoshita's voice.

"Yuigahama. You invited me to lunch and then failed to show up at our meeting place, making me seriously doubt you as a person. If you were going to be late, you should have at least contacted me. Am I wrong?"

Hearing those words, Yuigahama smiled in relief and faced Yukinoshita. "S-sorry. Oh, but I don't know your number, Yukinon…"

"Oh? Is that right? Then I suppose that one part was not your fault. I won't mention it again." Yukinoshita completely ignored the vibe in the room and conducted the conversation as she saw fit. It was refreshingly self-centered.

"H-hey! We're not done talking here!" Miura, finally defrosting, snapped at Yukinoshita and Yuigahama. The queen of flames stoked the fire even hotter and let her rage burn with a roaring fierceness.

"About what? I don't have the time to talk to you, though. I still haven't had my lunch."

"Wh-what? You can't come in here out of the blue and treat me like that! I'm *talking* to *Yui* right now."

"Talking? Don't you mean yelling? Was that supposed to be conversation? It looked to me like you were just getting hysterical and one-sidedly forcing your opinion on others."

"What?!"

"I apologize for failing to notice that you were talking. I'm unfamiliar with the particulars of your ecosystem, so I mistook it for the howling threats of an ape."

The seething queen of flames froze before the queen of ice. "Ngh…!"

Miura glared at Yukinoshita in unveiled rage, but Yukinoshita coldly shook it off. "You can play the king of the castle and bluster all you like, but please keep it to your own territory. Your pretense is as flaky as your makeup."

"Huh? What're you talking about? You're not making sense!" Clearly unable to admit defeat, Miura flopped back into her seat with a clatter. Her curls bounced up and down as she began to angrily fiddle with her phone. No one would talk to her when she was like that. Even Hayama, who got along with her, yawned to avoid the situation.

Right beside Miura, Yuigahama stood stock-still. Her fingers fretted the hem of her skirt as if she wanted to say something. Picking up on Yuigahama's intent, Yukinoshita moved to step out of the classroom.

"I'm going on ahead."

"Me too, I-I'll…"

"…You can do what you want."

"Yeah." Yuigahama smiled broadly. But she was the only one smiling.

Hey, come on… What's with this atmosphere in here? There was an unusual degree of anxiety in the classroom; it was even more awkward than usual. Before long, most of the students started formulating excuses like they were thirsty or had to go to the bathroom or whatever and left. The only people who remained in the end were Hayama and Miura's clique and some curious rubberneckers. I had no choice but to jump on the big wave rushing out of the room. Or rather, I should say that had it gotten any tenser, I'd have found myself unable to breathe. I'd die. Gingerly and making as little sound as possible, I passed by Yuigahama. When I did, I heard her whisper, "*Thanks for standing up earlier.*"

× × ×

When I left the classroom, I found Yukinoshita outside. She was leaning against the wall immediately beside the door, arms crossed and eyes closed. Perhaps due to her chilly aura, no one was around her. It was very quiet. And because of the silence, I could hear the conversation inside the class.

"Um...sorry. I'm just, like...anxious if I'm not fitting in with others...like, I just sort of pick up on what other people want without thinking...and maybe that can be irritating."

Miura said nothing.

"Well it's like...I dunno, I've just always been like that, you know? Like, even when we were playing *Ojamajo Doremi*, I actually wanted to be Doremi or Onpu-chan, but other girls wanted to be them, so I'd go with Hazuki... It's like...maybe it's because I grew up in an apartment complex, but there were always people around me, and that seemed like the obvious thing to do..."

"I have no idea what you're trying to say."

"Y-yeah, of course not. Well, I don't really get it myself, but...but you know, seeing Hikki and Yukinon, I noticed...even though there was no one around them, they looked like they were having fun, and they were always saying what they really thought, and even though neither of them are trying to fit together, they somehow do..." Her voice sounded like a stifled sob leaking out, stuttering along haltingly.

With each word, Yukinoshita's shoulders twitched, her eyes opening very slightly to glance into the classroom. *You idiot. You can't see it from here. If you're that worried, go in there. You're way too proud.*

"Seeing them, it's like all my desperate attempts to fit in were all wrong... I mean, like, Hikki's seriously a *hikki*. During lunch hour, he reads alone and laughs to himself... He's creepy, but he looks like he's having fun."

Hearing the word *creepy*, Yukinoshita chuckled. "I thought your strange habits were limited to the clubroom, but you're like that in your classroom, too, huh? That really is disgusting, so you should stop."

"If you think I'm being weird, then say so."

"It's so obvious. I just don't want to talk to you when you're so scary."

I'll take care for real from now on. I won't read any light novels with evil gods in them at school anymore.

"So that's why I thought maybe I could stop forcing myself and do what I wanted…or something like that. But it's not like I don't want to hang out with you or anything. So can we still…maybe…be…friends?"

"Hmph. Uh-huh. Sure, whatever." Miura snapped her cell phone shut.

"Sorry…thanks."

After that, there was no further conversation in the classroom, and I could hear the pitter-patter of Yuigahama's indoor shoes. Yukinoshita pushed herself off the wall she'd been leaning against, as if taking it as a sign. "Huh. So she can actually be honest." To my astonishment, she flashed a brief something that just barely counted as a smile.

It wasn't ironic or disparaging or sad; it was just a genuine smile.

But it disappeared in an instant, and she reassumed her usual cold, crystalline expression. While I was busy watching her smile, she strode briskly down the hallway and disappeared without paying me any regard at all. She was probably going wherever she was supposed to meet Yuigahama for lunch.

And right when I was thinking, *Now, what should I do?* and about to leave, the door of the classroom slid open with a rattle.

"Huh? Wh-why are you here, Hikki?"

I raised my right arm stiffly and gave her a jerky wave, like *'Sup*, in an attempt to evade the question. When I looked at her face, it was red.

"You heard?"

"Heard *what*?"

"You *were* listening! You were eavesdropping! You're such a creep! A stalker! A pervert! Um, um, um…and a creep! Unbelievable! You're such a creep. You're really *such* a creep."

"Hold back a little there." *Even I get a little sad if you unload all that venom right in my face. And don't say all that with such a sincere look. That's actually pretty hurtful.*

"What? I'm not gonna start holding back now. Whose fault do you think this is, you idiot?" Yuigahama stuck out her pink tongue at me and, with that cute provocation, ran away. *What are you, an elementary schooler? And don't run in the hallway.*

"Whose fault is that? Yukinoshita's, duh." I muttered to myself. There was no one else there, so of course it was to myself.

When I looked at the clock, there was only a little time left until lunch ended. That terribly parching lunch hour was over. I resolved to go buy a Sportop to soothe both my throat and my heart.

On my way to the school store, I suddenly changed my mind.

Nerds have their own nerd communities; they're not loners. In order to become a normie, you had to navigate your way through hierarchical relationships and power balances, and that was really tough. In the end, I was the only loner. Ms. Hiratsuka didn't have to go so far as to put me in an isolation ward. I was already a pariah in the class. There was no point in her quarantining me in the Service Club.

What a sad conclusion. Reality was just too harsh.

Sportop was the only thing that was sweet to me.

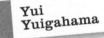

Yui
Yuigahama

Yukino
Yukinoshita

Birthday

June 18

Special skills:

Texting, karaoke, fitting in

Hobbies:

Karaoke, cooking
(I'm gonna try, anyway!)

How I spend my weekends:

Shopping with friends,
karaoke with friends,
photo booths with friends,
relaxing with friends

Birthday

January 3
(It's during winter vacation,
so I've never had the
experience of a birthday
party with classmates.)

Special skills:

Cooking, laundry, cleaning, house
chores in general, Aikido

Hobbies:

Reading (general literature,
English literature, classics),
horseback riding

How I spend my weekends:

Reading, watching films

In other words,
Yoshiteru Zaimokuza is rather off.

It's a little late to be going over this, but basically the purpose of the Service Club is to listen to any requests students have and then help them with their problems. I have to mentally confirm it this way, or I really wouldn't know what the point was anymore. I mean, usually Yukinoshita and I just read during club time, you know? And Yuigahama just fiddles with her phone.

"Hmm. Hey…so, like, why are you here?" She'd show up like it was only natural, and while I'd taken her presence for granted, Yuigahama wasn't actually a member of the club. I wasn't actually even sure if *I* was a member. Hey, seriously, was I in this club? I wanted to quit, anyway.

"Huh? Oh, you know, I just have nothing else to do today, know what I'm sayin'?" she said.

"No, I don't know, not if you use words like 'know what I'm sayin'.' What is that, a Hiroshima dialect?"

"What? Hiroshima? No, I'm a Chiba native."

Well, actually, "know what I'm sayin'" is from the Hiroshima dialect, and that makes a lot of people go, *Huh? That's the first time I've heard that.* The masculine register of the Hiroshima dialect has a reputation for sounding scary, but its feminine register is actually very cute. It's among my personal top ten ranking of cutest accents.

"Hmph. I'm not going to let you call yourself a Chiba native just because you were born in Chiba prefecture."

"Uh, Hikigaya. I have no idea what you're talking about." Yukinoshita gave me a thoroughly scornful look. But I ignored that.

"Let's go, Yuigahama. First question: What do you call internal bleeding from a blunt strike?"

"*Aonajimi!* Blue bruise!"

"Ngh! Correct. I never expected you'd have grasped even the Chiba dialect... Then, question number two: What comes with your school lunch?"

"Miso peanuts!"

"Oh-ho, it seems you really are a Chiba native."

"That's what I said." She put a hand to her hip and tilted her head to the side with a look on her face that said, *What's this guy's problem?*

Beside her, Yukinoshita had her elbows on the desk and her hands on her forehead as she sighed. "What's this about, now? Was there a point to that exchange?"

Of course there was no point. "It was just the Trans-Chiba Ultra Quiz. Trivia from all across the prefecture! Most specifically, from between Matsudo to Choshi."

"That's not covering much!" Yuigahama quipped.

"Fine, then how about from Sawara to Tateyama?"

"That's not across. That's north to south," said Yukinoshita.

You guys know all that from just the place names? Just how obsessed with Chiba are you?

"Okay, question number three. If you get on the Sotobo Line toward Toke, what rather uncommon animal will you see on the way?"

"Oh, speaking of Matsudo, Yukinon, there's supposed to be a lot of ramen shops in the area. Let's go sometime!"

"Ramen, huh? I haven't had it often, so I don't really know."

"It's okay! I haven't had it often, either!"

"Huh? What's okay about that? Could you explain?"

"Sure. So yeah, what was the name of that shop in Matsudo again? There's supposed to be a place that's really good..."

"Are you listening?"

"Hmm? I'm listening. Oh, but there's some good places in the area. It's in my neighborhood, so I'm really familiar with it. It's about five minutes from here on foot. There's this shop I pass by a lot when I'm walking my dog."

The correct answer was ostriches. Really, it was surprising to suddenly see an ostrich outside the train window... It was actually pretty exciting.

Sigh.

Ignoring the two girls and their one-sided conversation about ramen, I went back to my book. Why the heck was I all alone here even when there were two other people in the room? I guessed this was the kind of thing high school students were supposed to do, though. High schoolers take part in a broader range of activities than middle schoolers do, showing interest in clothing and cuisine and the like. Conversation about ramen shops is particularly high schooler–esque, don't you think?

I guess the Trans-Chiba Ultra Quiz isn't normal fare, though.

× × ×

It was the following day. When I went to the clubroom, I arrived to find the unusual sight of Yukinoshita and Yuigahama standing stock-still in front of the door. I studied them, wondering what the hell they were doing, when I noticed that the door was open just a crack and that they were peeking inside.

"What're you doing?"

" "*Eeeek!*" " Shrieking cutely and simultaneously, the two of them leaped into the air.

"Hikigaya... Y-you surprised me..."

"*You* guys surprised *me*." *What's with that reaction? You guys are acting like my cat does when I run into it in the living room in the middle of the night.*

"Could you not sneak up on us like that?" Even Yukinoshita's glare and her grumpy expression were just like my cat's. Now that I think of it, I was the only one in my family who my cat doesn't like. Another thing Yukinoshita and my cat shared in common.

"Sorry. So what're you doing?" I asked again, and Yuigahama, just like she had before, opened the door a crack and quietly peeped inside while replying, "There's a suspicious person in the clubroom."

"You two are the suspicious ones here."

"Just listen. Never mind about us. Could you go inside and see what's going on in there?" Yukinoshita ordered, looking sullen.

I stepped in front of the two of them as instructed, cautiously slid open the door, and went in.

Waiting for us was a gust of wind. The moment I opened the door, a sea breeze blew through the room. It scattered sheets of paper about the classroom, quite characteristic of the breeze that blew around this seaside school. It looked just like a flock of doves flying out of a silk hat used for magic tricks, and in the middle of that white world stood a man.

"Heh-heh-heh… I'm quite surprised to see you in a place like this. I've been waiting for you, Hachiman Hikigaya."

"Wh-what did you say?!" He was surprised, but he was waiting for me? What was that supposed to mean? I was the surprised one here.

Swiping aside the fluttering white papers, I sized up the intruder. Just as I suspected, he was… No, I didn't know him. Nope. I was unacquainted with Yoshiteru Zaimokuza.

Well, I suppose I wasn't acquainted with most of the students at this school. Within the category of people with whom I was unacquainted, though, this guy far and away topped the list of people I didn't want to know. Plus, he was sweating in a trench coat and wearing fingerless gloves even though it was almost summer. Even if I had known a guy like that, I wouldn't have cared.

"Hikigaya, he seems to know you…" Yukinoshita hid behind my back as she compared me and the interloper, a doubtful expression on her face.

He flinched for a moment under her discourteous gaze before immediately confronting me instead, crossing his arms with a low chuckle. He shrugged his shoulders dramatically, shaking his head arrogantly. "How could you forget the face of your partner? I'm absolutely offended, Hachiman."

"He's calling you his partner..." Yuigahama gave me a chilly look. Her eyes were saying, *All you pieces of garbage can go and die.*

"Indeed, partner. You have memories of those days, do you not? We survived hell together many a time."

"We were just paired up in gym class," I couldn't resist retorting, and a grimace inspired by loathing spread across his face.

"Hmph. That evil custom is nothing less than hellish. Pair with whomever you like, they say? Heh-heh-heh... I never know when I might perish, so I do not forge such bonds... I need not another such soul-rending farewell. If that was love, then I have no need of it!" His eyes glazed over as he stared out the window. He probably saw the image of some beloved princess of his floating in the sky. Or maybe everyone just likes *Fist of the North Star* too much.

Well, if you've come this far, no matter how thick you are, you've got to have noticed by now. This guy is a little...you know.

"What do you want, Zaimokuza?"

"Hngh, you have voiced the name that is carved on my soul. I am indeed the Master Swordsman General, Yoshiteru Zaimokuza." His trench coat fluttered vigorously, rustling as he stretched his chubby face into an exaggeratedly handsome expression and turned to face me. He was completely in character with the Master Swordsman General identity he'd created. Just watching him made my head throb. Actually, it hurt my soul more than it did my head, and Yukinoshita's and Yuigahama's daggerlike stares hurt even more than that.

"Hey...what's *that*?" Displeasure—or rather, discomfort—etched on her face, Yuigahama glowered at me. Why was I the one getting glowered at?

"This is Yoshiteru Zaimokuza... We're partners in gym class." Frankly, it was nothing more and nothing less than that. That was all there was to our relationship. I guess it wasn't entirely wrong to say that we were partners for the purpose of surviving that "hellish time."

Seriously, having to pick partners for stuff was hell.

And because Zaimokuza was so painful to watch, he understood the bitterness of that moment as well.

Zaimokuza and I had first paired up in gym class because we were the only two left, and ever since then, we've always been paired together. Frankly, he had such a bad case of M-2 syndrome that I wanted to trade him off to another team. Unable to manage it, though, I'd given up. I'd also thought about declaring myself a free agent, but unfortunately, signing someone of my caliber was just so expensive that it hadn't gone well. Wasn't that right? Yeah, no. It was just that neither of us had any friends.

Yukinoshita listened to my explanation while she compared Zaimokuza and me. And then, as if satisfied, she nodded. "This is what they call 'birds of a feather flocking together,' huh?" She'd reached the worst possible conclusion.

"Don't be stupid. You can't lump the two of us together. I'm not that painfully awkward. And we don't flock together, anyway!"

"Heh, I concur. We are indeed no friends... I'm so alone, hee-hee!" Zaimokuza smiled sadly in self-deprecation. Oh, he was back to normal now.

"Not that I care, but doesn't this friend of yours have some business with you?"

Her words brought me nearly to tears. The word *friend* hadn't sounded so sad since middle school. Not since Kaori-chan told me, *You're nice, and I like you, but I don't know about dating... Yeah, let's be friends.* I don't need friends like that.

"Mwa-ha-ha-ha-ha, I nearly forgot! Incidentally, Hachiman, is this the place of meeting for the Service Club?" Zaimokuza, back in character, looked at me while belting out an odd guffaw.

What the heck was with that laugh? This was my first time hearing it.

"Yes, this is the Service Club," Yukinoshita replied in my stead.

Zaimokuza glanced at her for an instant before immediately returning his gaze to me. Seriously, why did people keep looking at me today?

"I-is that so? If it is as the sage Hiratsuka advised me, then, Hachiman, you are obligated to grant my wish, are you not? To think that we would yet be master and servant, even after all these centuries… Is this the guidance of the great Bodhisattva Hachiman?"

"The Service Club will not necessarily grant your wishes. We can only help you to achieve your goals yourself," droned Yukinoshita.

"Heh. Mm-hmm… Then lend your aid to me, Hachiman. Heh-heh-heh… This reminds me of how we once attempted, as comrades in arms, to seize hold of the land."

"What happened to the master-and-servant thing? And why do you keep looking at me like that?"

"A-hem, a-hum! Between you and I, such trifling details are unimportant. I shall make a special exception in this case." Zaimokuza made some contrived throat-clearing noises in an attempt to cover up his inconsistency and regarded me as he had before. "My apologies. It appears that in this era, the hearts of men are corrupted, compared to the days of yore. I miss the purity of the Muromachi era… Don't you, Hachiman?"

"No. Go die."

"Heh-heh-heh. I do not fear death. On the other side, I would merely take the kingdom of heaven for mine own." Zaimokuza raised his hands up high as his coat rustled and fluttered.

The word *die* didn't seem to bother him that much.

I'm the same way. When you're used to getting insulted and abused, you just get good at striking back, or rather, compartmentalizing it. What a sad skill. I'm crying right now.

"Whoa…" Yuigahama was cringing, and she'd gone somewhat pale.

"Hikigaya, come," Yukinoshita said, tugging my sleeve and whispering in my ear. "What is that 'Master Swordsman General' stuff?" Such a cute face and pleasant smell so close to me, and yet her words completely lacked eroticism.

One word was enough to answer her question. "That's M-2 syndrome. M-2 syndrome."

"Em-too syndrome?" Yukinoshita cocked her head and gaped at

me. I noticed that the shape of the girl's lips when she made the *oo* sound was super-cute. What a mysterious discovery.

Yuigahama, who'd been listening intently, joined in the conversation. "He's sick?"

"He's not actually sick. It's just slang."

Put it simply, *M-2 syndrome* referred to a range of behaviors common to second-year middle schoolers who were too awkward to look at. But even within that category, Zaimokuza's case was terminal. We're talking full-blown "evil eye" territory.

He yearned for the kinds of abilities or special powers that appeared in manga, anime, games, and light novels, and he actually acted as if he possessed them. Of course, once you had powers, you had to create a premise where you were the reincarnation of a legendary warrior or chosen by the gods or a secret service elite in order to explain the origins of those powers. And then you would act based on that premise.

So then why did he do this?

Because it was cool.

I think most middle schoolers have fantasized about that sort of thing at least once. You've stood in the mirror before and practiced saying something like *All you ladies and gentlemen watching Countdown TV, good evening! Well now, tonight I've written the lyrics for this song on the theme of frank love…*right?

In a nutshell, M-2 syndrome was an extreme example of that.

I briefly explained the affliction, and Yukinoshita seemed to understand. It never ceased to impress me how swiftly her mind operated. It was as though if you explained one to her, she'd understand all the way up until ten. She had an aptitude for grasping the heart of the matter with little explanation.

"I don't get it," Yuigahama muttered. In contrast to Yukinoshita, Yuigahama stood with her mouth hanging open unpleasantly, as if she were saying, *Duuuuuh?* Well, even I wouldn't have gotten it from that brief an explanation. Yukinoshita was the weird one here for catching on so quickly.

"Hmph. So essentially, it's as if he's role-playing within a setting of his own design."

"That's basically it. He's basing his character off Yoshiteru Ashikaga, the thirteenth shogun of the Muromachi period. It was probably just easy for him to go with that because they have the same name."

"Why does he see you as his ally?"

"I think he's just taking the name Hachiman and thinking of the Bodhisattva Hachiman. The Seiwa Genji clan zealously worshipped him as a god of war. You know about the Tsurugaoka Hachiman shrine, right? The one in Kamakura?" I replied, and Yukinoshita suddenly went silent. When I cast her a questioning glance, she opened her big eyes wide and considered me.

"I'm surprised. You know a lot about it."

"I guess." I felt unpleasant memories rising within me, so I looked away and avoided the subject while I was at it. "Zaimokuza is incredibly anal over citations and historical facts, but at least his fantasies are history based, so they're not as bad as they could be."

Yukinoshita gave Zaimokuza a sidelong glare, and with a look of utter contempt, she asked, "It gets worse than *that?*"

"Yep."

"Just for my own reference, what sort of fantasies are we talking about?"

"Well, originally, there were seven gods in the world. Three gods of creation—Garan, the Wise Emperor; Methika, Goddess of War; Hearthia, Protector of Souls—three gods of destruction—Olto, the Foolish King; Rogue of the Lost Temple; Lai-Lai the Paranoid—and the eternally missing god, the Nameless God. These seven gods are eternally repeating cycles of prosperity and decline. This is the seventh time they've remade the world, and to make certain that this time they can prevent its destruction, the Japanese government is looking for the reincarnations of these gods. The most important god among these seven is the eternally missing god, the Nameless God, whose powers are yet unknown, and this missing god is me, Hiki... Hey, you're really good at leading questions! You really freaked me out there! I was just about to go into detail."

"I didn't prompt any of that."

"So creepy."

"Watch what you say, Yuigahama, or I might inadvertently kill myself."

Yukinoshita sighed, a look of disgust on her face as she again compared me and Zaimokuza and said, "In other words, you and *it* are of the same breed. So that's why you know so much about his 'Master Swordsman General' nonsense."

"No, no, no. What are you talking about, Yukinoshita? Of course that's not true. I just know a lot about it because of other stuff, you know? I chose to take Japanese history, okay? I played *Nobunaga's Ambition*, okay?"

"Mm-hmm?" Yukinoshita gave me a look that said, *Guilty until proven innocent.*

But even under her gaze, I would not falter, because I was not like Zaimokuza. I could confidently return Yukinoshita's gaze, as she was in error.

I am not the same as Zaimokuza. I was the same as Zaimokuza.

Hachiman is a fairly rare name, so I had a phase where I thought I might be special in some way. Having liked anime and manga since I was little, it was inevitable I'd fall prey to such delusions. Everyone, at one point or another, lies in bed at night and imagines they have some kind of hidden powers and that one day those powers will suddenly awaken—entangling them in a battle to determine the fate of the world—and keeps a Diary of the Celestial Realm in preparation for the time that will come, and writes a quarterly report for the government about it, right? You don't?

"Well, you know. Maybe I was like that as a kid, but not anymore."

"I'm not so sure about that." Yukinoshita smiled mischievously, leaving me and approaching Zaimokuza.

Watching her go, the thought suddenly crossed my mind: *Am I really so different from him?*

The answer was yes.

I don't have those stupid delusions anymore. I don't write in my Celestial Diary anymore or write reports for the government anymore. The most I write these days is a list of people I hate, and the first name on that list is, of course, Yukinoshita.

I don't assemble Gundam models and play with them while making action noises or combine clothespins to make the ultimate robot. I've also outgrown training with self-defense weapons made from rubber bands and aluminum foil. I've stopped cosplaying with my dad's long coat and my mom's fake fur scarf.

Zaimokuza and I were different.

While I uncertainly arrived at that conclusion, Yukinoshita stood before Zaimokuza, and Yuigahama whispered, "Yukinoshita, run!"

Pretty sad, am I right?

"I think I understand. Your request is for us to cure your mental illness, isn't that right?"

"Hachiman, I have come to this place so that my wish might be granted, as per my agreement with thee. I hath but a single wish to ask of ye, though it is a truly noble and sublime ambition." Zaimokuza turned away from Yukinoshita to address me directly. He was mixing up his second-person pronouns and throwing in *hath* to boot. How confused was this guy?

That was when I noticed something. Whenever Yukinoshita spoke to him, that idiot would turn my way instead. Well, I got why. If I didn't know what Yukinoshita was really like, she'd have flustered me every time she talked to me, and I wouldn't have been able to look her in the eye, either.

But Yukinoshita lacked the empathy of the average individual. She wouldn't treat a man and his innocent feelings with any kind of sensitivity. "I'm the one speaking here. Look at me when I'm talking to you," she said coldly, grabbing Zaimokuza's collar and forcing him to face forward. Yes, though completely lacking in manners herself, Yukinoshita was incredibly fussy over the manners of others. So fussy that

I'd even started giving her a formal greeting every time I walked into the clubroom.

When Yukinoshita let go of his collar, Zaimokuza hacked away, coughing for real. Apparently, this wasn't the time to be in character. "M-mwa...mwa-ha-ha-ha. You caught me with mine guard down!"

"And stop talking like that."

Her cold treatment caused Zaimokuza to fall silent and examine his shoes.

"Why are you wearing a long coat at this time of year?"

"Ahem-hem. This cloak is armor that protects mine body from miasma and is one of the twelve sacred treasures I have always had in mine possession. With each of my reincarnations, I change it to a form most appropriate for that body. Fwa-ha-ha-ha-ha!"

"Stop talking like that."

"Oh, okay..."

"Then what are those fingerless gloves? Is there a meaning to them? Your fingertips are left unprotected."

"Oh, yes. Um...I inherited these from my past life, and they're one of mine twelve sacred treasures, special gauntlets known as Overamd, from which I fire my Diamond Shot. 'Tis easier to use that skill with my fingertips free...and that's why! Fwa-ha-ha-ha-ha!"

"Stop."

"Ha-ha-ha! Ha-ha-ha...ha..." His laugh, which had begun as a hearty one, turned a little sad and wet sounding near the end. After that, he went quiet.

Then, as if she'd taken pity on him, Yukinoshita's expression did a one-eighty, turning kind. "Anyway, you want us to cure that illness of yours, I take it?"

"Uh, I'm not sick, though," Zaimokuza said very quietly, averting his eyes from her. He glanced at me uncomfortably. Now he was totally back to normal. Apparently, Zaimokuza lacked the capacity to stay in character with Yukinoshita staring straight at him, eyes blazing.

Agh! I can't stand to watch this anymore! Zaimokuza was just too pathetic. It made me want to throw him a rope or something. Anyway, when I took a step to separate myself from the two of them, I heard something rustle at my feet. It was the source of the paper blizzard that had whipped through the room.

"This paper…" Lifting my eyes from the page, I looked around. They were printed in a fixed grid of forty-two by thirty-two characters and were scattered everywhere. I picked them up, one by one, and sorted them numerically.

"Oh-ho, as expected, you understand with no explication. It seems we did not endure that hellish time together for nothing."

Completely ignoring Zaimokuza's dramatic muttering, Yuigahama studied the stack in my hands. "What's that?" I handed her the bundle of papers, and she flipped through, inspecting them. A question mark floated above her forehead as she attempted to read through it before she sighed deeply and returned the heap to me.

"I think it's a novel draft."

That got a reaction from Zaimokuza, and he cleared his throat to return us to the topic at hand.

"Your discernment obliges me. That is indeed the draft of a light novel. I'm thinking about submitting it to a contest for new writers, but as I have no friends, I have no one with whom to seek counsel. Please read it for me."

"I feel like I just heard something very sad delivered very casually," said Yukinoshita.

You could say that trying to write a light novel is the logical consequence of a case of M-2 syndrome. It is indeed reasonable to want to give shape to the things you've continually yearned for. It's also perfectly normal to think, *Well, I daydream a lot, so I can write!* Furthermore, if you can make a living doing what you love, that's a very fortuitous thing. So there was nothing mysterious about Zaimokuza writing a light novel. The mystery was why he was coming all this way to show it to us.

"There's submission sites and threads and stuff. Why don't you just post it online?"

"I cannot! Those people are without mercy. If I were to receive such harsh criticism from them, I think I'd die."

What a wimp.

But it's true that people on the Internet, whose faces you can't see, can be pretty blunt and inconsiderate, while friends will be kind and gentle and say placating things. Most people with the sort of relationship I had with Zaimokuza would find it hard to be harsh. There's something about looking someone in the eye that makes it hard to give them a biting critique. You'd probably put it as delicately as possible. That is to say, *most* people would.

"But you know…"

I glanced to the side with a sigh. When my eyes met Yukinoshita's, she looked puzzled. "I think Yukinoshita would be more merciless than a submission site."

X   X   X

Yukinoshita, Yuigahama, and I all took home copies of the draft that Zaimokuza had given us and decided to spend the night reading it.

If I were to categorize Zaimokuza's novel as a certain genre, I'd call it a school superhero story. Set in a certain urban region of Japan, it had secret organizations, people with superpowers and memories of their past lives, scheming, and then the main character—the kind of normal boy you'd see anywhere—has his hidden powers awaken. Finally, there's a big spectacle of the hero defeating one villain after another.

By the time I was done reading it, the sun was rising, so I ended up sleeping through most of my classes the next day. But even so, I somehow got through a listless sixth period, endured a short homeroom, and decided to go to the clubroom.

"Hey! Wait, wait!" Just as I was entering the special-use building, I heard a voice calling out behind me. When I turned, I saw Yuigahama running up to me with a thin bag over her shoulder. She seemed particularly energetic as she came up to walk beside me. "Hikki, you look tired! What's wrong?"

"Come on, of course I'm tired after reading that brick! I'm so sleepy. Actually, I'd like to know how you could read that thing and still have energy the next day."

"Huh?" Yuigahama blinked. "Oh, o-of course. Man, I'm *so* tired."

"You didn't read it, did you?"

Yuigahama didn't reply to my question. She just started humming something while looking out the window. She was trying to play dumb, but there was sweat dripping off her cheeks and the back of her neck. I'd have liked seeing her blouse turn transparent…

× × ×

Opening the door to the clubroom, I caught a rare glimpse of Yukinoshita dozing off.

"Long night, huh?" I commented, but she continued breathing softly in her sleep. She was almost smiling, an expression quite different from her usual flawless mask, and seeing this new side of her made my heart race.

I started feeling as though I wouldn't mind watching her tender, sleeping face forever…her gently swaying black hair…her smooth, pale, almost translucent skin…her large, misty eyes, and her well-shaped pink lips…

"You surprised me. That face of yours woke me up completely."

Ack… That remark right there just woke me up, too. I almost let her appearance deceive me and lost my head. I'd like to send this girl to an eternal sleep.

Yukinoshita yawned broadly like a cat, raising both hands above her head and stretching high.

"From the look of it, you had a pretty rough night, too."

"Yes, it's been a long time since I last stayed up all night, and I've never read anything of this nature before… I don't think I'll be able to get into this genre."

"Yeah, me either," Yuigahama said.

"You didn't even read it. Read it now, come on!" At my insistence, Yuigahama groaned and pulled said draft from her bag. It was in mint condition without a single crease. Yuigahama flipped through it at an unnaturally fast pace. She read it like it was the most boring thing in the world, seriously. Leaning in from the side to watch, I opened my mouth to speak.

"Zaimokuza's draft isn't representative of all light novels. There's a lot of good ones," I said, fully acknowledging that I wasn't being very supportive of Zaimokuza.

Yukinoshita tilted her head and listened. "Like the one you were reading the other day?"

"Yeah, that one's interesting. I recommend Gaga—"

"When I get the chance." There is a law that says, *People who say that will never actually read it.* I keenly felt that law come into effect at that exact moment as someone knocked wildly on the clubroom door.

"Good morrow." Zaimokuza entered with an archaic salutation. "Now then, let me hear your impressions." He sat down in a chair with a thud and crossed his arms arrogantly. His expression had an edge of smug superiority, his face brimming with confidence.

Opposite him sat Yukinoshita, looking unusually apologetic. "I'm sorry. I don't really know much about this sort of thing…," she prefaced.

Zaimokuza's response was generous. "I care not. I wanted to ask the opinions of normal folk. Say what you will about it."

Yukinoshita replied with a brief, "Sure," took a small breath, and readied herself.

"It was boring. It was actually painful to read. It was boring beyond anything I had imagined."

"Gagh!"

She cut the poor bastard down in a single strike. Rattling in his chair, Zaimokuza was thrown back in his seat, but he somehow managed to right himself again.

"First of all, your grammar is all over the place. Why do you constantly put sentences in reverse order? Do you know how to use grammar? Did you not learn that in elementary school?"

"Nghh… I used a simple style in order to give the reader an impression of intimacy…"

"Don't you think you should be capable of writing basic Japanese before you think about that? Plus, there are so many errors in the kanji readings you're sticking in there. You don't read the characters for 'ability' as 'strength.' And how on earth does something written with the characters for 'illusory red blade flash' get pronounced as 'bloody nightmare slasher'—in English? Where did that 'nightmare' come from, anyway?"

"Geh! U-ugh… No! These days they come up with distinctive names for superpowers."

"This is just self-indulgence. Nobody but you will understand it. Do you want people to actually read this? Oh yes, speaking of getting people to read it, it's so obvious what's going to happen in this book that it's not in the least bit suspenseful. And why does the heroine take off her clothes in this part? There's absolutely no need for it in that scene, and it's utterly dull."

"Ergh! B-but you need…elements like that in order to sell, um…"

"And these other sentences are too long, too verbose, have too many characters, and are too hard to read. Or perhaps I should just ask that you not make people read an incomplete story. Before acquiring some literary skills, you first should acquire some common sense."

"Gyagh!" Zaimokuza threw out all four of his limbs and emitted a shriek. His shoulders twitched spasmodically. His eyes rolled back to the ceiling, showing only the whites. His overreactions were starting to get annoying, and I thought it was about time for him to stop.

"That's enough," I said. "Laying that all on him at once is a little much."

"I'm still not done, but…fine, then. So next is Yuigahama?"

"Huh? M-me?!" Yuigahama replied in surprise. Zaimokuza turned to her and gave her a pleading look. His eyes were blurry with tears. Seeing this, and understandably feeling sorry for him, Yuigahama stared into space and tried to look for something to praise. "U-um... Y-you know a lot of difficult words, huh?" she squeezed out.

"So cruel—ngf!"

"You didn't have to finish him off there..."

Those words were practically taboo to an aspiring writer. I mean, saying that means there was nothing else praiseworthy about it, you know? It's something that people who don't really read a lot of light novels often say when asked to give their opinion, but saying that is basically the same thing as saying, *That was boring.*

"O-okay, you next, Hikki." Yuigahama stood from her seat and offered it to me as if making her escape. She sat me down directly opposite Zaimokuza and deposited herself daintily in a seat behind me and to the side.

Zaimokuza had already burned himself out. He was all pale, and I couldn't stand to look him in the eye. "G-gngh. H-Hachiman. You get it, right? You understand the world I created, the horizons of the book. None of these fools can comprehend it, but you understand the depth of my tale, don't you?"

Yes, I understand.

I nodded to put him at ease. Zaimokuza's eyes told me, *I trust you.*

It would have made me less of a man had I failed to reply here. I took a deep breath and said kindly, "So what're you ripping off here?"

"Bfft?! Gerk... eergh..." Zaimokuza rolled around writhing on the floor, and when he hit the wall, he stopped and lay still without a twitch. His empty eyes looked up at the ceiling, and a single tear streaked down his cheek. His message of *Oh, I guess I'll just die* was abundantly clear.

"You're merciless. That was even crueler than me." Yukinoshita was quite taken aback.

"Hey..." Yuigahama poked my side with her elbow. She seemed to be saying, *You have something else to say, right?* What should I have said...? I thought for a bit before remembered I'd forgotten to raise the most basic point.

"Well, the important part is the illustrations. Don't worry too much about the content."

X X X

Zaimokuza gasped in and out, going through some Lamaze technique to calm himself before pushing himself to his feet, trembling like a newborn baby deer. Then he smacked the dust off his clothes and turned straight to me.

"Will you read my work again sometime?" I doubted my ears for a moment. He repeated himself in a clearer, stronger voice. "Will you read my work again sometime?" He regarded both me and Yukinoshita expectantly.

"Are you—"

"—a masochist?" Yuigahama, hiding in my shadow, cast Zaimokuza a loathing leer. It was as if she were saying, *Die, you pervert.* No, that wasn't his problem.

"You still wanna do that after having your book chewed up like that?"

"Of course. Your criticism was indeed harsh. I even thought that maybe I should just die, because it's not like I can get girls, and I don't have any friends anyway. I was actually thinking that everyone but me should just die."

"Yeah, I'll bet. If someone said all that to me, I'd want to die, too." But having taken all those hits, Zaimokuza could still say that.

"But…but even so, it made me happy. I wrote that because I wanted to, and I'm glad I could have someone read it and give me their opinion. I cannot say as of yet what I should call this feeling I have right now, but…having someone read my draft does please me," he declared, smiling. It wasn't the Master Swordsman General's smile; it was Yoshiteru Zaimokuza's smile.

Oh, I get it.

He didn't just have M-2 syndrome. He was afflicted with a full-blown writer's fever. Wanting to write because you want to write, because you have something to say…feeling happy when what you've written moves someone, and then wanting to write over and over…carrying on even in the face of the disapproval of others… I think that was what they called the writing bug.

I *had* to read it. Because, I mean, this was his goal: the result of his M-2 syndrome. This was the vindication of his struggle to give shape to his fantasies. Even after being treated like a sicko, being frowned upon and laughed at, he never yielded and never surrendered.

"When I've written something new, I'll bring it here." He left those words behind and turned from us, leaving the club with dignified steps. The door he closed after him seemed awfully dazzling.

Even if it's twisted, childish, or wrong, if you can commit to it, it has to be right. If having someone deny your ability is enough to make you change, then it isn't your dream, and it isn't you. That was why Zaimokuza was fine the way he was.

Aside from the creepy parts.

X   X   X

A few days passed after that. It was sixth period. The final class of the day was gym. Zaimokuza and I were, as usual, paired up. That was nothing out of the ordinary.

"Hachiman. What divinely skilled artist is popular these days?"

"You're getting ahead of yourself. Think about that after you've won that contest."

"Hmm. 'Tis so. The problem is where I should make my debut…"

"Why do you keep assuming you're going to win?"

"If I get popular and it gets made into an anime, maybe I can marry a voice actress?"

"Come on. Enough of that. First, write your draft. Okay?"

That was basically how Zaimokuza and I started talking during gym class. If anything changed, that was the extent of it. It's not like we talked about anything important. Our conversations weren't especially uplifting, and we didn't burst into laughter like the people around us. The things we talked about were neither fashionable nor cool. It was nothing but pathetic nonsense. Even I thought it was dumb. I honestly wondered what the point of these conversations was.

But, at the very least, I didn't hate gym class anymore.

That was basically it.

Guidance Counseling Survey

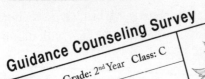

Soubu Secondary School   Grade: 2nd Year   Class: C

Name:

Yoshiteru Zaimokuza

Ⓜ / F

Attendance no. 12

What is a personal value you hold dear?

I am a blade, always ready for battle.

In your grad yearbook, what did you write as your dream for the future?

Elementary school → Manga artist
Middle school → Novelist

What are you doing now to prepare for your future?

Always equipping a 1 kg weight on my arms in order to
be prepared for the battles to come.

Teacher's comments:

Who are you fighting? You know, even if you do take off those
weights, you're not going to develop any hidden powers. And did
you change your dream from manga artist to novelist because
you can't draw or what?

"Zai...something or other. I feel so sorry for you...for your brain, I mean."

"Zaimokuza, you need to consolidate your life and your role-playing into a cohesive whole. Come on."

But **Saika Totsuka** has one.

My little sister, Komachi, held a slice of toast slathered in jam in one hand as she enthusiastically pored over a fashion magazine. I was peeking at it from the side while drinking my morning black coffee. The articles in the magazine were filled with extremely irritating terms like *safe sex* and *super-hot*. I felt like I was getting stupider just reading it, my coffee dribbling out the corners of my mouth as I went *bleagh*. Come on, was this for real? Is Japan gonna be okay? It seemed to me that if you were to grade the intellect of this article on a bell curve, it would only come out to around the twenty-fifth percentile. What's more, my sister was nodding along as she read it. *Just what part of this is resonating with you?*

I was told that this fashion magazine, *Heaventeen*, is the number one magazine among middle-school girls, and in fact, those who don't read it actually get bullied. Komachi went *ooh* appreciatively as she dropped crumbs on the page. *Are you doing a solo Hansel and Gretel or what?*

It was seven forty-five. "Hey. Look at the time." My sister was deep into the magazine, so I poked her shoulder with my elbow and let her know it was about time to go.

Komachi raised her head with a gasp and checked the clock. "Ack! Crap!" she yelled, immediately closing the magazine with a slap and standing up.

"Hey, hey, hey. Look at your mouth, look! There's stuff on it."

"Huh? No way. I'm jammed?"

"Is your mouth an automatic rifle? That word does not mean what you think it means."

My sister swiped her mouth with a pajama sleeve while grousing, "Oh, crap!" She was quite a handsome man, my sister.

"You know, Bro, sometimes I don't get what you're talking about."

"That's you. You mean you!"

Completely ignoring me, Komachi began panicking and flailing her way into her school uniform. She threw off her pj's, baring smooth white skin, a white sports bra, and white panties.

Don't undress here. Not here.

Little sisters are mysterious creatures. No matter how cute they are, you don't really feel anything toward them. I can only regard her underwear as mere pieces of cloth. She was cute, but all I could think about her was *I guess it's because she looks like me.* This is how it is with real little sisters.

I gave Komachi a sidelong glance as she covered herself in a sloppily arranged uniform. She flashed her panties below her knee-length skirt as she pulled on her socks and rolled them down twice to her ankles. I pulled the milk and sugar toward me.

Maybe she was trying to make her boobs grow this month or something, because lately she'd been drinking a lot of milk. I didn't really give a damn. But putting the phrase *the milk my sister drank* in meaningful-sounding italics makes it sound kind of lewd and depraved. But who really cared? I didn't pull the sugar and milk toward me because it was *the milk my sister drank.* I just wanted to put it in my coffee.

I was a natural-born child of Chiba, the kind they say gets marinated in MAX Coffee for their first bath and is suckled on the stuff instead of breast milk, so my coffee had to be sweet. Condensed milk would have been even better. But I could drink it black, too, okay?

"Life is bitter, so coffee at least should be sweet," I muttered to myself, tossing back the heavily sugared drink. That line could have been a MAX Coffee slogan.

So good… The ad copy I just came up with, I mean. They should actually use it.

"Bro! I'm ready!"

"Bro is still drinking his coffee." I replied, doing an impersonation that did not remotely resemble something I'd seen in reruns of *From the Northern Country*.

But of course Komachi didn't notice. She just cheerfully sang, "I'm late! ♪ I'm late! ♪" It made me wonder if she actually wanted to be late or what.

This was something that happened a few months ago, but this one time, my idiot of a sister slept in and was running late for school, so I ended up taking her on the back of my bike. Ever since then, I've gradually been taking her to school more and more often.

Nothing is less trustworthy than a woman's tears. Komachi in particular had that special knack for crying that younger girls do, and she was a master at manipulating her older brother. She was vicious. Thanks to her, the idea that *women* = "people who use men like my little sister Komachi does" is imprinted on my brain. "If I can't trust women anymore, it'll be your fault. What'll I do when I'm old if I can't get married?"

"Then I'll take care of you somehow, okay?" She grinned. I'd always thought of her as a child, but something about that look on her face was mature. I felt my heart skip a beat. "I'll work hard, save money, and put you in an old folks home or something."

Maybe less mature and more just your typical adult.

"You really are my little sister." I sighed. I gulped down the rest of my coffee and stood. Komachi prodded my back:

"It's already this late because you're so slow! I'm gonna be late!"

"You brat…" If she weren't my sister, I definitely would have given her a punt. Usually, it was the other way around, but in the Hikigaya household, things are different. My old man was abnormally fond of my sister, and his famous saying of *I'll kill any man who comes near her, even her brother* had gotten even me to back off. If I'd tried to kick her, I would have been beaten and thrown out of the house.

Well, in other words, I was of the lowest caste in my own home. Nevermind about school.

I walked out the door and threw my leg over my bicycle, and Komachi climbed on the back. She put her arms firmly around my waist and held on tight. "Let's go!"

"You're not even gonna say thanks?" Riding with two people on a bicycle violated traffic laws, but as Komachi was basically an infant on the inside, I'd like to beg leniency on this one matter.

I lightly set us rolling, and Komachi nagged, "Don't get into an accident this time. Because I'm riding with you today."

"You don't care if I get into an accident when I'm riding alone?"

"No, no, no. Bro, I'm just worried because sometimes you get this rotten-fish look in your eyes and start zoning out. This is sisterly love, okay?" she placated, smushing her face into my back like a pest. Had it not been for that preceding line, it would've come off as cute, but at this point, it just felt manipulative.

Still, it wasn't my intention to cause my family needless worry. "Yeah, I'll watch out."

"Especially when I'm riding with you. For serious."

"I'll ride over every bump on the road, you brat." Despite my remark, I didn't want to hear her griping *Ow!* and *You bumped my butt!* and *I'm damaged goods now!* so I chose even ground. Those exclamations of hers made everyone in the neighborhood give me the stink-eye. In any case, it was a safe ride.

On the day of my entrance ceremony, I'd gotten into a traffic accident. I'd been so excited about the ceremony and my new life, I'd left the house an hour early, but it was not to be my lucky day.

It was around seven AM, I think. A girl had been walking her dog in the neighborhood, and it had gotten off its leash. Unfortunately, just then, a fancy-looking limousine drove up. Before I knew what I was doing, I raced over as fast as I could. In the end, I'd been carried away in an ambulance and hospitalized. That incident sealed my fate as a loner at my new school.

As a result of that accident, my brand-spanking-new bicycle got totaled, and my golden left leg got fractured. Had I been a soccer player, it would've thrown a shadow over the entire future of soccer in Japan. It was a good thing I didn't play soccer.

I was saved in the sense that my injury hadn't been that severe. There was no saving me, though, from that fact that nobody came to see me in the hospital except my family. They visited me every three days. *Hey, you should visit every day!*

After I was hospitalized, it had apparently become a family tradition for my parents to take my sister to go out to eat. With each visit, they regaled me with the details, saying things like *We ate sushi the other day* or *We had barbecue.* I considered snapping my sister's pinky.

"But you know, it's a good thing you got better quick. I'm sure it was because you had a good cast. Casts really work well on liniments, huh?"

"You idiot, that's *ligaments*. Plus, I didn't injure my ligament. It was a bone fracture!"

"You're being incomprehensible again, Bro."

"No! You're the one being incomprehensible! It's you!"

But nothing I said had an impact, and Komachi changed the subject as if that was the reasonable thing to do. "S'yeah…"

"Huh? A reference to Issei Fuubi Sepia? That's way too old, come on."

"I was saying 'so, yeah,' Bro. You're bad at listening."

"You're bad at talking."

"So yeah, after your accident, the owner of that doggy came to our place to say thanks."

"I didn't know that…"

"You were unconscious. So we got some sweets. They were yummy."

"Hey, I definitely didn't get any of that. Why'd you eat 'em all without telling me?" I demanded, turning, but Komachi just smiled coyly, giggling like *tee-hee* ☆. She was so infuriating.

"But you go to the same school, you know? Haven't you met? They said they were gonna say thanks to you at school."

Without thinking, I screeched to a halt. Komachi yelled, "Ah!" and buried her face in my back. "Why'd you stop so suddenly?!"

"Why didn't you tell me that earlier? Didn't you get a name?"

"Huh? I think it was 'the sweets person'?"

"What, are you buying treats for the office? And don't say it like you'd say 'the ham man.' What was the actual name?"

"Hmm, I forgot. Oh! We're at school. I'm off!" No sooner were the words out of her mouth than she hopped off my bike and dashed off toward the school gates.

"What a brat." I glared at her receding back.

Right before she disappeared into the school building, she spun around and saluted me. "See you later! Thanks, Bro!" she said, waving her hand and smiling. Despite what a terrible sister she was, I felt like she was a little bit cute just then. I waved back at her, and when she saw, she added, "Watch out for cars!"

I sighed lightly in exasperation, turned my bicycle around, and headed to school...the very school where the aforementioned dog owner was presumed to be.

I didn't have any particular desire for a meeting. I was just a little bit curious. But if we hadn't met after attending the same school for over a year, the disinterest in a reunion was probably mutual. Well, that's how it goes. I'd saved someone's dog and gotten a fracture. Coming to my house to say thanks was probably enough.

Glancing at the basket on the front of my bike, I noticed a black school bag inside that wasn't mine. "That idiot." I promptly turned around and started pedaling back to find Komachi running after me with tears in her eyes.

×   ×   ×

The start of a new month came with new gym activities. At my school, three gym classes were merged into one, so you had a total of sixty boys who were subsequently split into two units. Until recently, we'd been doing volleyball and track. This month, it was tennis and soccer.

Neither Zaimokuza nor I were really team players. We were more like solo superstars who focused on individual technique. And so, judging that we'd actually be a hindrance in a soccer scenario, we both chose tennis.

I *was* the man who threw away his soccer career due to that old leg injury after all. Not that I'd ever actually played soccer. But apparently, a lot of people wanted to play tennis this year, so following a fierce rock-paper-scissors tournament, I remained alive on the tennis side while Zaimokuza lost, getting consigned to the soccer side.

"Heh, Hachiman. 'Tis tragic I will have not the opportunity to unveil my magic strike. With whom am I supposed to practice passing with if you're not around?!" His sentence had started firm and resolute, but by the end of it, his expression was tearful and pleading. It was quite moving. And I was likely to have the same problem.

Then tennis practice started. After some half-assed warm-ups, the gym teacher, Atsugi, gave us a lecture on the basics. "Okay then, try doing some rallies. Split into groups of two, one person on either side of the net," he ordered, and everyone paired up, moving to either end of the court.

How can you guys react so quickly, finding partners without even looking around? Are you masters of the no-look pass or what?

My loner radar pinged, detecting a public shaming on the horizon. Fear not. I keep a secret plan in my back pocket precisely for situations such as this. "Um, I'm not really feeling well, so can I just hit a ball against the wall? I think I'd just be a bother to the others," I announced, and without waiting for Atsugi's reply, I swiftly proceeded to rebound a tennis ball with the wall as my partner. Once I got started, Atsugi had missed his opportunity to reply, so he didn't say anything.

Absolutely perfect.

The synergistic objection combo of *I don't feel well* plus *I'd be a bother* is so effective because of the implication that you really want to participate in the given activity. After many long years as a loner, I'd finally mastered the ultimate technique for dealing with pairing off in gym class. *I'll teach it to Zaimokuza, too, eventually. He'll weep tears of joy.*

I passed the time serving the ball, chasing it, and returning it deftly in an almost mechanical fashion. Meanwhile, I could hear the cheers of raucous boys celebrating fancy rallies.

"Hya! Whoa! Nice, huh? Pretty sweet, huh?"

"That was *so* sweet! There's no way he's gonna get it! You've got this one in the bag!" they exclaimed, looking like they were having fun as they practiced volleying.

I turned in their direction, thinking, *Shut up and die*, to find Hayama among them.

Hayama's group was less a pair and more of a quartet. There was the blond guy he often hung out with in class, but who were the other two? I didn't recognize them, so they were probably from Class C or Class I. Either way, they were exuding a cool-kid aura. It was the most boisterous spot in the court.

The blond who'd failed to return Hayama's smash suddenly yelled "Whoa!" and everyone around glanced his way to see what was going on. "Oh man! That hit just now, Hayama! That was so hard-core! Did it spin? It just spun, right?"

"Nah, I just hit a slice by accident. Sorry, I messed up," Hayama apologized, one hand raised.

The blond completely overreacted, drowning out Hayama's apology. "No way! A slice?! That's, like, a miracle ball! That's seriously crazy. You're hard-core, Hayama."

"Oh, you think?" Hayama matched his friend's energetic attitude and smiled cheerfully.

Then the two who'd been practicing beside them chimed in. "You're pretty good at tennis, Hayama. Teach me how to do that slice you just did." The sycophant approaching Hayama had brown hair and a quiet expression. He was probably in the same class. I didn't know his name and, given that, figured he was no one important.

In a flash, Hayama's group had become a sextet. It was the largest party ever to grace this class. You know, the word *sextet* sounds rather like *sexroid*. Yes, yes, it's dirty, very dirty.

Anyway, that was how the tennis lessons became the Kingdom of Hayama. It began to feel like *if thou art not in Hayama's group, thou shalt not participate in PE*. Naturally, everyone who wasn't in Hayama's little circle got all quiet. *This is censorship. Bring back free speech.*

You'd rightly assume that Hayama's group was rowdy, but it wasn't Hayama himself actively starting conversations. It was the people around him who were noisy. Actually, it was the self-appointed cabinet minister of their contingent, the blond one, who was loud.

"*Sliiiice!*"

See? He was loud.

The shot the blond had just made wasn't a slice at all. It went wide past Hayama into a corner of the court, flying to a dark, dank place where the sun did not shine. In other words, right at me.

"Oh! Sorry! Pardon, for real. Um…uh…Hi? Hikitani? Hikitani, can you get me the ball?"

Who the hell is Hikitani? I didn't care enough to correct him, so I just picked up the ball from where it was rolling around and threw it back to him.

"Thanks!" A brilliant smile on his face, Hayama waved at me.

I returned his greeting with a slight bow. Why was I bowing here? I'd apparently instinctively judged Hayama to be my social superior. Even I had to admit that was beta of me. I was feeling so inferior, I even wondered if there were other, better betas out there than me. My feelings growing increasingly gloomy, I smacked them against the wall.

With youth, there comes walls.

Speaking of walls, why is the slang term for a girl with small breasts *nurikabe*? I wonder. According to one theory, *nurikabe* are actually magically transformed tanuki—you know, the wild Japanese raccoon dog—and the barrier spirit is actually the tanuki's balls stretched out wide. What kind of wall is that? Certainly a surprisingly soft one! And doesn't that means that, paradoxically, that small-breasted girls being belittled as *nurikabe* are actually really soft? QED, proof complete. Stupid.

At any rate, that wasn't the kind of thing Hayama could figure out. That miraculous hypothesis was only made possible by my extraordinary sensibilities.

Yeah, I'd call today a draw. Let's do that.

X   X   X

Lunch time.

I was eating lunch in my usual spot, outside the first floor of the special-use building, right by the nurse's office, diagonally from the rear of the school. It was situated in such a way that I could look over at the tennis court. I munched away at a sausage roll, a tuna rice ball, and a Neopolitan bun. I was at ease.

A rhythmic thumping like a hand drum seduced me into drowsiness. Apparently, during lunch hour, a girl from the girls' tennis club practiced on the court. She always faced the wall, served, and then gallantly chased after the ball before returning it. I watched her running around while scarfing down every last bite of my meal.

Lunch hour would likely be over soon. I slurped lemon tea from a juice box as the wind whooshed by. Its direction had changed.

It depended on the weather, but because the school was right by the sea, the direction of the wind generally shifted around noon. In the morning, a sea breeze blew off the water, but then it would change to blow back the other way, as if returning from whence it came. Feeling that breeze on my skin as I sat alone wasn't a bad way to spend lunch.

"Huh? Oh, it's you, Hikki." The air current carried a familiar voice to my ears. When I turned to look, Yuigahama was standing there, holding down her skirt against the blustery wind. "Why're you in a place like this?"

"I always eat my lunch here."

"Oh, really? Why? Wouldn't you rather eat in the classroom?" she asked, the look on her face telling me that she was sincerely baffled.

I replied with silence. *If I could do that, I wouldn't be eating here, duh. Get a clue, seriously. Let's change the subject.* "Anyway, why are you here?"

"Oh, that's right! Actually, Yukinon beat me at rock-paper-scissors, so this is, like, my punishment?"

"Talking to me is your punishment?" *Hey, that's really mean. Maybe I'll just go off and die.*

"N-no, no! The loser just has to go buy juice!" Yuigahama got all flustered, flailing her hands around in denial.

Oh, that was good to hear. I'd almost gone and killed myself there. I sighed in relief, and Yuigahama plunked herself down daintily beside me.

"Yukinon didn't want to at first, though. She was like, 'I can obtain my own sustenance myself. Why should fulfilling a mild desire for conquest bring me pleasure?'" For some reason, she imitated Yukinoshita's voice as she said it. It was stunningly accurate.

"Well, that sounds like her."

"Yeah, but when I said, 'You don't think you can win?' she accepted."

"That sounds like her." Yukinoshita tried to act cool, but she really was a sore loser when it came to competitions. I mean, she'd taken on Ms. Hiratsuka's challenge the other day, too.

"So, like, the minute Yukinon won, she silently did this tiny fist pump. It was actually really cute." Yuigahama sighed in satisfaction. "I kinda feel like this is the first time I've had fun getting punished for losing a game."

"You've done that stuff before?" I asked, and Yuigahama nodded.

"Just a bit."

The moment she said it, I suddenly remembered. Oh yeah, there was always that dumb-looking group in the corner of the classroom around the end of lunch making a fuss after a game of rock-paper-scissors…

"Hmph. Fun times with your in-crowd, I guess."

"Why d'you have to act like that? You're so mean. So you hate that stuff?"

"Of course I hate stuff like in-crowds and in-jokes. Oh, I like in-fighting, though. Because I'm never part of the 'in.'"

"That's a sad reason, and you're a terrible person."

Leave me alone.

Yuigahama smiled, holding her hair back as the wind blew past her. The expression on her face was different from the one she'd had when she was with Miura and her friends in the classroom.

Oh, I saw why.

I couldn't be entirely certain, but I thought her makeup wasn't as heavy as before. She'd changed it to a more natural look. Or maybe she'd changed it at some other point before. But I never go staring at girls' faces, so I don't really know. I suppose this was proof that she'd changed. It was a pretty small change, though. With nearly no makeup on, her eyes relaxed when she smiled, making her seem younger and more guileless.

"But you've got your own in-crowd, Hikki. You always look like you're having fun when you're chatting with Yukinon at the club. Man, sometimes I feel like I can't join in." Yuigahama pulled her legs in and hugged them as she spoke, burying her face in her knees as her eyes darted toward me questioningly. "I'd like to talk more and stuff... N-not in a weird way, though! I-I mean with Yukinon, too! You get that, right?!"

"Relax. I'm not going to get the wrong idea about you."

"What's that supposed to mean?!" Yuigahama jerked her head up, huffing mad.

When I saw her get ready for a punch, I thrust out a hand, trying to get her to calm down before I spoke. "Well, Yukinoshita is different. She's a force majeure."

"She's what?"

"Hmm? Oh, *force majeure* means 'powers or circumstances that cannot be resisted with human ability.' Sorry for using such difficult words."

"That's not what I meant! I understand what the words mean! And don't treat me like I'm stupid! I did pass the entrance exams to get into this school, you know!" Yuigahama chopped me in the throat with her hand. It was a clean hit on my Adam's apple, and I choked.

A faraway look clouded her eyes. "Hey, speaking of the entrance exams, do you remember the day of the entrance ceremony?" she asked me earnestly.

"Huh? *Khoff khak khak*… What? Oh, I was in a traffic accident that day."

"An accident…"

"Yeah. On the first day of school, I was biking there when some idiot let go of their dog's leash. The dog was about to get hit by a car, so I protected the dog with my own body. I was so gallant and heroic and super-cool."

I guess I was dramatizing it a bit, but as nobody else knew about the incident anyway, nobody would care. More importantly, since nobody knew about it, nobody else was gonna bring it up, so I had to make myself look good.

On hearing that, though, Yuigahama's face twitched, and she stiffened. "S-some idiot…? Y-you don't…remember who, Hikki?"

"Well, I wasn't really in a frame of mind to be thinking about that. I was in a lot of pain. Whoever it was didn't leave much of an impression on me, anyway, so it was probably somebody pretty bland."

"Bland…? I-it's true I wasn't wearing any makeup that day… My hair wasn't dyed, either, and I was wearing some pajamas or something I just threw on, but… Oh, but the pattern on my pj's was teddy bears, so maybe it was a little dumb-looking…"

Yuigahama's voice was so quiet I couldn't hear what she was saying at all. She barely opened her mouth as she chewed on her words, face downcast. Did she have a stomachache or what?

"What's wrong?"

"N-nothing… Anyway! You don't remember that girl, right?!"

"Like I told you, I don't remember… Huh? Did I say it was a girl?"

"Huh?! Uh…you did, you did! You totally said it! Actually, you said nothing but *girls*!"

"How creepy do you think I am?" I retorted, and Yuigahama tittered as if hiding something as she turned to look at the tennis court, a smile still on her face. Her movement drew me to face that direction as well.

The tennis club girl who'd just been practicing by herself was coming back, wiping off her sweat as she walked.

"Hey! Sai-chaaaan!" Yuigahama called out, waving. Apparently, it was someone she knew. When the girl noticed Yuigahama, she ran to us at a trot. "Hey. Practicing?"

"Yeah. Our team is really bad, so I have to spend my lunches practicing, too… I asked if I could please use the court at lunch, and I finally got the okay. What are you and Hikigaya doing here, Yuigahama?"

"Aw, nothing much." Yuigahama said, turning to me like *Right?*

No, I was eating my lunch, and you were in the middle of running an errand, weren't you? What kind of birdbrain are you? Don't forget stuff so fast.

The girl, whose name was apparently Sai-chan, giggled, as if to say, *Oh, really?*

"You're practicing at lunch even though we're doing tennis in class, huh, Sai-chan? That's got to be rough!"

"Oh, no. I'm doing it because I like it. Oh, and Hikigaya, you're good at tennis, aren't you?"

The conversation unexpectedly turned toward me, and I naturally fell silent. *What? This is news to me. And actually, who are you? How do you know my name?* A number of questions sprang to mind, but before I could say anything, Yuigahama made a drawn-out *ooooooh* noise, like she was impressed.

"Really?"

"Yeah, his form is really good."

"Aw, you're making me blush! Ha-ha-ha! So who is she?" I was considerate enough to say that last part very quietly so that only Yuigahama could hear. But Yuigahama was all about smashing apart that consideration.

"Whaaaat?! But you're in the same class! And, like, you have gym together! Why don't you know?! I can't believe it!"

"D-don't be dumb. I totally remember! It just slipped my mind for a second! And hey, the girls have gym separately!" She'd completely squandered my tact. Now it was totally obvious that I didn't remember this girl's name. Her eyes were too much to handle. If she'd been a dog, she'd have been Chihuahua level. Had she been a cat, she'd have been up there with Munchkins. She came off just that cute and loveable.

"Ah, aha-ha. So you don't remember my name, huh…? I'm in your class. I'm Saika Totsuka."

"O-oh, sorry. It hasn't been long since we last switched classes, so I just sort of…you know? Right?"

"We were in the same class in first-year, too… I guess I'm just forgettable…"

"No, that's not true! It's just…you know… I don't really talk to the girls in our class, so I never get to know their names…"

"Just remember it already!" Yuigahama hit my head with a smack. Watching us, Totsuka looked reproachful as she mumbled, "You two sure are close, huh…?"

"Wh-what?! W-we're not close at all! All there is between us is the urge to kill! It's like I'm gonna kill Hikki and then kill myself or something like that!"

"That's right. Wait—what?" I spluttered. "That's scary! You're scaring me! I don't want your lover's suicide or whatever! That stuff is too heavy!"

"Huh?! Don't be stupid! I didn't mean it that way!"

"You really are close…," Totsuka said softly, this time turning back to me again. "I'm a boy, though. Do I look that delicate?"

"Huh?" Both my body and my mind ground to a halt. I jerked my head over to look at Yuigahama, asking her with my eyes, *You're kidding, right?* She nodded, her cheeks still tinged red as if her anger still hadn't cooled.

Huh? For real?! No way! You're kidding me, right?

Totsuka, noticing my dubious expression, looked down, his face also red. Turning up his eyes, he glanced at me. He slowly tucked his hands into the pockets of his shorts. It was an awfully bewitching gesture. "I can prove it to you if you want?"

Something twitched inside my heart.

Devil Hachiman whispered into my right ear. *Why not? Have him show you! You might get super-lucky, ya know?* Well, yeah, that was true. This wasn't the sort of chance you'd get every day after all.

Hold it right there! Oh, here he is, the angel's here. *If he's offering, why not just have him take off his shirt?*

Don't talk to me like that. You're no angel.

In the end, I decided to trust in my own rationality.

Indeed, androgynous characters such as this one are brilliant precisely because of their androgyny. Rationality led me to this perspective, and it prodded me toward more level-headed judgment. "Anyway, yeah, sorry. Even if I didn't know, I still hurt your feelings." I waffled, and Totsuka shook his head, flinging away the tears that had welled up in his eyes as he smiled.

"No, it's okay."

"But anyway, Totsuka. I'm surprised you know my name."

"Huh? Oh, yeah. I mean, you stand out, Hikigaya."

Yuigahama stared at me. "Huh? He's pretty plain. I didn't think you'd recognize him without some special reason."

"You jerk, I stand out! I stand out like a field of glittering stars against the night sky."

"No, you don't," she replied with an incredibly serious look on her face.

"I-if you're all alone in the corner of the classroom, it actually makes you stand out, though."

"Oh yeah, that's true...oh, uh, sorry." After that, Yuigahama looked away. That kind of attitude hurt more, though.

Right when it seemed as though the mood would turn heavy again, Totsuka made a save. "So anyway, you're pretty good at tennis, Hikigaya. Do you play a lot?"

"No, the last time I played it was *Mario Tennis* back in elementary school. I've never done it in real life."

"Oh, that's the one everyone plays together at parties," Yuigahama said. "I've played that before. The doubles and stuff are really fun."

"I've only ever played it alone, though."

"Huh? Oh…uh, sorry."

"What, are you part of the land mine disposal team in my heart now? Is it your job to dig up every single bit of trauma I have?"

"You're just full of too many bombs!"

Totsuka watched our exchange with an amused smile. Then the bell rang, signaling the end of lunch hour. "Let's head back," Totsuka said, and Yuigahama followed after him. I watched them, feeling rather odd.

I see. They're in the same class, so it's obvious they would go together, huh. That sort of thing always left an impression on me.

"Hikki? What're you doing?" Yuigahama turned and gave me a puzzled glare. Totsuka stopped as well, turning to face me.

I can come with you? I started to say and then stopped.

Instead, I said this: "You're not gonna get her that juice?"

"Huh? …Ahh!"

×   ×   ×

A few days went by, and it was gym class again. My frequent wall practice was slowly turning me into a wall-shot master. Now I could do a serious rally with the wall without even taking a single step.

And starting the next day, we would be playing matches for a few classes. In other words, this was my final day of rally practice. Since it was my last, I figured I'd smack that ball with all I had, but just as that thought crossed my mind, I got poked in the shoulder.

What was this, a guardian spirit, prodding me from behind? Since nobody would talk to me, it had to be a supernatural phenomenon, right? Or so I thought as I turned to find a finger jabbing my right cheek.

"Aha! I got you!" The source of that cute laugh was Saika Totsuka.

Huh? No way. What was this feeling? My heart was pounding in my chest. I felt like if he wasn't a guy, I'd have been confessing feelings to him immediately only to be rejected just as quickly.

Wait, I'd be getting rejected?!

Well, once I'd seen Totsuka in his uniform, it was clear he was a guy, but when he was wearing something like gym clothes—which were the same for both boys and girls—for a minute there, you weren't quite sure. Had he worn black knee-highs instead of ankle socks, I definitely wouldn't have been able to tell.

His arms, waist, and legs were all slender, and his skin was transparently white.

Well, he didn't have boobs, obviously, but Yukinoshita was lacking to about the same degree in that department, too.

Whoa, just thinking about her made me shiver in terror. Thankfully, though, that thought sobered me enough to reply to the broadly grinning Totsuka.

"What's up?"

"Hey. The person I always partner with isn't here today. So... maybe...you could do it with me?"

Hey, stop looking up at me like that. It's so cute. Don't blush like that. Hey.

"Oh, sure. I'm alone, anyway." I replied. *Sorry I couldn't whack you with a ball, wall...*

After I apologized to the wall, Totsuka exhaled in relief and quietly mumbled, "I was so nervous!"

If you start saying stuff like that, I'm gonna be the one getting nervous here. For real, too cute. I'd heard from Yuigahama that a faction among the girls were calling him the prince because he was so cute. Did the word *prince* imply the desire to protect him, then?

And so Totsuka and I began our rally practice. He was in the tennis club, so he was actually pretty good. My serves had reached an unparalleled level of accuracy through my wall practice, but he skillfully received them, returning them directly in front of me.

We repeated that hit and return over and over again, and perhaps feeling as if it was even becoming monotonous, Totsuka spoke. "You really are good, Hikigaya." We were pretty far apart, so his voice was drawn out and slow.

"Because I've been practicing against a wall. I've mastered tennis."

"That's squash! It's not tennis!"

We both continued talking in our drawn-out yells as our rally continued. Other students were hitting and then missing, receiving and then missing, and we were the only ones who kept it going for a long stretch.

Then the rally stopped. The ball bounced toward Totsuka, and he caught it. "Let's take a little break."

"Sure."

We sat down together. *So why are you sitting beside me? I guess it's not weird. Usually, when guys sit together, they face each other or sit diagonally from each other, right? Isn't this kind of close? It's close, isn't it?*

"Hey, I'd like to ask you for some advice, Hikigaya." Totsuka pronounced, looking serious.

I see. He'd have to sit this close if he wanted to talk about something secret, huh? That's why he's so close, right? "Advice, huh?"

"Yeah. It's about the tennis club. We're really bad, you know? And we don't have enough people. Once the third-years graduate after the next tournament, I think we'll get even worse. A lot of the first-years only started in high school, and they're not really very good yet... Plus, because we're so bad, it feels like we can't get motivated. And when you don't have many people, every member automatically makes the team, too."

"I see."

That made sense. I think it's something that often happens with tiny clubs. A weak club couldn't scrape together enough members, and a club without enough members would have no competition to make it to the slot of a regular. So even if members took the day off or skipped, they'd still be able to go to the tournaments, and if you go to competitions, you pretty much feel like you're on the team.

I bet there's quite a few people out there who would be satisfied with that even if they didn't win. A club like that would never get any better, and because they weren't any good, they couldn't recruit members, and thus the downward spiral would continue.

"So…would you mind possibly joining the tennis club?"

"Huh?" *Why are you asking me that?* I asked with my eyes alone.

Totsuka sat there with his legs drawn up in front, making himself seem smaller, occasionally glancing at me with pleading eyes.

"You're good at tennis, Hikigaya, and I think you can get even better. Plus, I think it will be a shot in the arm for everyone else. And…if you're with me, I think I can try harder, too. U-um, I don't mean that in a weird way! I-I just want to get stronger."

"You can just stay weak. I'll protect you."

"Huh?"

"Uh, sorry. Slip of the tongue."

Totsuka had been so adorable right there, I'd just let slip something I shouldn't have. I mean, he was just so cute! I'd been extremely close to just joining the club right there. I'd been about to raise my hand so fast, you'd have thought it was a race to get pudding instead of school lunch.

But no matter how cute he was, there were some things I just couldn't agree to.

"Sorry. I can't."

I knew my personality quite well. I didn't really see the point of going to a club every day, and running around early in the morning was a little unfathomable to me. The only people who get up that early are those old geezers in the park doing tai chi. My motto was *I canna keep this up!* like some kind of Korosuke imitation, so I'd definitely quit the club. I mean, I quit my first part-time job after three days.

If I joined the tennis club, I'd only be guaranteeing Totsuka's disappointment.

"Oh…," he droned, sounding sincerely let down.

I searched for the right words. "Well, how about this? I'll think about a way to help you out." *Not like I can do anything, though.*

"Thanks. I feel a bit better just having talked to you about it." He smiled at me, but I could tell he was merely trying to console himself.

If he was just trying to make himself feel better, though, I thought that was okay.

X   X   X

"No."

That was the first thing out of Yukinoshita's mouth.

"No? Hey, come on—"

"No means no." Her second refusal was even colder.

This had all started because I'd mentioned Totsuka's problem to Yukinoshita. I'd been planning to steer the conversation in a convenient direction, smoothly quit the Service Club, and then put on a show of joining the tennis club before slowly fading out, but she'd cut that option clean off for me.

"I think Totsuka has the right idea about me joining the tennis club, though. Basically, we just have to give the club members a little jolt. I mean, if they get the bomb dropped on them that there's a new member, that'll mix things up, right?"

"Do you think you are capable of operating in a group? A creature such as yourself would never be accepted, am I wrong?"

"Ngh…"

She was right; I totally couldn't. It was true that I'd probably quit, but also, just seeing the others having fun and chilling together as a club might force me to whack them with a racket.

Yukinoshita laughed in a way that was a lot like a sigh. "You have absolutely no understanding of group psychology, do you? You're a master loner."

"I don't want to hear that from you."

She ignored me completely and continued speaking. "Though they may band together against you as a common enemy, they'd only expend the necessary effort to get rid of you, making no effort to improve themselves, so it wouldn't solve anything. Source: me."

"I see… Huh? Source?"

"Yes. In middle school, I returned from abroad to Japan. Of course, I was transferring in, and all the girls in the class, or rather, the whole school, were desperate to eliminate me. Not a single one of them attempted to improve themselves in order to best me. Those imbeciles…," she reflected, and as she spoke, something like black fire swelled at her back.

Oh, crap, I might have stepped on a land mine.

"W-well, you know. When a cute girl like you shows up, it's inevitable that sort of thing would happen."

She paused. "Y-yes, well, I suppose. It's true that I am far more attractive than any of them, and I'm not so mentally weak on that front to put myself down. Therefore, you could say that it was a forgone conclusion, in a way. But still, Yamashita and Shimamura were quite cute, you know? It seems they were fairly popular with boys, too. But that's just appearance. When it came to academics, sports, arts, etiquette, and even spiritually, they most certainly never approached someone of my caliber. If you just can't beat someone no matter how hard you try, it's no surprise you would try to hold them back and drag them down."

Yukinoshita had appeared to be at a loss for words for a moment, but soon she was right back to tooting her own horn. Her praise wasn't just fluid. It rushed along like the bright blue crashing waves of Niagara Falls.

I was impressed she'd managed to say all that without faltering once. Perhaps this was her own way of hiding her shyness? So there was a speck of cuteness within her after all. Maybe all that talking was what had made her face so red.

"Can you do me a favor and not say anything weird? You're giving me unpleasant chills."

"It's a relief to hear you say that. Yeah, you're not cute after all."

Actually, Totsuka was way cuter than any of the girls I knew. What the hell was with that? Oh yeah. We were supposed to be talking about Totsuka.

"Is there nothing we can do to help the tennis club get better?" I asked.

Yukinoshita's eyes widened as she stared at me. "This is rare. When did you start worrying about other people?"

"Well, you know. This is the first time anyone's ever asked me for help, so it just kind of happened." Having someone rely on you was a very pleasing thing indeed. Plus, Totsuka was so cute, so I just… A relaxed smile slipped onto my face.

"I've been consulted on romantic matters quite often, though," Yukinoshita said, as if to counter me. She was puffing out her chest and speaking as if it was a point of pride, but her expression slowly darkened. "That said, girls essentially tell you about their crushes for the sake of deterrence."

"Huh? What do you mean?"

"If you tell people you like someone, everyone else has to be careful around them, right? It's like you're emphasizing your ownership of them. Once you know she likes him, if you lay a hand on him, you'll be treated like a home-wrecker and excluded from the girls' clique, and then even if he says he likes you, he'll just take off after. Why do I have to take all that abuse from them?"

Yet again, black flames began rising from her body. I'd expected having girls talk to you about their crushes was a super-bittersweet thing, but this was just plain bitter. *Why must she crush the pure dreams of boys like that? Is this fun for her?*

Yukinoshita suddenly smiled in mild self-deprecation, as if to wash away her unsavory memories of the past. "What I'm saying is that it's not necessarily a good idea to listen to anyone and everyone about every little problem. You know that old saying: 'A lion throws its own young off a cliff and kills it.' "

"He's not supposed to kill it!" The correct version was *A lion hunts its child with all its might.*

"What would you do?"

"Me?" Yukinoshita blinked her big eyes with a pensive look that said, *Oh, yes.* "I suppose I'd make them all run until they died, do practice swings until they died, and play tennis until they died." She was smiling a little as she said that. So scary.

While I was getting rather seriously freaked out, the door to the clubroom opened with a rattle.

"Yahallo!" The stupid-sounding greeting reached my ears. Carefree compared to her counterpart, Yuigahama was brimming with birdbrained, bimbo smiles, as usual, looking as if she had not a worry in the world. But behind her stood someone who looked timid and serious.

His eyes were downcast, as if he lacked confidence. His fingers weakly grasped the hem of Yuigahama's blazer, and his skin was translucently white. He was such an ephemeral existence, it seemed as though he would disappear like a fleeting dream if the light shone on him.

"Oh…Hikigaya!" Instantly, the color returned to his clear skin, and he smiled like a flower bursting into bloom. When he smiled, I finally realized who he was. Why had he looked so glum?

"Totsuka, huh."

He stepped delicately toward me, squeezing the cuff of my sleeve instead now. *Hey, hey, you're not allowed to do that! But he's a guy, though…*

"Hikigaya, what're you doing here?"

"Well, this is my club… What are you doing here?"

"Today *I* brought someone with a request, heh-heh," Yuigahama announced proudly, pointlessly puffing out her chest. *I'm not asking you. I wanted to hear the answer from Totsuka's cute lips…*

"Well, like, listen! I'm a member of the Service Club, too, aren't I? So I thought I'd do my job for once. And Sai-chan seemed to have a problem, so that's why I brought him here."

"Yuigahama."

"Yukinon, you don't have to thank me or anything at all. I just did my duty as a club member."

"Yuigahama, you're not actually a member, though."

"I'm not?!"

She's not?! That was a surprise. I had thought for sure this was a thing where she just gradually ended up being in the club.

"No. I haven't gotten an application form from you or consent from our supervisor, so you're not a member."

Yukinoshita was pointlessly strict about these rules.

"I'll fill one out! I can fill out as many applications as you want! Lemme join you!" With tear-filled eyes, Yuigahama began to write *application form* on a sheet of loose-leaf paper in rounded, childish, phonetic hiragana characters. She could at least have written it in kanji…

"So, Totsuka, was it? What did you need?" Ignoring Yuigahama scribbling away on her application form, Yukinoshita turned to Totsuka.

Pierced by her cold gaze, Totsuka twitched for a moment. "U-um… you can help me…get better…at tennis, right?" At first, he'd been looking at Yukinoshita, but as he got toward the end of his sentence, Totsuka's gaze shifted over to me. He was shorter than me, so he was looking up at me, seeing how I'd react.

Hey, don't look at me like that… You'll get me all worked up. Stop giving me that look.

Then, though it likely wasn't her intention to save me, Yukinoshita replied in my place. "I don't know how Yuigahama explained it to you, but the Service Club is not your personal genie. We only provide a little assistance and encourage your independence. Whether you improve or not is up to you."

"Oh… I see…" Discouraged, Totsuka's shoulders drooped.

Yuigahama had probably promised all sorts of things. I glared at her. She was muttering, "My seal, my seal," as she rummaged around in her bag for the personal stamp she would sign the form with. She noticed my attention and lifted her head.

"Huh? What?"

"Don't give me that. Your irresponsible remarks have crushed this boy's slim hopes to smithereens." Yukinoshita attacked her mercilessly, but Yuigahama just tilted her head.

"Hmm? Hmm? But, like, you and Hikki can figure something out, right?" Yuigahama asked bluntly, a completely blank expression on her face. Depending on how you interpreted that remark, it could have meant something disparaging, like *So you can't do it?*

Unfortunately, there was someone in that very room who would take it that way. "Hmph. You've become a lot more forthright these days, Yuigahama. Never mind that boy… I can't believe *you* would try to test me." Yukinoshita smirked. Agh, Yuigahama had flipped that weird switch in Yukinoshita's brain. Yukino Yukinoshita would accept any challenge head-on and beat it down with all she had. She'd beat you down even if you didn't challenge her. She was the kind of person who would even oppress me, and I never resist. I'm like Gandhi. "Fine. Totsuka, I accept your request. You want me to improve your abilities in tennis, is that correct?"

"Y-yes, that's right. I-if I get better, everyone else will try harder, too, I think," Totsuka replied from behind my back. Perhaps he was overwhelmed by how widely Yukinoshita's eyes flared. He gently peeked out from behind my shoulder. His expression was fearful and uneasy. He was just like a trembling wild rabbit, which made me want to put him in a bunny girl costume.

Well, I think an ice queen like this one declaring she's going to help you would scare most people. At this rate, I wouldn't have been surprised if she had said, *I'll make you stronger, but in exchange for your life!*

Are you some kind of witch or what?

I took a step forward in an attempt to protect Totsuka and ease his anxiety. When I drew near him, I smelled shampoo and deodorant intermingled: the indescribable scent of a high school girl. *What kind of shampoo is he using?* "Well, I don't mind helping, but what are we going to do?"

"I just told you, didn't I? Don't you remember? If you have no confidence in your memory, I suggest you take notes."

"Hey, you can't mean you were serious…," I said, remembering her *something something until you die* remarks, and Yukinoshita smiled as if to say, *Oh, you're so insightful.* That smile was scaring me…

Totsuka's white skin went even paler, and he began trembling like a leaf. "A-am I going to die?"

"It's okay. I'll protect you," I said, patting him on the shoulder.

Totsuka's cheeks flushed, and he gazed at me feverishly. "Hikigaya…do you really mean that?"

"Oh, sorry. I just wanted to try saying that." It was one of the top three lines I'd wanted to try saying once, as a man. By the way, number one is *You go on ahead. Leave this to me.* There was no way I'd ever protect Yukinoshita from anything, though, or protect anyone at all, for that matter. But, well, now that I'd tossed off that remark, if I didn't say something to wiggle my way out of that statement, he'd leave still feeling uneasy.

Totsuka let out a short sigh and pouted his lips. "I don't understand you sometimes, Hikigaya…but…"

"Hmm, you have tennis club practice after school, right, Totsuka?" Yukinoshita cut him off. "Then let's do some special training during lunch. Are you fine with meeting at the court?" She briskly decided the arrangements for the next day.

"Roger!" Yuigahama replied as she finally finished writing out her application form. Totsuka nodded, too. And that meant…

"You mean…me, too?"

"Of course. You don't have any plans during lunch, anyway, now, do you?"

Indeed I did not.

× × ×

The training from hell was scheduled to begin at lunch hour the next day.

I wondered why I was going along with them. At the end of the day, all this community known as the Service Club did was scrape together a bunch of weaklings, and all these weaklings were doing was doze off inside that little walled garden. The teacher had just gathered together this group of losers and given them a temporary comfortable shelter. And how was that any different from the classic teen experience that I hated so much?

Maybe that was the very purpose for which Ms. Hiratsuka had created this sanatorium for excising the sources of our respective sicknesses.

But if what ailed us was something that could be wiped away through such a shoddy effort, none of us would have been sick in the first place.

That was how it was for Yukinoshita.

I didn't know what her deal was, but I didn't think it was something that could be healed here. And even if my wounds could have been mended, the only way that could have happened was if Totsuka were a girl. If, through this tennis episode, something that could be called a romantic comedy were born between Totsuka and me, then it might have been different.

As far as I could tell, the cutest one there was Saika Totsuka. He had an open personality, and above all, he was nice to me. If I took the time to nurture this love, there was a possibility I might grow some humanity.

But, like…he was a boy. God was such a jerk.

Though I was in the midst of a mild bout of despair, I still took the trouble to change into my gym sweats and head out to the tennis court. I would wager it all on the tiny hope that Totsuka might actually be a girl!

The gym uniform at my school was an unfortunate shade of pale neon blue, and it stood out dramatically. The color was uncool to the point of being sublime, and all the students hated it, so no one wore it of their own volition outside of gym class or club time. Everyone was in their regular uniforms at lunch, and I was the only one sticking out like a sore thumb in my gym clothes. My conspicuousness led to my capture by a certain annoying individual.

"Ha! Ha-ha-ha-Hachiman!"

"Don't segue from a bellowing laugh into my name."

Even in a school as large as Soubu High, there was only one person here who would laugh so creepily: Zaimokuza. He folded his arms and blocked my path.

"How unexpected to encounter you in a place like this! I was just thinking about going over to hand you my newly conceived plot. Come and feast your eyes upon it!"

"Oh, uh, sorry. I'm a little busy right now." I slipped past him and casually ignored the proffered bundle of papers.

But Zaimokuza kindly grabbed my shoulder. "Give me not such sad lies. There's no way you'd have any plans."

"I'm not lying. And I don't want to hear that from you!" Why was everyone saying the same thing? Did I look like I had that much free time on my hands? Well, I guess I actually did have a lot of free time on my hands.

"Heh. I understand, Hachiman. You just wanted to look cool, so you told a little white lie, huh? And then, in order to prevent that lie from being exposed, you spun further lies. And then you will desperately do so again. It's a tragic infinite spiral, but you know, at the other end of that spiral is emptiness. To be specific, human relationships are emptiness.

But there is yet time to turn back! What? You saved me! This time, 'tis my turn to save you!" Zaimokuza delivered this line, which was number two on my list of the things I wanted to try saying once, as a man. He was giving a thumbs-up and had an irritating, contrived look on his face.

"I really do have plans…" I could actually feel the muscles in my face spasm in irritation as I attempted to convince Zaimokuza. But just then…

"Hikigaya!" I heard that cheerful soprano voice, and Totsuka leaped into my arms. "You came at just the right time. Let's go together?"

"Y-yeah…"

There was a racket case slung over his left shoulder, and his right hand was, for some reason, grasping my left. Why?

"H-Hachiman… Who is that person…?" Zaimokuza looked back and forth between Totsuka and me in astonishment. Gradually, his expression changed, transforming into something I felt I'd seen before. Oh, I knew. Like in Kabuki? With a flourish that almost made me think I'd heard a Kabuki actor cry out and bang his drum, Zaimokuza's eyes flared open, and he assumed a pose. "Y-you fiend! Have you betrayed me?!"

"Betrayed you? How?"

"Silence! You half-handsome failure of a hot guy! I took pity on you because you were a loner, but now you've gotten cocky!"

"That 'half' and 'failed' part was unnecessary." The loner part was true, so I couldn't argue that.

His face distorted in rage, Zaimokuza growled and glared at me. "Unforgivable..."

"Hey, calm down, Zaimokuza. Totsuka isn't a girl. He's a guy... probably," I said, without conviction.

"P-p-p-pullshit! There's no way such a cute girl could be a boy!" Zaimokuza objected, messing up his words.

"He is cute, but he's a guy."

"Hey...calling me cute and stuff...it makes me a little...uncomfortable." Right beside me, Totsuka's cheeks went red as he averted his face. "Um, is this...your friend, Hikigaya?"

"Oh, I dunno..."

"Hmph. Someone like you could never be my eternal rival." Zaimokuza was in full sulk mode. Man, what a pain in the ass.

But I could get where he was coming from. It's only natural that when someone you've felt slight sympathy for turns out to be possessed of completely different qualities than those you assumed, you feel a tinge of sadness much like betrayal.

I wondered what could I say at a time like this in order to bring our relationship back to normal. Unfortunately, I was lacking in EXP, so I didn't know. But I did feel a little bit sad. It was because I felt like maybe he and I had some kind of understanding, and maybe one day we could laugh about it and accept each other or something.

But I guessed that sort of thing was never gonna happen after all.

A friendship where you're always trying to be considerate of the other person, always worrying about what they think, always responding to every single text, always seeking their approval and then finally connecting with them, isn't friendship at all. If that troublesome process was what they called youth, then I didn't need any of it. Enjoying your-self among some tepid community is basically just stroking your own ego. It's deceit. The worst sort of evil.

Plus, Zaimokuza was really obnoxious when he got jealous.

I swore I'd prove my righteousness, my own justice, and chose the path of loneliness.

"Let's go, Totsuka." I pulled Totsuka's arm.

But after replying, "Oh...yeah...," he didn't move from the spot.

"Zaimokuza, was it?"

Zaimokuza acted a little weird at being addressed, but he nodded.

"If you're Hikigaya's friend, maybe...you can be my friend, too? I'd be glad if you would. Because...I don't have many guy friends," Totsuka said, smiling shyly.

"Heh... Ngh... Heh...heh-heh-heh. Indeed, Hachiman and I are bosom buddies. No, *brothers*. No, no, no, I am the master, and he is the servant. Well, if you're going to be like that, then I suppose I have no choice. I'll be your...u-um...friend? Then. Or lover, if you wish."

"Yeah, I don't think...that's possible. So let's be friends."

"Hmm, I see. Hey, Hachiman, does this mean this person likes me? Am I a babe magnet now? Are chicks finally gonna start digging me now?" Zaimokuza immediately sidled up to me and whispered into my ear.

Yeah, no. Zaimokuza wasn't my friend after all. Someone who'd immediately change his attitude after discovering he could befriend a pretty girl through me could never be my friend. "Let's go, Totsuka. If we're late, Yukinoshita will freak out."

"Hmm, we cannot have that. Then let us hurry. That lady...is really scary," Zaimokuza said, following me and Totsuka. Apparently, Zaimokuza was now with us. We were all walking in a line for some reason, so to someone seeing us, we might have seemed rather *Dragon Quest*–ish... No, he was less *Dragon Quest* and more like King Bonbii from Momotetsu, I think.

×　×　×

Yukinoshita and Yuigahama were already at the tennis court. Yuki-noshita was still in her uniform, and only Yuigahama had changed into her gym clothes. They must have been eating lunch at the court. When they saw us, they quickly packed away their tiny meals.

"Then let's get started."

"Th-thank you for doing this." Totsuka faced Yukinoshita and gave her a little bow.

"First of all, let's build up that muscle that you are so fatally lack-ing. In order to comprehensively build your biceps, deltoids, pectorals, abdominals, obliques, dorsals, and femoral muscles, first, do push-ups… For now, just go at it until you're *nearly* dead."

"Whoa, you sound so smart, Yukinon…huh? *Nearly* dead?"

"Yes. Muscle repairs itself to the degree that you have torn it, but every time it repairs itself, the fibers bind more strongly, and this is known as overcompensation. In other words, if you do it until the point of near death, you'll power up all at once."

"Come on, he's not a Super Saiyan…"

"Well, he won't get that muscle immediately, but there is another point to this training: to raise his basal metabolism."

"Basal metabolism?" Yuigahama asked, tilting her head with a question mark.

You don't even know that?

Yukinoshita looked somewhat astonished, but perhaps figur-ing it would be faster to explain than to criticize Yuigahama, she briefly added: "To put it simply, it means to make the body fit for physical activity. When the basal metabolism rises, it becomes easier to burn calories. It increases the efficiency of the transformation of energy."

Yuigahama nodded. Abruptly, her eyes lit up. "It makes it easier to burn calories…in other words, lose weight?"

"Indeed. It makes it so you can expend even more calories when breathing and digesting, with the result that you get skinnier just by being alive."

At Yukinoshita's words, the sparkle in Yuigahama's eyes grew. For some reason, she was bubbling with even more vigor than Totsuka.

Then, as though Yuigahama's enthusiasm had set him off, Totsuka clenched his fist as well. "Th-then I guess I'll just try doing it."

"I-I'll do it with you!" Totsuka and Yuigahama got into plank position and slowly began doing pushups.

"Ngh......gh! Ahhh, phew!"

"Ugh...ngh! Ngah! Phew, phew, nnnngh!" Stifled panting leaked from both of them. Distorting their faces in anguish, they broke a light sweat, and their cheeks flushed.

Totsuka's arms were apparently pretty sore, because occasionally, he would shoot me a pleading glance. Gazing at him leisurely from above made me feel, um...odd.

When Yuigahama bent her arms, shining skin peeked out from the collar of her gym clothes. Oh no. I couldn't look straight at that. My heart rate had been up pretty high for a while, and there was a good chance it was irregular now.

"Hachiman... Why is it...that I feel so at peace right now...?"

"What a coincidence. I feel the same way." I leered down at the occasional flashes of skin below us until a voice came at me like ice water down my back.

"Why don't you two shake off those appetites of the flesh by doing some exercises?" When I turned, Yukinoshita was giving me a look of utter contempt. She said I had *appetites of the flesh*. She noticed?!

"H-hmph. A warrior never shirks his training. Well then, I shall join you!"

"Y-yeah. Not getting enough exercise is a scary thing. There's, like, diabetes and gout and u-uh...cirrhosis of the liver and stuff!" We flung ourselves on the ground with incredible speed and began our push-ups.

Yukinoshita circled around deliberately to stand in front of us.

"Seeing you like that, it looks rather like a new kind of groveling," she said, and she chuckled.

What did you say, you bastard? You'll awaken anger within even my most peaceful of hearts. Oh, forget it. The only thing that's going to awaken within me is a kink for push-ups.

What on earth are we doing?

I'm sure you know the saying, "If you pile up enough dust, it'll make a mountain." Or even "Two heads are better than one." Basically, I'm talking about the idea that people become stronger when they gather together. But we were just gathering a bunch of failures to enact more fail.

In the end, we were made to do push-ups for the whole lunch hour, and I writhed around in bed late that night in muscle pain.

Saika Totsuka

Birthday

May 9

Special skills:

Tennis,
jigsaw puzzles

Hobbies:

Handicrafts

How I spend my weekends:

Taking long baths,
going for walks

Yoshiteru Zaimokuza

Birthday

November 23

Special skills:

Sword fighting, writing, meditation

Hobbies:

Reading (manga, light novels),
gaming (RPGs, simulation, dating sims),
watching anime,
Internet

How I spend my weekends:

Writing,
wandering around Akihabara

"Wait, do you like me, Totsuka? Have I become a babe magnet now? Can I call myself a babe magnet now?"

"Totsuka, you're fine staying weak. Because I'll protect you."

Guidance Counseling Survey

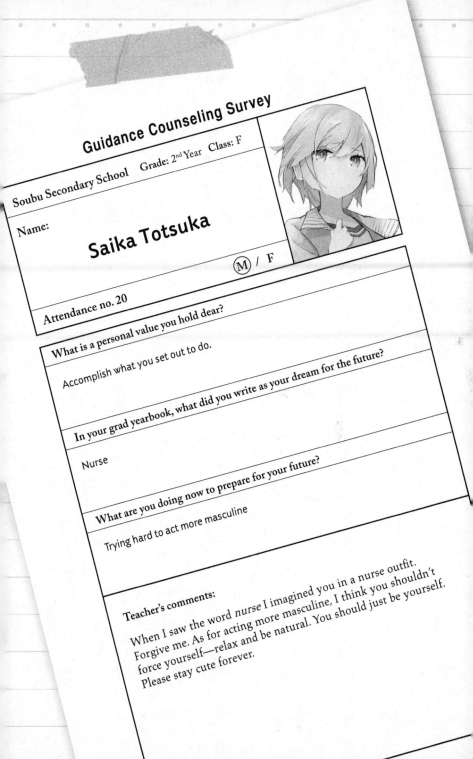

Soubu Secondary School   Grade: 2nd Year   Class: F

Name:

Saika Totsuka

(M) / F

Attendance no. 20

What is a personal value you hold dear?

Accomplish what you set out to do.

In your grad yearbook, what did you write as your dream for the future?

Nurse

What are you doing now to prepare for your future?

Trying hard to act more masculine

Teacher's comments:

When I saw the word *nurse* I imagined you in a nurse outfit. Forgive me. As for acting more masculine, I think you shouldn't force yourself—relax and be natural. You should just be yourself. Please stay cute forever.

Sometimes, **the gods of romantic comedy** are kind.

Days of this and that passed, and our tennis program plunged into phase two. I made it sound cool right there, but essentially, we just finished doing basic workouts and finally started practicing with a ball and racket.

I say *we*, but actually, the only one practicing was Totsuka. He was on his own as he desperately pitted himself against a wall under the instruction of the drill sergeant from hell—er, Yukinoshita.

Well, the rest of us didn't have to do this tennis club practice or whatever, so each of us just passed the time however we wanted. Yukinoshita was reading a book in the shade while occasionally glancing over to see how Totsuka was doing and yelling at him to snap to it, as if just remembering why she was actually there. Yuigahama had started out practicing with Totsuka but had gotten sick of it almost immediately and was spending most of her time napping near Yukinoshita. She was like a dog taken on a walk to the park only to get tired and flop down by the water fountain.

Then there was Zaimokuza, fully intent on developing his magic strike. *Agh, geez, don't throw acorns. And don't dig up the clay court with your racket, either.*

Gathering together a bunch of failures only results in a greater fail after all.

Me? I was zoning out in a corner of the court while observing some ants. Fun times.

No, really, it's fun. I don't know what those little things are think-ing as they scurry around, but they live a pretty harried lifestyle. I dunno. Maybe looking down from a tall office building in Tokyo would elicit the same feeling. The shapes of the salarymen in black suits, com-ing and going, and the shapes of the worker ants seemed to be one and the same. Eventually, I'll become just like one of those ants, a black speck seen from above. I wonder how I'll feel about life then.

I don't mind salarymen, and actually, I'd even like to be one. It's a pretty secure life. It's number two on the list of things I'd like to be in the future after househusband. Number three is a fire engine. Yeah, like I'm gonna be a car.

Of course, I know full well that being a salaryman isn't all fun and games. When I see my father's face after he comes home from work, he's exhausted from life, and I salute him for that. I think it's noble to keep on going to work even when bad things happen. So I unconsciously pro-jected my father onto those ants as I mentally cheered them on.

You can do it, Dad. Never surrender, Dad, and don't surrender your hair follicles, either, Dad. I prayed silently as I dreamed of my future and worried about the prospects of my hairline in the years to come. Perhaps my prayers were heard, because the ant was marching back to the hole from whence it had come. I'm sure that was what it was doing. I was so moved, I sniffled and wiped away a tear.

Just then…

Smash!!

"Dad!!"

The ant suddenly disappeared along with a tennis ball, leaving no trace behind. Eyes burning with rage, I glared back in the direction the ball had come from.

"Hmm…so I toss up dust to dazzle my opponent and then take that opportunity to drive the ball in their direction. It seems my magic strike is complete! This is my fecund illusory earth, *Blasty Sandrock*!"

So it was you, Zaimokuza… You were the one who did this to my father (the ant)…but whatever. It's just an ant. I put my hands together in a light prayer for the deceased.

Basking in the lingering memory of his successful technique, Zaimokuza spun his racket around before slinging it over his shoulder and posing. It looked like he'd just gained some EXP.

Well, I didn't give a damn about Zaimokuza or that ant. *Guess I'll watch Totsuka being cute to kill some time.*

I could see Yuigahama, who'd woken up at some point, laboriously dragging around the ball cart under Yukinoshita's direction. She tossed out balls one after another as Totsuka struggled to hit them all back.

"Yuigahama, give him some more difficult tosses, like over here and over there. It's not real practice unless you do."

Totsuka received balls near the lines and by the net, his ragged breathing contrasting sharply with Yukinoshita's calm voice. Yukinoshita was serious. A serious jerk.

No, I mean you're seriously training him. You're scaring me, so don't look this way… How do you know what I'm thinking?

Yuigahama's throws not only had terrible form, her aim was all over the place, and the balls flew unpredictably. Totsuka tried to run after them all, but after about the twentieth ball, he skidded and fell.

"Ahh! Sai-chan, are you okay?!" Yuigahama halted her throw and ran up to the net.

Totsuka smiled with teary eyes as he stroked his scraped knee. He's so brave. "I'm fine, so keep going."

But Yukinoshita grimaced. "You wanna keep going?"

"Yeah… You're all helping me with this, so I want to try a little more."

"I see. Then you take it from here, Yuigahama," Yukinoshita said and spun around, striding away to disappear into the school building.

Totsuka watched her uneasily and mumbled, "D-did I maybe say something to make her angry?"

"No, she's always like that," I replied. "In fact, she's not calling you foolish or incompetent, so there's a fair chance she's in a good mood."

"Aren't you the only one she talks to like that, Hikki?"

No, I think she talks to you like that a lot too, Yuigahama. You just don't notice.

"Maybe…she's fed up with me… No matter how much we keep doing this, I never get any better, and I can only do five pushups…" Totsuka's shoulders slumped as he looked down. Well, that did sound like the sort of opinion Yukinoshita would have. But…

"I don't think so. Yukinon doesn't give up on people who look to her for help," Yuigahama said, rolling a tennis ball around in her hands.

"Yeah, that's true. I mean, she even helped you with your cooking. She went that far for you, and there's still some hope for Totsuka, so she's not going to give up on him."

"What's that supposed to mean?!" Yuigahama threw the tennis ball she'd been fiddling with at my head. It made a stupid-sounding thunk; a clean hit on my noggin. *Hey, you've actually got nice aim. You'll get snapped up in the next draft.*

I picked up the ball as it bounced away and tossed it lightly toward Yuigahama. "She'll be back soon enough. I think you can just keep going."

"Okay!" Totsuka replied cheerfully, returning to his practice. After that, he didn't grumble once or voice a single complaint. He tried really hard.

"Man, I'm tired! You do the throwing now, Hikki!"

Yuigahama's giving in first? Come on.

Well, it wasn't like I had anything better to do. All I was doing was dedicated ant observation, and that ant had been murdered by Zaimokuza, leaving me with completely loose ends. I had nothing to do.

"All right. I'll trade."

"Yay! Oh, this is the first time I've given up after five throws, so watch out."

Five throws? That was way too fast. Just how bad was her endurance? I moved to take the balls from Yuigahama, but then her expression, which had been a cheery smile, grew shadowed.

"Oh, they're playing tennis! Tennis!" I heard the squeal of a chittery voice and turned to see a great crowd walking our way with Hayama and Miura at the center. They were just passing Zaimokuza and had apparently noticed Yuigahama and me.

"Oh… So it's Yui-chan and her friends," a girl beside Miura observed quietly.

Miura glanced at Yuigahama and me, casually ignored us, and called out to Totsuka. It seemed she hadn't even noticed Zaimokuza from the start. "Hey, Totsuka. Can we play here, too?"

"Miura, I'm not exactly…playing… This is practice…"

"Huh? What? I can't hear you."

Miura seemed unable to hear Totsuka's too-quiet protests, and her retort silenced him. Well, if she'd asked for me to repeat myself like she'd just asked him, I'd have fallen silent, too. She's seriously scary.

Totsuka scrabbled together what little courage he had and opened his mouth once more. "I-I'm practicing…"

But the queen didn't give a damn about that. "Hmph. But, like, these guys aren't part of your club. So that means it's not, like, just the boys' tennis club using the court now, right?"

"Y-yes, that's true, but—"

"Then it's okay for us to use it, too, right? Hey, how about it?"

"But…," he began and then looked at me like he wanted help.

Huh? Me? Oh, well, I guess there was only me. Yukinoshita was still off somewhere, Yuigahama was awkwardly looking away, and no one cared about Zaimokuza. So that left just me, eh?

"Oh, sorry, but Totsuka asked for permission to use the court, so others can't use it."

"Huh? Like I said, you guys aren't in the club, but you're using it."

"Yeah, but we're just helping Totsuka out with his practice. It's sort of like subcontracting or outsourcing."

"Huh? What are you even talking about? Creepy."

Wow, she had no intention of listening to me at all. This is why I hate idiot sluts like her. If words don't get through to her, does she still even count as a primate? I could have more of a conversation with some dog.

"C'mon, don't pick a fight." Hayama came between us as if to smooth things over. "Listen, the more the merrier. Can't everyone play?"

Those words sparked something. Miura had cocked back the hammer, and Hayama had pulled the trigger. All that was left was to let the bullet fly.

"Who's this *everyone*? Is that the same *everyone* as the one you bring up when you pester your mom to buy you something by saying, '*Everyone's* got one!'? Who the hell are these guys? I have no friends, so I've never used that tactic."

The bullet flew for its target after passing right through my foot. A brilliant shot! A miraculous attack!

Even Hayama was shaken by my quip. "Uh, well, I didn't mean it that way. Hey, I'm sorry. Um, if you need someone to talk to, I'm here, if you want." He rushed to comfort me with dazzling speed.

Hayama is a good guy. I almost said, "Thanks..." or something with tears in my eyes. But. If that small amount of sympathy were enough to save me, my personality wouldn't have gotten this bad. If that one line could solve someone's issues, no one would have any issues in the first place.

"Hayama, I appreciate your kindness. I know you're a good guy. *And* you're the ace of the soccer team. You're even good-looking to boot. You must be *so* popular with the ladies."

"Wh-where's this coming from?" Hayama was visibly shaken by the sudden flattery.

Hmph, just keep thinking you're so great. I'm sure you have no idea. Why do you think people praise one another? It's in order to raise them up even higher so it's easier to knock their feet out from under them and drag them down from their pedestal! This is known as death-by-praise.

"You're talented and have so much, and yet you want to take even the tennis court from me, who has nothing? Aren't you ashamed, as a human being?"

"He speaks truth! Whatever-your-name-is Hayama! Yours is the most reproachable form of conduct and a violation of ethics! This is an invasion! The right of vengeance is mine!" At some point Zaimokuza had come up to us and launched into a dramatic speech.

"S-seeing both of you together is twice as annoying and pathetic…" Yuigahama, beside us, was at a loss for words.

Hayama scratched his head and then gave a short sigh. "Hmm, oh, okay…"

A wicked smile slipped onto my lips. That was it. Hayama didn't like stirring up trouble. And at that moment, the players involved in the scene were myself, Zaimokuza, and Hayama. Hayama was trying to calm down the situation while being faced down by superior numbers.

"Hey, Hayato!" A bored-sounding voice slipped in from the side. "Why're you taking so long with these guys? I wanna play tennis."

Agh, here come the stupid curls again. Are your brain cells twisted up like that, too? Keep up with the topic at hand. People like you step on the accelerator when they mean to hit the brakes.

Miura actually had mixed up the accelerator and the brakes just then.

Her words had given Hayama a moment to think. In that brief interval, his mind turned the key in the ignition. "Hmm. Okay then, how about this? Us non–club members will play a match, and the winner will be able to use the tennis court at lunch from now on. Of course, they'll help Totsuka with his practice. It'll be better for him to practice with people who are better at tennis, anyway. And everyone can have fun."

What's with that flawless logic? Are you a genius?

"A tennis match? Whaaat, that sounds totally fun." Miura gave that ferocious smile, appropriate for the queen of fire.

Instantly, their hangers-on cheered excitedly. That was the moment we burst into phase three, swept along by the fever of competition in wild enthusiasm and mayhem. I made it sound cool right there, but basically, we were having a match with the tennis court as the stakes.

Why was this happening…?

×　×　×

I was being somewhat facetious when I tossed out the phrase "wild enthusiasm and mayhem," but that was how things unfolded. This tennis court in the corner of the schoolyard was now crowded and bustling with commotion. Had I bothered to take a head count, I'm sure it would easily have been over two hundred people. Of course, Hayama's clique was there, and a lot of others had heard rumors from somewhere and had descended upon us. The majority of them were Hayama's friends and fans. They were mainly second-years, but there were some first-years mixed in, and I could see a few third-years sprinkled in, too.

For real? He's more popular than most politicians.

"HA-YA-TO! *WOO!* HA-YA-TO! *WOO!*" After the audience cheered his name, they started a wave.

This was totally like a pop idol concert. I don't think all that cheering was completely sincere. The majority of them were just rubbernecking to see a spectacle. Right? I wanted to believe that. Either way, from an outsider's perspective, their enthusiasm seemed rather cold, and there was an almost religious air to it. It was a truly fearsome teenage religion indeed.

In that crucible of chaos, Hayato boldly strode to the center of the court. Even with this many spectators gathered around, he wasn't the least bit hesitant. He was probably used to that degree of attention. Surrounding him were not only his usual hangers-on but also boys and girls from other classes. We were completely engulfed by them. Gazes flitted here, there, and everywhere, and when I closed my eyes, I ended up dizzy from the earsplitting tumult of it all.

Hayama was already holding a racket and standing on the court. He gazed at us as if deeply interested to see who would step forward.

"Hey, Hikki. What'll we do?" an anxious-looking Yuigahama asked.

"We're not doing anything." I glanced toward Totsuka. And speaking of Totsuka, he was acting like a pet rabbit abandoned at someone else's house. He walked up to my side, timidly pigeon-toed.

What the hell? So cute. Apparently, I wasn't the only one who thought so, and I could hear the shrill sound of girls' cheering *Prince!* and *Cutie-Sai!* flying at the figure who stimulated such protective urges. But every time Totsuka heard those cheers, his shoulders trembled. Seeing his reaction, the Totsuka fans freaked out even harder and wailed. Even I freaked out a bit.

"Totsuka isn't going to play, huh…?" Hayama had said it was a match between non–club members. In other words, this was a match with Totsuka and the tennis court on the line.

"Zaimokuza, can you play tennis?"

"Leave it to me. I read the entire series, and I even saw the musical. I have a slight advantage in this quaint game of ball and net."

"I was stupid for asking you. And if you're gonna think up a lame way to say *tennis*, then come up with one for *musical*, too."

"Then there is naught but for you to play, Hachiman. And how would I say *musical* in an old-fashioned way, then?"

"Good point."

"Do you have a chance at victory? And what would be an old-timey way to say *musical*?!"

"No, I don't. And shut up. If you can't find a way to change it into something else, then change that character you're playing. You're already out of characters, anyway."

"I-I see… You're so smart." I impressed him so much, he snapped out of character. It appeared Zaimokuza's problem was solved now, but mine was not, not by a long shot. Agh…what a mess.

As I was coming to my wits' end, a certain someone tossed a rude and irritated remark at me. "Hey, can you hurry it up?" I raised my head, thinking, *Shut up, you slut*, and there was Miura, grasping her racket as if she was checking it.

It seemed I wasn't the only one surprised to see her holding a racket. Hayama was, too. "Huh? You're gonna play, Yumiko?"

"What? Of course I am. I've been *saying* I want to play tennis."

"Well, but they're probably going to have boys play. You know, um, Hikitani, was it? That guy. Then you'll be at a disadvantage," Hayama said as if in warning.

Who's Hikitani? Hikitani isn't going to be playing. Hikigaya is playing. Probably.

Miura thought a bit while she sproinged her ringlet-curl things. "Oh, then, we should just make it a boys-girls mixed doubles match. Oh man, I'm so smart. But, like, are there any girls who would even pair with you, Hikitani? That would be *too* funny." Miura guffawed in crass, shrill cackling, and the hangers-on all burst out laughing with her. Even I laughed before I realized what I was doing. Heh-heh-heh…*feh-huh-huh.* Frustrating to admit it works, but extremely effective nonetheless. I was engulfed by darkness.

"Hachiman. This is dire. You have no female friends. And if you were to try asking some girl you don't know, none of them would help a nondescript, lonely bastard like you. What'll you do?"

Shut up, Zaimokuza. He was completely right, though, so I couldn't tell him to take it back.

It was too late to say, *Sooorry, forget all that stuff I said!* ☆ at this stage of the game. I glanced toward Zaimokuza, wondering what I should do, and he looked away awkwardly, avoiding my eyes as he whistled voicelessly. When I let slip a sigh, Yuigahama and Totsuka followed suit as if part of a chain reaction.

"Hikigaya. I'm sorry. This would have worked out if…I were a girl…"

It's true. I wonder why he's not a girl. He's so cute. "Don't worry about it." I kept my thoughts to myself and patted Totsuka's head. "And…don't you worry about it, either. You have a proper place where you belong, so you should keep it safe," I said, and Yuigahama's shoulders twitched as she bit her lips apologetically.

Yuigahama had a position within the class. Unlike me, she was capable of forming proper human relationships. She still actually wanted to be friends with Miura and her clique. Though I am indeed a loner, it wasn't like I was jealous of crowds who were friendly with one another. It wasn't like I was praying for their misfortune… I'm not lying, okay? Really.

Ours was neither a close circle nor a group of friends. We were just a ragtag band brought together by fate, or rather, dragged together by fate.

I just wanted to prove this one thing: that loners are not pitiful people, and that being a loner does not make you inferior. I was completely enlightened by the knowledge this was purely for the sake of my own ego. I was super-enlightened. So enlightened I could teleport and breathe fire and stuff.

But I didn't want to deny the validity of who I was then or who I was in the past. I would never say that my time spent alone was a sin or that being alone was evil. And that was why I would fight in order to prove the truth of my justice.

I walked alone to the center of the court.

"...it." I heard a tiny sigh, so tiny it was nearly lost in the crowd.

"Huh?"

"I said I'll do it!" Groaning quietly, Yuigahama's face was bright red.

"Yuigahama? You idiot. Don't be stupid. Forget about it."

"What's so dumb about this?!"

"Why're you doing this? Are you stupid? Or do you like me?"

"Wh...what? You're the stupidhead talking nonsense. You're so stupid!" A terrible, menacing look on her face, Yuigahama yelled, "Stupid, stupid" at me over and over, so mad she was turning crimson. She stole the racket from me and swung it violently.

"S-s-s-sorry!" While somehow managing to dodge her swipes, I immediately apologized. That whooshing sound skimming by my ear was really scary. As I apologized, I pleaded *Why?* with my eyes.

Yuigahama apparently picked up on that, and she looked away shyly.

"Well...like...y'know? I'm in the Service Club, too...so it's normal for me to do this, right? It's...where I belong and stuff."

"Hey, calm down. Take a good look at this situation, okay? Our club isn't the only place you belong. Look, the girls in your clique are giving you the stink-eye."

"Huh? Actually for real?" Face twitching, Yuigahama glanced over toward where Hayama and the others stood. Her neck turned around so jerkily, you could almost hear it creak. It was so unnatural, I wanted to tell her to put some WD-40 on it.

The girls of Hayama's group, with Miura at their head, crossed their arms and glowered our way. *Of course they would. You made such a loud declaration, they could obviously hear you.*

Miura's unnaturally large eyes, colored pitch-black in mascara and eyeliner, were filled with hostility, and her blonde hair, curled in drill-like whirls, swayed in displeasure. Was she Madame Butterfly or what?

"Like, Yui, if you're gonna stick with those guys, it means you're going up against us. Are you okay with that?" Queen-like Miura folded her arms and tapped her foot on the ground. It was a pose of royal rage.

Overpowered, Yuigahama gently shut her eyes. Her fingers gripped the hem of her skirt, and nervousness made them tremble. The ogling onlookers burst into an exchange of whispers. This was no different than a public execution. But Yuigahama lifted her head and squared off against the other girl.

"Th-that's not what I… I mean, it is like that, but… But…my club is important to me, too! So I'm gonna do it."

"Huh… Oh, really? Don't embarrass yourself," Miura replied bluntly. But there was a smile on her face. A smile that blazed like the flames of hell. "Get changed. I'll lend you a girls' tennis uniform, so why don't you come, too?" Miura jerked her chin toward the tennis club's room to the side of the court. She was probably trying to be nice, but that gesture only gave the appearance of saying, *Why don't I end you in the clubroom?*

Yuigahama followed her, her expression stiff, and everyone around issued expressions of pity as she walked away.

Well, you know. My condolences.

"Hey, Hikitani." Hayama spoke to me as I was pressing my hands together in prayer. He must have had some pretty strong communication skills if he was talking to me. Even though he got my name wrong.

"What?"

"I don't really know the rules of tennis, and doubles are pretty hard. So maybe we could not take this too seriously?"

"Well, this is amateur tennis. We just hit it back and forth and keep score, right? Like in volleyball."

Hayama smiled brilliantly. I smiled along with him, a rather unpleasant smirk.

While we were at it, our partners returned. Yuigahama's face was all red as she drew nearer, trying as hard as she could to pull her hem down over her legs. She was wearing a uniform that was like a polo shirt with a skort. "Like...this tennis outfit is embarrassing... Isn't this skort kinda short?"

"Uh, don't you usually wear your skirt about that short?"

"What?! What d'you mean?! Y-you mean you're always looking?! That's creepy, so creepy! You're such a creep!" Yuigahama glared at me in rage and raised her racket.

"It's okay! I don't look at all! I don't even notice! Relax! And don't hit me!"

"That...kind of makes me mad, too...," she mumbled, slowly lowering the racket.

Zaimokuza cleared his throat dramatically as if he'd been waiting for that moment. "Hmm. Hachiman. What about our strategy?"

"Well, I guess a good plan would be to aim for the girl." A dumb-looking girl like that would probably be an instakill. She was definitely the weak point, anyway. Going for her would be a much better idea than taking Hayama head-on.

But when Yuigahama heard me say that, her tone turned wild. "What? Don't you know, Hikki? Yumiko was in the tennis club in middle school, you know? She went to Regionals."

I observed the Madame Butterfly known as Yumiko. It was true. Her stance looked legit, and her movements were extremely light.

Watching her, Zaimokuza mumbled, "Heh, so those sausage curls of hers are not just for show, huh?"

"They're more of a loose wave, though," said Yuigahama.

Who cares.

X   X   X

The match was a fierce back-and-forth with sparks flying.

At first, there were constant, passionate roars and shrill cheers from the audience, but as the breathtakingly close match continued, more and more they were just following us with their eyes and then exhaling and cheering exuberantly when a point was made. It was just like a pro match on TV.

We were in a long rally, and tensions ran high. As the match progressed, it was as though each smack of the ball took a little bit out of each of us.

What broke the equilibrium was Sausage Curl's serve. By the time I heard the *thwock*ing sound of ball against racket, the shot was already in the middle of the court like a bullet and bouncing behind me.

What was that? Did the ball just do a sausage curl, too?

I'll get to the point. Madame Butterfly is a pretty high-level player. "She's really good," I muttered.

"I told you so." For some reason, Yuigahama sounded proud. Was she even on my side?

"Wait, you haven't been touching the ball at all!"

"Well, I've never really played tennis before." She laughed, like *ta-ha-ha!* as if to try to distract me from what she'd just said.

"Why are you here if you've never played tennis?"

"Ngh! Well, sooo*rry!*"

You idiot, you've got it backward. *I* should be sorry. Just how much of a ridiculously good person are you? You've never even played this game, but you're still saying you'll play a match in front of a huge crowd for Totsuka's sake. Not many people can do that. If she were actually good at tennis, it would be incredibly cool, but, well, things don't always go well, and that's life, I guess.

At first, it was a pretty even contest between the unparalleled accuracy of my serves and Miura's flawless receives, but as we got closer to the latter half of the match, the gap between us slowly widened. Well, that was because the opposing pair was concentrating on aiming for Yuigahama, though. Perhaps surprised by my string of surprisingly good plays, they had changed their target. There is also the possibility that they were just completely ignoring me.

"Yuigahama. You guard the front. I'll try to manage the rear."

"Okay. Thanks."

We confirmed our basic plan, and I settled into my prescribed position.

Hayama's serve came fast and hard. It hit the farthest possible point, the corner of the court, with pinpoint accuracy, and bounced away even farther. But I leaped to the side and desperately reached for the ball. I stretched my racket as far as it would go, and when it touched the ball, I swung with all my might. The ball returned to our opponents' side of the court, but Madame Butterfly smacked it right back with careful aim.

I didn't even look; I just rolled to my feet and ran at full speed to where I thought she might be directing it.

I frantically ordered my legs forward, and somehow, they were still listening to me. I ran past the ball and arrived at the point of descent, and when the ball connected with my racket, I aimed for the barest margin of the court and hit it forcefully.

But apparently, Hayama had anticipated that, because he was waiting right there, and with a swipe, he let fly a drop shot right between Yuigahama and me, as if testing us.

I'd lost my balance on that last swing and couldn't possibly get there in time. I sent Yuigahama a pleading glance, and she ran where the ball was coming down and returned it. But a glancing blow was the best she could do, and the ball soared up high, falling square in front of Madame Butterfly.

Miura fired it back at us at full power. A sadistic smile rose to her lips, and the ball skimmed past Yuigahama's cheek before disappearing far behind her to bounce in an empty spot on the court.

"Are you okay?" I called out to Yuigahama where she had plopped down on the court instead of going to retrieve the ball.

"That was so scary...," Yuigahama mumbled, her eyes practically drowning.

Madame Butterfly's expression softened with concern for a brief moment.

"You're such a jerk, Yumiko," joked Hayama.

"What? No way! This kind of thing is normal in a match! I'm not that bad!"

"Oh, so you're just a sadist, then." Laughter followed as Hayama and Madame Butterfly teased one another. As if in compliance, the spectators joined in.

"Hikki, we have to win, okay?" Yuigahama said, standing and picking up her racket. Then she let out a tiny "Ow!"

"Hey, are you okay?"

"Sorry. I think I might have pulled something." She went *tee-hee*, a coy smile on her face. In a heartbeat, her eyes were overflowing with tears. "If we lose, Sai-chan'll be in trouble, huh...? Aw, man... This could get nasty... We can't fix this by just apologizing, huh? Ah, geez!" Yuigahama bit her lip in frustration.

"Well, it'll all work out somehow. Worse comes to worst, we'll put Zaimokuza in a girls' uniform."

"They'll be able to tell right away!"

"I guess. Then let's do this: You just stay in the middle of the court. I'll handle the rest somehow."

"What're you gonna do?"

"Since antiquity, there has been a forbidden move in tennis. It is known as *Whoops, my racket turned into a rocket!*"

"That's just rough play!"

"Well, in a pinch, I'll get serious. When I get serious, I'm more than capable of groveling and shoe licking."

"That's some weird stuff to get serious about..." Yuigahama sighed in exasperation, then giggled. Maybe it was her injury, or maybe she'd just laughed so hard that now she was crying, but when she gazed at me, her eyes were moist and red.

"Oh, you're terribly stupid, Hikki. You've got a terrible personality, and you're even terrible at giving up. You're just terrible all over. You never gave up back then, either. You just went all the way, yelling so hard it was creepy. You looked so desperate... I remember."

"Hey, what're you talking about?"

Yuigahama cut me off. "I just don't think I can keep up with you," she said, blown away. She delivered it like a parting remark as she turned her back to me and walked away. She shoved through the confused crowd, saying, "Hey, hey, you're in the way. You're in the way!" and then disappeared.

"What was that about?" I was left standing alone in the middle of the court. When I glanced over where Yuigahama's back had vanished into the crowd, a grating laughter rang through the air.

"What's wrong? Had a little scrap with your *friend*? Did she *abandon* you?"

"Don't be stupid. We've never fought once. We're not close enough to get into a fight in the first place."

"Uh…" Hayama and Madame Butterfly actually flinched.

What? That was supposed to be funny.

Oh, I get it. I guess you need a certain degree of intimacy with most people before you can make self-deprecating jokes with them, huh? If you don't, they just get really weirded out.

Zaimokuza was the only one who got it, and he stifled a laugh. I whirled around, clicking my tongue, and he pretended he had nothing to do with any of this as he mumbled something to himself and disappeared into the crowd. The bastard was running away, huh? Well, if our positions were reversed, I'd most certainly have done the same thing.

His expression growing glum, Totsuka looked at me sadly.

Oh well. I guess it was time to start groveling. I'll show you serious. If you're going to suck up, you've got to throw away your pride and suck up with all you've got, and that's something I take pride in.

Alone on the tennis court, I felt so helpless it was unbearable, or maybe I'll just say I was stuck in a painfully awkward atmosphere. Abruptly, the crowd began murmuring.

And then it parted on its own.

"What kind of nonsense is going on here?" Appearing before us was an incredibly displeased-looking Yukinoshita clad in her gym top and a skort. In one hand, she was carrying a first aid kit.

"Oh, hey, where'd you go? And what's with that outfit?"

"Who knows? I really have no idea. Yuigahama simply asked me to put this on," Yukinoshita said, and when she turned, Yuigahama popped out at her side. It seemed they had exchanged clothes, and now Yuigahama was wearing Yukinoshita's uniform. *Where did you guys change? No way, not outside?! Mm-hmm...*

"I didn't want us to lose like this, so I got Yukinon to step in."

"Why me?"

"I mean, you're the only friend I have who I can ask to do this, Yukinon."

Yukinoshita twitched. "Fri...end?"

"Yeah, friend." Yuigahama replied instantly.

Oh, I dunno about that.

"Do you usually ask your friends to handle trouble for you? I feel like you're just conveniently using me."

"Huh? I wouldn't ask if you weren't my friend. I couldn't ask someone I didn't care about to do something important," Yuigahama stated nonchalantly, as if it were completely obvious.

Oh-ho, so that's how it works... I've been manipulated into doing cleaning duty before by the phrase *we're friends, right?* so I hadn't gotten that impression at all. I see... So me and those guys had actually been proper friends. Yeah, no way.

Yukinoshita must have felt precisely as I did on that point. She gently pressed a hand to her lips and pondered silently. Her doubts were reasonable. I wouldn't have taken that so easily, either. But Yui Yuigahama was a special case. I mean, she was an idiot.

"You know, I think she's being serious. Because she's an idiot."

Yukinoshita softened in reaction to my remark. She smiled her usual unyielding smile and brushed off the hair falling over her shoulders. "Do not underestimate me. It may surprise you to hear this, but believe I'm a good judge of character. There's no way someone who can be nice to the two of us could be a bad person."

"That reason is too sad," I remarked.

"But it's the truth."

Indeed it was.

"I don't mind playing tennis, but…could you wait for a moment?" she asked, moving over to Totsuka. "You can at least treat your wounds yourself, right?"

Totsuka took the first aid kit being offered to him with a confused expression. "Huh? Oh yeah…"

"Yukinon, you went all the way to get that… You really are nice after all, huh?"

"Perhaps. It seems that a certain boy is secretly calling me the ice queen, though."

"H-how did you know that?! Ah! No way, did you read my list of people I hate?!" Crap. That was a diary that contained every single insult I could possibly hurl at Yukinoshita.

"I'm shocked. You really call me that? Well, not that I care what anyone thinks of me," she said, turning in our direction. But her demeanor wasn't her usual calm one, and it had a slight bewildered tinge to it. At first, her voice sounded strong, but it grew quieter until finally she averted her eyes. "So…I don't really…mind if you…think of me as a…friend."

Yukinoshita's cheeks went so red that you could hear the sound of her blush. She held the racket she'd received from Yuigahama and stood with her head downcast, glancing at the other girl. Her unbelievable display of cuteness earned her a sudden embrace.

From Yuigahama.

"Yukinon!"

"Hey…could you not cling to me like that? It's stifling…"

Huh? This isn't the part where I'm supposed to come in, then? She's always getting blushy around Yuigahama, isn't she? Is that how it is? Is this

a guy-guy girl-girl rom-com or what? Are all the gods of romantic comedy total idiots?

She somehow pried off Yuigahama and then cleared her throat before speaking. "I'm extremely reluctant to play doubles with that boy, though. But I have no choice, do I? I shall accept your request. I just have to win this match, correct?"

"Yeah! Well, Hikki can't win with me as a partner, so."

"Sorry for causing you trouble." I bowed my head, and Yukinoshita glared at me frigidly.

"Don't get the wrong idea. It's not like I'm doing this for you."

"Ha-ha-ha! Again with the *tsundere* lines!" Oh man. Geez. Ha-ha-ha-ha! No, no, you didn't hear those types of clichés anymore, you know?

"*Tsundere*? That sounds like quite the repulsive piece of vocabulary."

Of course. There was no way Yukinoshita would know what a *tsundere* is.

But most importantly, she never lied. The things she said might be incredibly cruel, but they were always true. So she honestly wasn't doing it for me.

That doesn't necessarily mean that she didn't like me, so I was okay with that. Yep.

"Anyway, show me that list of yours later. I'll correct it for you." She burst into an absolutely brilliant smile, like a flower blooming.

I wonder why that smile didn't warm my heart even the slightest bit. I was terrified. I felt as if there were a tiger right in front of me. And if there was a tiger in front of me, then... Of course, you know how the saying goes. There was a wolf behind me. Or a horse.

"Yukinoshita, was it? Sorry, but I can't go easy on you. You seem like a delicate girl, so, like, if you don't wanna get hurt, you should back out, mmkay?" I turned to see Miura with her curls spinning around even tighter, a bold smile on her face. Oh, you idiot, Miura. Provoking Yukinoshita is a death flag...

"Relax. I'll be the one going easy on you. I'll reduce that cheap pride of yours to dust," Yukinoshita said, an invincible smile on her face. At the very least, she seemed invincible to me. Yukinoshita was someone you really didn't want to make your enemy, but it was reassuring to have her as an ally. That was why I was so astonished to see someone make an enemy of her. Hayama and Miura were ready to square off with us.

The fierce smile on Yukinoshita's face was so cold and beautiful it forced you to snap to rigid attention.

"You've harassed my friend..." Yukinoshita stopped there, blushing very slightly. Saying that word out loud had to be pretty embarrassing. She silently shook her head and began again. "...No, my fellow club member. Are you ready to face the consequences? Just so you know, though I may not look it, I'm quite a vindictive person."

No, you look very much like a vindictive person.

×　×　×

Somehow or other, all the players had assembled for the tennis match, and we were entering the real-deal final phase at last. The Hayama-Miura pair made the first move. First serve went to Madame Butterfly, aka Sausage Curls, aka Miura. "Like, I dunno if you know this, Yukinoshita, but I'm *real* good at tennis," she bragged as she dribbled the ball like a basketball, bouncing it off the ground, catching it, and bouncing it again.

With her eyes alone, Yukinoshita indicated that Miura should continue.

Miura smiled. It was a completely different expression from the one Yukinoshita had displayed. It was the aggressive leer of a beast. "Sorry if I scrape your face or anything."

Whoa, scary. This was the first time I'd ever heard anyone give advance notice that their volleys would be physically dangerous. The moment that thought crossed my mind, I heard a sharp *whoosh*ing sound cut through the air, followed by the light bounce of a ball. The strike whizzed at high speed toward Yukinoshita's left side. Yukinoshita was right-handed, so the ball was out of her reach, plunging just barely in-bounds by the left-hand line.

"Not good enough." By the time I heard her murmur, she was already in position for a counterattack. She took a step with her left foot and spun on that axle as if she were dancing a waltz, connecting with the ball with a right-handed backhand. It all came in a single flash, as if she were drawing a blade from its sheath and striking in one smooth motion.

Miura let out a tiny shriek as the ball bounced in her court and sprung up again at her feet. It was an eye-opening, ultra-high-speed hit that was impossible to return.

"I'm sure you didn't know, but I'm quite good at tennis myself." Thrusting out her racket, Yukinoshita stabbed the other girl with the sort of frosty glare you'd use on a louse.

Miura took a step back, regarding Yukinoshita with fear and animosity. Her lips twisted slightly, and she spat out a curse. Yukinoshita was fearsome indeed to extricate that kind of expression from the queenly Miura.

"Nice one."

That look from Miura was a bluff, and Yukinoshita completely ignored it. To be precise, her focus was entirely fixated on the ball. "She had exactly the same look on her face as the girls in my class who used to harass me. It's painfully simple to read lowlifes like them." Yukinoshita smiled proudly and then began her attack.

Even her defense was an attack. I'm not talking about that tired cliché of *the best defense is a good offense*. Her defense actually doubled as an offense. When a serve approached, it was unfailingly thrust back into our opponents' court, and when hits were returned to her, she would force them back without flinching.

The audience was enthralled by her flawless performance.

"Aha-ha-ha-ha-ha! Our army is unstoppable! Mow them down!" Apparently, he'd sensed victory in the air, because Zaimokuza had returned at some point and was trying to hitch his wagon to the winning team. It was infuriating. But the fact that he was with us also meant that the tide had turned. When it had been Yuigahama and me playing, we'd totally been treated like the away team, but gradually, the audience had begun favoring Yukinoshita. Or rather, a lot of the guys were shooting Yukinoshita heated glances.

Yukinoshita was in a separate curriculum, so most people didn't know what she was really like, and of course, she was good-looking. She had a mysterious air about her, like that of an unattainable idol. It wasn't that people were scared of her; it was more like there was just this taboo around talking to her.

You could say that Yuigahama was actually fairly courageous to break through that barrier. She was also quite the idiot. But she was straightforward, sincere, and honestly kind, and that had resonated with Yukinoshita. It was unlikely that anyone other than Yuigahama could have gotten Yukinoshita to come here. And because this was for brave Yuigahama's sake, Yukinoshita was giving it all she had. If I'd been the one doing the asking, she probably wouldn't have shown up.

The gap between our scores shrank before our eyes. Yukinoshita whirled freely about the court, almost fairylike in her movements. Her dancing footwork was the greatest show this stage had ever seen. A minor actor like myself just occasionally popped the ball back. Every time I touched it, I was on the receiving end of painful stares of *No, not you!*

Arousing the expectations of the spectators, it came again to be Yukinoshita's turn to serve. She squeezed the ball and threw it high into the air. It seemed as though it would be sucked into the blue sky as it flew toward the center of the court. It was clearly far from Yukinoshita's position. Everyone thought that she'd made a mistake.

Yukinoshita jumped.

She took a step forward with her right foot, threw out her left leg, and at last took off with both legs. Her pace was light and staccato. She fluttered splendidly in the air, like a falcon gliding calmly through the sky, and none who watched her were left unmoved. She was beautiful and fast. Onlookers forgot to blink as though the image of her were burned into their retinas.

There came a particularly loud slam, and then the ball bounced and dribbled to a roll. Neither I, the audience, Hayama, nor Miura could move.

"A-a jump serve...," I stammered, utterly shocked. Yukinoshita's crazy move had left my mouth gaping open, and I couldn't shut it again. We'd been so far behind, but she had caught up basically on her own. Now we were two points in the lead. One more point, and victory would be ours. "You really are unbelievable. Just keep doing that, and we'll end this in a snap," I complimented in all sincerity.

Suddenly, Yukinoshita grimaced. "If I could, I would like to...but I cannot."

I was about to ask, *What?* But then Hayama got into a serving stance.

Oh well. Yukinoshita would just make some flawless return, and we'd win anyway. I wasn't being flippant about it; I just had absolute confidence in our victory and slid into a sloppy stance.

Hayama was already losing interest in the game, and this serve wasn't as strong as his previous one. It was reasonably fast but still exceedingly average. It arced between Yukinoshita and me.

"Yukinoshita," I called out, thinking to leave it to her, but she didn't reply. Instead, I heard an exhausted *plop*, and the ball landed between us.

"Hikigaya. May I brag a bit?"

"What? And what was that just now?"

Apparently, she had no interest in hearing my reply. She sighed deeply and sat down right there on the court. "You know, I've always been good at everything, so I've never done anything for a very long time."

"Where's this coming from?"

"I had someone teach me tennis, once. I learned it in three days, and I beat my instructor. In most sports...no, not just sports; it's the same in music, too—I can generally master it all within three days."

"So you're the opposite of a three-day quitter? And this really is just bragging. What's your point?"

"The only thing I lack confidence in is my endurance."

I heard a stupid-sounding *splonk* noise as the ball bounced past her. Too late to be discussing this now.

Because Yukinoshita could do anything, she never persisted, never kept on with anything, and she was fatally lacking in stamina. Looking back, when we were practicing during lunch hour, she had only watched.

Well, when you thought about it, maybe it was obvious. If you feel like you want to get better, you practice, and if you practice more, you gain that much more endurance. But if you can master anything from the start, you would never even practice in the first place, and naturally, you would never build up any staying power.

"Hey, don't say that so loud," I chided, glancing toward Hayama and Miura.

The beast queen smiled ferociously. "I heard all of it, you know," she said in an aggressive tone as if venting all of her pent-up anger. At her side, Hayama chuckled.

The situation was dire. We had only been in the lead for the briefest instant, and all too quickly, they'd caught up and brought us to deuce. This was an amateur match with irregular rules. After deuce, victory would only come with a decisive two-point lead. I'd been relying on Yukinoshita, but now she was out of energy and listless. What's more, the opposing team knew it. We were already fully aware that my serves wouldn't work on them. The moment I tried, they'd casually return the ball, and it would all be over.

"Well, you came and stuck your nose in our business, but it's over for real now, huh?"

I had no comeback for Miura's provocation. Yukinoshita was silent, too. She actually seemed pretty tired and was starting to nod off. *Who are you, Hiei?*

Chuckling deep in her throat, Miura eyed us with snakelike contempt. Seriously, she's got to be an anaconda of some kind.

Picking up on the sketchy vibe, Hayama intervened. "Well, we all did our best. Let's not take this too seriously. We had fun, so why don't we just call this a draw?"

"C'mon, Hayato, what're you talking about? This is a match, so we've got to take it seriously and settle this."

In other words, having beat us in the match, she would then formally steal the court from Totsuka. Still, the way she said *settle this* was actually scary... *I wonder if she's gonna do something to me... Man... I really can't handle pain.*

As I waffled, I heard the sound of someone clicking their tongue. "Could you be quiet for a moment?" Yukinoshita demanded, annoyed. Before Miura could speak, she quickly continued, "This boy will settle the match, so please be quiet and accept your loss."

Everyone doubted their ears on hearing that. Of course, I did, too. Actually, I was the most surprised one there. All at once, all eyes were on me. It goes without saying, but none of them had ever noticed me before, and now that they were treating me like *Why are you here?* the value of my existence skyrocketed.

I met Zaimokuza's gaze. *Why are you giving me the thumbs-up?*

I met Totsuka's as well. *Why do you look so hopeful?*

I met Yuigahama's gaze. *Don't cheer me on so loud. It's embarrassing.*

I met Yukinoshita's ga—she looked away. Instead, she threw the ball at me. "Did you know? I may spit venom and abuse, but I've never once spat out a lie." Because of the way the wind was blowing, I heard her voice loud and clear.

Oh, I know. The only liars here are them and me.

X   X   X

In a silence so deep it was unnatural, the only noise I could discern was that of the ball bouncing against the ground. In that unique air of tension, I buried my consciousness deeper and deeper within myself. I made myself believe *I can do it, I can do it.* No, I *do* believe in myself. I mean, there was no way I could lose.

My life here at school has been worthless, sad, difficult, and nothing but garbage, but I've survived it all on my own. I've gotten through a painful and pathetic young adulthood all by myself, so I could never lose to someone who has always lived with the support of the crowd.

Lunch hour was almost over. Any other day, I would have been in my spot across from the tennis court and to the side of the nurse's office eating my lunch. I recalled the time when Yuigahama talked to me and the place where I first met Totsuka.

I listened. I couldn't hear Miura's mockery or the clamoring of the audience. *Fwoo,* it went. I could hear that noise. For the whole year, it was me, and probably only me, who had ever heard that sound.

That was when I served.

My hit was gentle and slow, like it was floating up. I saw Miura gleefully bounding forward. Hayama swiftly came in to support her. The audience looked disappointed. I could see in the corner of my vision Totsuka slowly closing his eyes. I overlooked Zaimokuza clenching his fist. My eyes met Yuigahama's, and she seemed to be doing something like praying. And then my eyes reflected Yukinoshita's victorious smile.

The ball swayed along on an unreliable, frail trajectory.

"*Yesss!*" Miura hissed just like a snake, positioning herself where the ball would come down.

When suddenly came a gust of wind.

Miura, you don't know. You don't know about the special wind that only blows here around Soubu High.

That breeze buffeted the ball along, blowing it wide. It strayed from Miura's spot and hit the edge of the court. But Hayama was running toward it.

Hayama, you don't know. That wind blows twice.

Only I knew. I'd spent my lunches there quietly, all alone, without ever talking to anyone, for a whole year. Only that wind knew about my lonely and tranquil time.

This was my very own magic strike.

The wind whooshed again, blowing the ball even after it bounced. The ball sailed to a corner of the court, landed with a *tump*, and rolled away.

Everyone fell silent and listened, their eyes opened wide.

"Oh yeah... I've heard something... They say there is a legendary technique used to control the wind... It is known as the heir of wind: *Eulen Sylphide*!" Zaimokuza exclaimed loudly, painfully awkward as usual.

Don't name it. You've basically just ruined it.

"No way...," Miura whispered in abject shock. That triggered a rustle of susurration among the audience, and before long, that rustle was turning into the phrase *Eulen Sylphide, Eulen Sylphide. Hey, you're not allowed to accept that name!*

"You got us... That really was a magic strike." Hayama faced me and smiled broadly. He regarded me as though we'd been friends for years.

Under the full brunt of his smile, still clenching the ball, I just stood there. I really didn't know how to reply at times like these. "Hayama. Did you play baseball when you were little?"

"Yeah, a lot. Why do you ask?" Hayama seemed suspicious at my unexpected question, but he'd unfailingly answered. Maybe he really was a good guy after all.

"How many people did you play it with?"

"Huh? You need ten people to play baseball, don't you?"

"Of course... But you know, I did it a lot alone."

"Huh? What do you mean?" Hayama asked.

I'm sure you wouldn't understand even if I explained.

It wasn't just about this.

Do you get how hard it is to ride your bicycle to and from school like an idiot in the middle of hot summer days or winter days so cold if feels like your fingers might fall off? You guys lie, deceive, and distract yourselves from it all by chattering It's so hot *and* It's so cold *and* No way *with your friends, but I endured that all on my own. There's no way you could get it. You couldn't get how scary it is every time there's a test and you have no one to ask what's on it; you just silently study and then face your results head-on. You all get together and compare answers and show each other your grades and call each other dunces and study freaks and run away from reality like that, but I'm always taking it straight in the face.*

How do you like my awesome power?

Following my heart, I fell into a serving stance. I arched my upper body back like a bowstring and threw the ball high, gripping the handle of the racket in both hands and laying it against the back of my neck.

The blue sky. The departing spring. The arriving summer. I'd send all of that flying.

"YOUTH SUCKS!"

With all my might, I smacked the descending projectile with an uppercut.

The ball connected squarely with the frame of the racket, producing a *thonk* sound as it was sucked into the faded blue sky. The ball climbed and climbed until all you could see was a tiny speck, far in the distance, smaller than a grain of rice. That was probably the ball.

"Th-that's...the airborne god of destruction, *Meteor Strike!*" Zaimokuza shouted, leaning forward. *Seriously, why are you naming this stuff?*

"*Meteor Strike...,*" every mouth recited. *Seriously, why are you guys accepting this stuff?!*

It wasn't that big a deal. It was just a fly ball.

Let me explain. When I was of a tender age, I didn't have any friends, so I developed the new sport of solo baseball. I would pitch the ball by myself, hit it by myself, and catch it by myself. I had to devise a way to continue the game for long periods of time, so I realized that I could have fun for the longest amount of time if I hit the ultimate maximum fly ball.

If I caught it, I was out, and if I missed and caught it after one bounce, it was a base hit. If I hit it really far, I treated it as a home run. The flaw in this game was if you got too invested in either the offensive or the defensive side, it became rather one-sided. Your mind needed to be as clear of thought as if you were playing rock-paper-scissors by yourself.

Good little boys and girls, don't copy this: You should play baseball with your friends.

But this was the very symbol of my isolation: my ultimate weapon.

The ball fell from the empty sky, an iron hammer upon those youth-worshipping bastards.

"Wh-what's that?" Still looking up at the sky, Miura was dumbfounded.

Hayama was the same, looking at the sky as if dazzled, but then his expression grew concerned. "Yumiko! Watch out!" he yelled to Miura, who was still standing stock-still in mute amazement. Of course, he may have known what was coming...but it was already too late.

The ball, meteoric though it may have been, gradually lost momentum, drawn downward by gravity, and the split instant those two forces were in balance, it hung in the air. When that balance was broken, the potential energy was converted into kinetic energy. The ball was in free fall. At the point of impact, it would explode.

SLAM! The ball detonated, blowing up a dense cloud of dust. Ending its long, long journey through the sky, it kicked up detritus and dirt, rising once more into the air.

Miura ran to try to hit it back, chasing after it uncertainly through the particulate debris. The ball wobbled toward the back of the court bordered by a chain-link fence.

Oh, watch out.

She collided with it. "Ngh!"

Hayama threw away his racket and ran to her with a leap.

Would he make it? Would he make it?! The pair disappeared from the audience's view in the dust storm.

A moment of stillness. I heard the sound of someone gulping down their spit. It might actually have been my throat making that noise. Then the dust cleared, revealing them. Hayama had thrown his back against the fence, wrapping his arms around Miura to protect her from the impact. Blushing, Miura was shyly clutching him, curled up against his chest.

Instantaneously, the spectators erupted in loud cheers and ear-splitting applause. It was a full-on standing ovation.

Hayama patted Miura's head as she nestled against his chest, and her face turned even redder.

The audience screamed and surrounded the pair. "HA-YA-TO! *WOO!* HA-YA-TO! *WOO!*"

Instead of a fanfare in their celebration, the bell signaling the end of lunch rang through the courtyard. At this rate, it felt like they would just kiss and the end credits would roll. Everyone was enveloped in the strange sense of accomplishment and the sort of despondency that you feel after watching a fun, epic movie or finishing a really good teen romantic comedy novel. Hoisting the pair of them high into the air, the crowd disappeared into the school.

FIN.

What the hell.

X   X   X

In the aftermath, we were the only ones left.

"I suppose this is what you call winning the battle and losing the war," I heard Yukinoshita say, bored, and I couldn't help but smile.

"Don't be stupid. Between us and them, it was never a contest in the first place." The youth worshippers are always in the lead roles.

"Well, that's true. That wouldn't have happened with anyone but you, Hikki. Getting totally ignored even though you won—that's majorly sad."

"Hey. Yuigahama. You really need to watch what you say. You need to realize that honest opinions hurt more than malicious remarks," I advised, giving her a reproachful look, but she didn't look like she felt bad about it at all.

Well, nothing she was saying was untrue, so there was no reason for her to feel bad after all. People like Miura and Hayama totally wouldn't have cared about something like this match or competition or whatever, anyway. They'd turn even this pathetic loss into a beautiful memory of their youths, and they'd hold on to that memory with religious zeal. It was awe-inspiring.

What the hell. Die in a fire, youth. Die in a fire.

"Gah, come on. What's so great about Hayama? I'd be like that if I'd been born and raised differently."

"Then you'd be a different person. Honestly, I do think your life could do with a reset, though." Yukinoshita gazed at me coldly as she indirectly told me to go die.

"B-but, you know… Um, it's sort of like it worked out because it was Hikki, um…it makes him seem sort of okay…," Yuigahama mumbled, barely opening her mouth. I couldn't hear her at all. *Speak properly, come on. You're acting like me when a clerk at a clothing store tries to talk to me.*

But her comment did seem to have reached Yukinoshita, who smiled very slightly and quietly nodded. "Well, it seems there are occasions when people may be saved by your depressingly twisted methods. Unfortunately," she added, eyes darting to one side. She was looking at Totsuka, who was walking slowly, nursing his scraped knee, as Zaimokuza followed him like a stalker.

"Hachiman, well done. I would expect nothing less of my partner.

But the day may yet come when we must settle things between us…"
For some reason, he got this faraway look in his eyes and started talking
to himself, so I ignored him for the moment and spoke to Totsuka.

"Is your knee okay?"

"Yeah…"

Before I realized it, I was surrounded by just guys. I don't know if
it was because Zaimokuza had show up, but at some point, Yukinoshita
and Yuigahama had disappeared. Hayama had gotten a James Bondian
ending, complete with getting the girl, but for me, it was just guys. It
was like an ending from the A-Team. Such injustice! Rom-coms are
nothing but an urban legend.

"Hikigaya… Um, thanks." Totsuka stood gazed at me. Then he
averted his eyes coquettishly. Frankly, I thought about just embracing
him right there and giving him a kiss, but you know, he's a guy…

This rom-com scenario was all wrong, and Totsuka's gender was
wrong, too. Incidentally, Totsuka was also thanking the wrong person.

"I didn't really do anything. If you're going to thank anyone, thank
them…" I glanced around for the girls, perusing the area. Then I spot-
ted a pair of ponytails bobbing along near the tennis clubroom. So that's
where they were.

Thinking I'd offer them a word of thanks, I headed over. "Yuki-
noshi…oh."

She was in the middle of changing.

The front of her blouse was open, and her pale lime-green bra
was peeking out. Her panties were still underneath her skort, but that
imbalance only emphasized how balanced the proportions of her slim
body were.

"Wh…wh-wh-wh-wh—"

*…what, I was thinking, I'm concentrating, shut up, what if I fail to
remember this…* And then for some reason, there was Yuigahama.

She was in the middle of changing.

Apparently, she was one of those people who started buttoning
her shirt from the bottom, and it was open wide at her chest, her pink

bra and cleavage peeking out. The skirt she grasped in one hand was being extended to Yukinoshita. Well, basically, she wasn't wearing it. The thighs stretching out from pink panties that matched her top were slim and long, and her calves were covered in knee-high navy-blue socks.

"Just die, for real!" She took a full swing at my face with her racket, connecting with a *thunk*.

Of course. If you're gonna have a teen rom-com, you need some of this. Not bad, god of rom-coms. *Guh.*

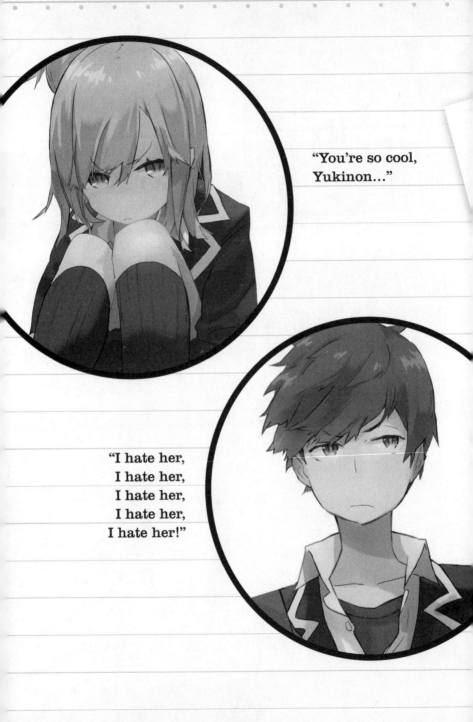

Guidance Counseling Survey

Soubu Secondary School   Grade: 2nd Year   Class: J

Name:
Yukino Yukinoshita

M / Ⓕ

Attendance no. 38

What is a personal value you hold dear?

"Absolute justice."

In your grad yearbook, what did you write as your dream for the future?

To run for political office using my father's influence.

What are you doing now to prepare for your future?

Winning the hearts and minds of the people.

Teacher's comments:

I like how straightforward you are, but why don't you consider your other options? Also, you're terrible at "winning the hearts and minds of the people." Let's try a little harder on that one.

And then **Hikigaya** ponders.

Youth.

The word is a mere five letters, but it fiercely moves the hearts of men. For adults out in society, it elicits a sweet pain and nostalgia. For young women, it elicits eternal longing. And for people like me, it elicits strong jealousy and dark hatred.

My life in high school was nothing like the technicolored mental image described above. It was an ashen, gloomy, monochrome world. It was somber from the very beginning, when I got into a traffic accident on the day of the entrance ceremony. After that, I commuted between my house and school, going to the library on weekends, and generally spending my days in a manner quite dissimilar from your average student. It was far removed from any sort of romantic comedy.

But I had fun.

Diligently going to the library to finish brick-sized fantasy novels, listening rapturously to radio personalities speaking when I happened to switch on the radio in the middle of the night, fishing for heartwarming articles within the wide electronic ocean ruled by text… I found all of that, encountered all of those things, precisely because I spent my days alone.

I was grateful and moved by every single one of those experiences, and though they brought me to tears, they weren't tears of lamentation. I will never deny the validity of the time I spent, those days of my youth known as *the first year of high school. I will vigorously affirm it. I doubt my stance on the matter will ever change.*

Nevertheless, I do want to point out that my position is not to deny the validity of the experiences of others currently celebrating their youths. In the midst of the teen experience as they are, they manage to turn even failure into wonderful memories. They look at their squabbles and fights as a time of youthful worry.

Through their youth filter, their world changes.

And that being the case, perhaps my teen years may be seen through those rose-tinted rom-com glasses as well. And maybe it isn't wrong. Maybe the place I'm in now may one day appear to glitter. Even my rotten, dead-fish eyes may one day sparkle. To the degree that I have those hopes, I feel that something is gradually growing inside me. Indeed, in the days I have spent in the Service Club, I have learned one thing.

In conclusion:

I got that far, and my pen stopped.

Left all alone in a classroom after school, I stretched out my arms above my head with a groan. It wasn't like I was being bullied or anything. I was just redoing that assignment as ordered by Ms. Hiratsuka. It was true, okay? I wasn't being bullied, okay?

I'd gotten about halfway through my essay at a good pace, but the conclusion just wasn't coming out right, and it had grown rather late.

I guess I'll write the rest in the clubroom, I thought, quickly tossing my paper and pens into my bag, putting the empty classroom behind me. The hallway to the special-use building was empty, and the sounds of students in sports clubs yelling reverberated through the halls.

Yukinoshita was probably reading again in the clubroom today. I could continue my essay without any interruptions, then. It wasn't like the club actually did anything, anyway. Very occasionally, strange people would show up, but those really were rare events. Most students talked about their problems or whatever among more approachable peers, people they were close to—or they just bottled it all up.

That was probably the correct thing to do, the desirable stance.

However, sometimes there are people who can't do that. People like me or Yukinoshita or Yuigahama or Zaimokuza.

I'm sure things like friendship and love and dreams and so forth are wonderful to many people. Even feelings of skittishness or anxiety can be seen in a positive light, I'm sure. That very outlook is what they call *youth*.

But at the end of the day, that's exactly why contrary sorts like me wonder if maybe people just enjoy being enraptured by the buzz of youth or whatever. My sister would say something like *Youth? Like, youth guys better get outta here? That's youse guys*, got it? You watch too much TV!

× × ×

When I opened the door to the clubroom, Yukinoshita was in the same place as always, unchanged from her usual posture as she poured over a book. She noticed the sound of the door creaking and raised her head. "Oh. I thought you wouldn't come today," she said, wedging a bookmark in her paperback. When you consider how she used to just keep reading her book and totally ignore me, she'd made incredible progress.

"Well, I thought about skipping out. I just had something to do today." I pulled out a chair at the long table diagonally in front of Yukinoshita and sat down. We were both at our regular posts. I pulled out the paper from my bag and spread it out on the table.

Looking intently at what I was doing, Yukinoshita raised an eyebrow in mild displeasure. "Hey. Just what do you think this club is for?"

"You're just reading, though," I pointed out, and Yukinoshita looked away awkwardly. It appeared that no one had come with requests today, either.

In the quiet room, the only sound was the second hand of the clock. Now that I think about it, it had been a long time since I'd last experienced this kind of silence. It was probably because a certain noisy individual wasn't around.

"Oh yeah, where's Yuigahama?"

"She's apparently going to spend some time with Miura and her friends."

"Huh…" That was surprising. Or not. They were originally friends, and ever since that tennis match, Miura's attitude had softened in a way apparent even to an outsider. I don't know if it was because Yuigahama was more open now or not.

"What about you, Hikigaya? Your partner isn't with you today?"

"Totsuka is with his team. I don't know if it's thanks to your special training or what, but he's all fired up about his club activities." And that meant he wasn't spending much time with me. It was so sad.

"Not Totsuka, the other one."

"Who?"

"Who…? There's another one, isn't there? That thing that's always lurking around you."

"Hey, don't scare me… Wait, can you sense ghosts?"

"Agh, ghosts? What nonsense. There's no such thing." Sighing, Yukinoshita gave me a look that said, *I'll turn* you *into a ghost if you like.* It was a rather nostalgic exchange. "I mean, you know. Za…Zai, Zaitsu? Was that it…?"

"Oh, Zaimokuza. He's not my partner, though." It was actually doubtful if he was even a friend. "He said, like, 'Today has been a scene of carnage… My apologies, but I shall prioritize my deadline' and went home."

"He certainly *talks* like he's a best-selling novelist," Yukinoshita muttered with an open expression of disgust.

No, no, no, stand in my shoes. I was the one being forced to read his stuff. He didn't even write the main text; he just brought me ideas for illustrations and plot outlines, you know? *Hey, Hachiman! I just thought up a cutting-edge new scene! The heroine has a body made of rubber, and the subheroine has the power to nullify those powers! This'll sell!* You idiot. That wasn't cutting edge; that was a disappointment. That was just a rip-off.

Well, at the end of the day, we'd just been part of a lukewarm temporary community, and once that time together had passed, we each went back to where we belonged.

It was what they call a once-in-a-lifetime encounter.

So if you're going to ask if this place was where me and Yukinoshita's belonged, it wasn't particularly. Our conversation was on and off, rambling, and awkward as usual.

"I'm coming in." Suddenly, the door opened with a rattle.

"Agh." Perhaps Yukinoshita had given up. She put her palm to her forehead lightly and sighed.

I see now. When you're in a quiet space and suddenly the door opens, you do want to say something sour. Huh.

"Ms. Hiratsuka. Please knock when you come in," I chided.

"Hmm? Isn't that usually Yukinoshita's line?" A baffled expression on her face, Ms. Hiratsuka pulled over a nearby chair and sat down.

"Do you need something?" Yukinoshita asked, and Ms. Hiratsuka's eyes sparkled in their usual boyish way.

"I thought I'd do a midterm announcement regarding that competition."

"Oh, that…" I'd totally forgotten. Actually, I had no memory of us solving one thing or anything, so of course it was easy to forget.

"Your current score is two wins each. Right now, it's a draw. Mm-hmm, a close contest is what makes a battle manga! Personally, I'm expecting Hikigaya's death to lead to Yukinoshita's awakening."

"Why am I dying in this plot? Um, you said we each won two, but we haven't really fixed anything. And only three people came to ask us for help." Can she not do arithmetic?

"According to my count, it was definitely four people. I said it would be biased and arbitrary."

"It's refreshing to see you go that far with your made-up rules." Are you Gian or what?

"Ms. Hiratsuka. Would you tell us on what basis these points were decided? As he just pointed out with his whining, we never resolved any of the worries people consulted us on."

"Mm-hmm…" In response to Yukinoshita's question, Ms. Hiratsuka fell silent and thought for a while. "Indeed…the kanji for *worry* has the symbol for *heart* on the left—in other words, you write heart to the side of bad fortune. Then on top of bad fortune, you put a lid."

"What grade are you in now?"

"When you're worried about something, you're always hiding what you really want on the side. The things that people consult you on aren't necessarily what they're really worried about. That's what I'm saying."

"The first part of that explanation was completely unnecessary," observed Yukinoshita.

"It wasn't particularly witty, either," I added.

Yukinoshita cut her down with a slice, and Ms. Hiratsuka withered a bit. "I see… I tried to think hard about it, though…" Well, the point was her standards for victory and defeat were entirely made up. The teacher sulked, glancing between myself and Yukinoshita as she opened her mouth. "Geez… You two get along well when you're being mean… It's like you've been friends for years."

"What? I would never be friends with that boy," Yukinoshita said, shrugging her shoulders. I thought she'd give me a sidelong glare, but she didn't even look at me.

"Hikigaya, don't feel too depressed. It's like that saying… 'Some insects prefer to eat knotweed.' There's no accounting for taste," the teacher said as if to console me.

I'm not depressed, though. Man, her kindness hurts.

"Indeed…" Surprisingly, Yukinoshita agreed. *Wait, you're the one who was trying to depress me!* But Yukinoshita didn't lie, and she never faked her feelings, so her words were surely trustworthy. She had a kind smile on her face. "Someday there will come a bug who will like you, Hikigaya."

"At least make it a cute animal!" I didn't say *Make it a human*, which was pretty modest of me, if I do say so myself.

In contrast, arrogant Yukinoshita was clenching her fist with a look on her face like *I sure let him have it!* Her eyes were sparkling at having said something witty, and she looked like she was enjoying herself.

Being the butt of her jokes, I wasn't enjoying myself at all. I mean, like, isn't talking with a girl supposed to be more *titter titter hee-hee flirt flirt smooch smooch*? This was just weird. Thinking to record the emotions that had just crossed my mind, I grabbed a mechanical pencil, and when I did, Yukinoshita peered at me.

"Oh yeah. What have you been writing?"

"Shut up. It's nothing." And then I scribbled off the last line of my essay.

There's something wrong with my youth romantic comedy.

Afterword

Long time no see. I'm Wataru Watari. And nice to meet you. I'm Wataru Watari.

This may sound sudden, but the *youth* you generally hear society describe is all wrong. It's all total lies. Going on a date to a big mall like LaLaport in your school uniform with your cute girlfriend or getting introduced to a girl from another school through your friend and going out to eat and stuff...none of that ever happens. It's fiction.

In a teen rom-com, they add this line at the end, right? *This is a work of fiction and has no connection to any real incidents, persons, or groups.* In other words, any teen rom-com like that is a pack of lies. Everyone is being deceived.

Real youth is when two guys stop by a fast-food joint like Saizeriya after school and loiter around until evening, surviving only on fountain drinks and focaccia, desperately bad-mouthing people and complaining about school to kill time. Stuff like that. That is the real teen experience. I've gone through it myself, so it's absolutely true.

But that kind of experience wasn't so bad.

Mixing melon soda and orange juice and calling it melonge and getting excited about it, going on field trips and playing mah-jongg in a brutal atmosphere with three other guys, seeing the girl I had a crush on with her boyfriend and me suddenly going quiet... Now I consider those good memories.

Sorry, that's a lie. I hated it. I wanted to go on a date with a high school girl in uniform, too. No, I still want to now. I wrote those feelings into this. I hope you enjoyed it.

Now, my acknowledgments.

To my manager, Hoshino-sama: If I were to write all my feelings here, I'd write a whole book, so I'll abridge it. You helped me with everything, big and small. Thank you very much.

To Ponkan⑧-sama: Your extremely cute and wonderful illustrations gave me strength every time I felt as if I would falter. I'm sincerely glad that I asked you to illustrate the book. Thank you very much.

Though she didn't know me at all, Yomi Hirasaka-sama wrote a blurb for me. When I felt as if I would be crushed by anxiety and worry, Hirasaka's comments gave me courage. Thank you very much.

To my friends: My friends! You only ever talk about money when I see you! I'm disappointed in you! Talk about your life and stuff!

To all my readers: The author Wataru Watari couldn't exist without you. Every single word you send me gives me energy. Thank you so much!

And finally, to myself in high school: This work was born precisely because you were so bitter in those days, always saying stuff like *This is so boring; this is so stupid.* Please be proud. Your youth was all wrong, but I'm sure it was totally right. Thanks.

Now, the story. Whether it continues or not is up to certain factors, but I trust I will see you all again. While I polish the next plot, I think I'll end it right about here.

On a certain day in February,
In a certain place in Chiba,
Feeling nostalgic for how I was so long ago,
While sipping on sweet, sweet coffee.

Wataru Watari

Chapter 1 ··· Anyway, **Hachiman Hikigaya** is rotten.

P. 11   **"That's some long-nosed sniper material. Are you one of the Straw Hat Pirates or what?"** In Eiichiro Oda's *One Piece* manga, the long-nosed sniper Usopp is both a chronic liar and a member of the Straw Hat Pirates.

P. 11   **"I'll start looking for a mechanical body and then end up as a bolt."** In Leiji Matsumoto's *Galaxy Express 999* manga, the protagonist, Tetsuro Hoshino, longs to replace his human body with an immortal machine body, but Queen Promethium, ruler of the machine empire, plans to remake him into a simple bolt.

P. 15   **"…just like those animals that chomped on Tomoko Matsushima."** Tomoko Matsushima, a Japanese singer and actress, was attacked by both a lion and a leopard in the space of ten days during the filming of a documentary in Kenya in 1986.

P. 16   **"This is a gambling apocalypse!"** *Gambling Apocalypse Kaiji* is a manga by Nobuyuki Fukumoto that chronicles the harrowing gambling travails of Kaiji, a feckless young man whose life of poverty leads him to become entangled in ever more dangerous games of chance.

P. 18   **"Even without some bespectacled elementary school student to tell me, 'Huh? Something's not right!'"** *Detective Conan*, also known as *Case Closed*, is a long-running mystery manga series by Gosho Aoyama that follows the cases of Shinichi Kudo, a brilliant detective whose strange reaction to a poison turns him into a small child. In his new guise, he solves cases as Conan Edogawa.

P. 18   **"More like Demon Superhuman."** *Akuma Choujin*, or "Demon Superhuman," is a reference to a group of villains from the *Kinnikuman* manga by Yoshinori Nakai and Takashi Shimada.

P. 21   **"'The Nighthawk's Star'? How obscure can you get?"** "The Nighthawk's Star" is a short story by Kenji Miyazawa, about an ugly bird bullied so badly and rejected so thoroughly that he ultimately dies and becomes a star in the night sky.

P. 21   **"The only other person I could think of who did that was a Saiyan prince."** Akira Toriyama's *Dragon Ball* manga involves a race known as the Saiyans—the prince of whom, Vegeta, is notoriously arrogant.

P. 24   **"Are you Golgo or what?!"** Golgo is the main character in Takao Saito's *Golgo 13*, a long-running manga about a taciturn, invincible assassin. Golgo's guard is never down.

P. 24   **"Think of it as the Hyperbolic Time Chamber."** In Akira Toriyama's *Dragon Ball* manga, the Hyperbolic Time Chamber is a training room where time passes more slowly, allowing years of training to take place in mere days of real-world time. In Japanese it's known as the *Seishin to Toki no Heya* or "Room of Spirit and Time."

P. 24   **"Or would it be easier to understand if I just called it *Revolutionary Girl Utena*?"** *Revolutionary Girl Utena* is a 1997 anime directed by Kunihiko Ikuhara. It involves a sinister student council scheming to "crack the world's shell."

P. 26   **"It's sort of like *Shonen Jump*!"** *Weekly Shonen Jump* is the most popular manga serialization magazine in Japan, serializing many popular adventure, action, and sports titles. Their main demographic consists of young boys or *shonen*. Most of the titles have themes revolving around the "Jump triangle" of friendship, competition, and hard work. They're generally about good old-fashioned heroes saving the world and achieving their dreams.

P. 26   **"Gundam Fight! Ready? Go!"** The *Mobile Fighter G Gundam* incarnation of the Gundam series involves organized battle tournaments between various mecha, which begin with this line. Like all of Ms. Hiratsuka's favorites, it's from the 1990s.

P. 26   **"It would have been easier to understand if I said 'Robattle,' huh?"** "Robattle" refers to battles between robots in the *Medabots* anime series, which is much more obscure than Gundam.

P. 29   **"Thinking that naughty, rage-inducing girl's a *tsundere*…"** *Tsundere* is a Japanese term that combines the terms *tsun-tsun* ("prickly") and *dere-dere* ("bashful"). It refers to a character who is prickly and irritable on the outside but secretly sentimental.

Chapter 2 ··· **Yukino Yukinoshita** always stands firm.

P. 33   **"She's like something out of Alcatraz or Cassandra. Why couldn't a Savior of Century's End show up right about now?"** Alcatraz is one famous prison, but Cassandra is another—at least, in the manga series

Fist of the North Star. Its hero, Kenshiro, is known as the Savior of the Century's End.

P. 35   **"Maybe you're so twisted up, it reversed all your meridians."** Another *Fist of the North Star* reference, this time to Souther, a villain whose internal organs are positioned in a mirror image from normal anatomy. One of his villainous projects is the construction of the Holy Emperor Cross Mausoleum, a pyramid built by child slave labor.

P. 35   **"You have a full-blown case of second-year head swell."** *Second-year head swell* (*kounibyou*, literally, "second year of high school disease") is a term Ms. Hiratsuka invents here to tease Hikigaya. However, it's based on an existing term, *chuunibyou* (literally, "second year of middle school disease, translated in this book as "M-2 syndrome").

P. 35   **"Do you like Keigo Higashino or Koutarou Isaka?"** Keigo Higashino and Koutarou Isaka are famous mystery authors.

P. 36   **"Gagaga and Kodansha BOX."** Gagaga Bunko published the *My Youth Romantic Comedy* series in Japan, while Kodansha BOX publishes NisiOisiN's *Monogatari* series.

P. 37   **"...it was as if she'd told me, *I think you should give up on 'Concrete Road.'*"** In the 1995 Studio Ghibli film *Whisper of the Heart*, Seiji Amasawa tells the protagonist Shizuku Tsukishima that she should give up on "Concrete Road," her lyrical rewrite of John Denver's song "Country Road." In response to this, she repeats "He's a jerk!" over and over.

P. 39   **"Foul play on the level of Maradona's Hand of God."** In the 1986 World Cup semifinal, Argentina defeated England thanks to a notorious goal scored by Diego Maradona in which he illegally used his hand.

P. 41   **"Are you friends if you meet someone once and siblings if you see them everyday? Mi-Do-Fa-Do-Re-Si-So-La-O?"** The opening song to the children's TV show *Do-Re-Mi-Fa Donuts* states that "if you meet someone once you're friends; if you see them every day you're siblings."

Chapter 3 ⋯ **Yui Yuigahama** is perpetually glancing around furtively.

P. 59   **"What was this, a Ryuu Murakami novel?"** Ryuu Murakami is a writer of literary fiction whose 1976 debut work, *Almost Transparent Blue*, chronicles the drug-fueled hedonism of a group of Japanese teenagers.

P. 66   **"There's no way my little sister could be this incompetent."** Very likely a reference to Tsukasa Fushimi's light novel *Ore no Imouto ga Konna ni Kawaii Wake ga Nai* ("There's No Way My Little Sister Could Be This Cute").

P. 74   **"What color is your patisserie?!"** Natsumi Matsumoto's *Yumeiro Patisserie* ("Dream-Colored Pastry Chef") follows the travails of clumsy but talented Ichigo Amano, who loves cake and dreams of turning pro.

P. 79   **"There is a certain saying... *If you have love...love is okay!*"** This is a catchphrase for *Apron of Love*, a novelty cooking show wherein female celebrities attempt to cook dishes in a kitchen full of unlabeled ingredients for a panel of male celebrity judges. Love is frequently not enough to ensure edible outcomes.

Chapter 4 ⋯ Even so, **the class** is doing well.

P. 92   **"And by 'those guys,' I was referring to the ones who'd brought their PSPs for a hunt..."** A reference to the Monster Hunter series of video games.

P. 97   **"This was an inquisition, and Yuigahama was being forced to step on a cross…"** When Christianity was outlawed during the Tokugawa period, people suspected of being Christian were forced to step on a crucifix in order to prove their innocence.

P. 97   **"Meals should have been more joyous and fun than this. If you subscribed to the ideology of the Lonely Gourmet, anyway."** *Kodoku no Gurume* ("The Lonely Gourmet") is a manga series written by Masayuki Qusumi and drawn by Jiro Taniguchi. It follows the gustatory life of Goro Inogashira, a salaryman whose greatest pleasure comes from solitary enjoyment of cuisine.

P. 102 **"Like even when we were playing *Ojamajo Doremi*…"** Yuigahama is referencing *Ojamajo Doremi*, a magical girl anime. Hazuki is the shyest and most passive of the main cast of characters.

P. 102 **"I won't read any light novels with evil gods in them at school anymore."** The *Jashin Oonuma* ("Evil God Oonuma") series of light novels follow the adventures of a boy who decides to become an evil deity with the help of an instruction manual and starter kit. It's published in Japan by Gagaga Bunko—which also publishes *My Youth Romantic Comedy*.

Chapter 5 ⋯ In other words, **Yoshiteru Zaimokuza** is rather off.

P. 113 **"I miss the purity of the Muromachi era…"** In Japanese history, the Muromachi period refers to the time between the mid-1300s to the mid-1500s, during which Japan was ruled by the Muromachi shogunate. The period ended with the collapse of Japan into smaller factions, a violent era known as the Sengoku or "warring states" era, to which Zaimokuza is referring here.

P. 115 **"I think he's just taking the name Hachiman and thinking of the Bodhisattva Hachiman."** Hachiman is a god of war in the Shinto tradition; with the arrival of Buddhism in Japan he was integrated into that faith as a bodhisattva, a human who has attained Buddhahood.

P. 115 **"The Seiwa Genji clan zealously worshipped him as a god of war."** The Seiwa Genji were a powerful line of the Minamoto clan of Japanese nobility for hundreds of years, tracing their lineage back to the Emperor Seiwa. The Kamakura and Ashikaga shogunates were both descended from the Seiwa Genji, and the Tokugawa shogunate claimed the lineage as well.

P. 116 **"I played *Nobunaga's Ambition*, okay?"** Nobunaga's Ambition is a series of turn-based strategy video games set during the Sengoku period. They follow Oda Nobunaga's quest to unify Japan.

P. 119 **"They were printed in a fixed grid of forty-two by thirty-two characters..."** Gagaga Bunko, the imprint that publishes the *My Youth Romantic Comedy* series as well as many others, requires submissions in this format.

Chapter 6 ··· But **Saika Totsuka** has one.

P. 132 **"...the kind they say gets marinated in MAX Coffee..."** MAX Coffee is a type of extra-sweet coffee available in cans and bottles. At one point it was marketed only in the Chiba, Ibaraki, and Tochigi prefectures of Japan.

P. 133 ***From the Northern Country*** is a long-running series of Japanese dramas set in the town of Furano, on Hokkaido, the northernmost island of Japan.

P. 135 **Issei Fuubi Sepia** was a performance group that was active in the 1980s. One of their most popular songs was called "Zenryaku, Michi no Ue Yori" ("Preface: From Above the Road") in which the exclamation "*Soiya!*" is repeated many times.

P. 136 **"What, are you buying treats for the office?"** Hachiman is referencing *chuugen*, a period in July when workers bring in gifts (usually edible) to give to their superiors as tokens of appreciation.

P. 136 **"…like you'd say 'the ham man.'"** This is a reference to a series of TV ads positioning Marudai-brand ham gift sets as good *chuugen* gifts. The first ham man was actor Tetsuya Bessho.

P. 139 **"Hikitani."** The second kanji character in Hachiman Hikigaya's name means "valley" and can be read as "tani." Hayama is therefore misreading his name as "Hikitani."

P. 151 **"My motto was *I canna keep this up!* like some kind of Korosuke imitation…"** Korosuke is a character from *Kiteretsu Encyclopedia* with a very peculiar way of talking.

P. 162 **"…he was less *Dragon Quest* and more like King Bonbii from Momotetsu, I think."** In classic *Dragon Quest*, all the characters follow behind the leader in a line. Momotetsu is another long running video game series that's sort of like a board game, and King Bonbii is an annoying character who follows behind the player and harasses them.

Chapter 7 ··· Sometimes, **the gods of romantic comedy** are kind.

P. 179 **"I read the entire series, and I even saw the musical."** The popular tennis manga *Prince of Tennis* had a stage musical adaptation, which is what Zaimokuza is probably talking about.

P. 182 **"Was she Madame Butterfly or what?"** Madame Butterfly was a voluminously-coiffed character in *Ace wo Nerae!* ("Aim for the Ace!"), a famous 1970s *shoujo* manga about tennis.

P. 197   **"Who are you, Hiei?"** Hiei is a character from *Yu Yu Hakusho*, whose Black Dragon special attack leaves him unconscious after its completion.

Chapter 8 ··· And then **Hikigaya** ponders.

P. 214   **"The heroine has a body made of rubber…"** This is a reference to the hero of *One Piece*, whose body has rubberlike properties.

P. 215   **"Are you Gian or what?"** Gian is the bully character in the famous manga series *Doraemon*.

Afterword

P. 219   **"Real youth is when two guys stop by a fast-food joint like Saizeriya after school and loiter around until evening…"** Saizeriya is a Japanese Italian fast-food chain. Its budget menu and relaxed atmosphere make it popular with students and families.